SPLIT

SPLIT

SWATI AVASTHI

EMBER

Text copyright © 2010 by Swati Avasthi
Cover art copyright © 2012 by Shutterstock

Ember and the colophon are trademarks of Random House, Inc.

Visit us on the Web! www.randomhouse.com/teens

Educators and librarians, for a variety of teaching tools,
visit us at www.randomhouse.com/teachers

The Library of Congress has cataloged the hardcover edition of this work as follows:
Split / Swati Avasthi. — 1st ed.
p. cm.
Summary: A teenaged boy thrown out of his house by his abusive father gets to live with his older brother, who ran away from home years ago to escape the abuse.
ISBN 978-0-375-86340-0 (trade) — ISBN 978-0-375-96340-7 (lib. bdg.) —
ISBN 978-0-375-89526-5 (ebook)
[1. Child abuse—Fiction. 2. Family violence—Fiction. 3. Brothers—Fiction.] I. Title.
PZ7.A931Sp 2010
[Fic]—dc22
2009022615

ISBN 978-0-375-86341-7 (tr. pbk.)

RL: 8.0

The text of this book is set in 11-point New Baskerville.

Printed in the United States of America

10 9 8 7

First Ember Edition 2012

This book is dedicated to my parents,
Pushpa and Pratap S. Avasthi.
All my life, they've given me seeds, water, and sunshine.
Then they waited patiently to see what I might grow.

now I have to start lying.

While I stare through the windshield at the building my brother lives in, I try to think up a good lie, but nothing comes to mind. "I was in the neighborhood"? Yeah, right. It's nineteen hours from Chicago to Albuquerque. If you drive all night. If you only stop for Mountain Dews and KFC extra crispy. By the way, KFC closes way too early in Oklahoma.

Maybe I should try "I'm just here to borrow a cup of sugar." Pathetic. How about "One more stop in the eternal quest for the perfect burrito"? Unless Christian has gone blind in the last five years, no lie is gonna cut it. My split lip might tip off Clever Boy. I run my tongue over the slit and suck on the blood.

My face will tell half the story. For the other half, I'll keep my mouth shut and lie by omission. Someday I'll fess up, tell him the whole deal, and then he can perform a lobotomy or whatever it takes. But right now, I just need Christian to open his door, nudge it wider, and let me stay.

When I open the car door, a *ding-ding, ding-ding* sound makes me pause. I search the dashboard for clues. Oh— headlights. I'm not used to driving at night. My license is only a couple of months old, but after making it here despite pissy Missouri drivers, tired Oklahomans, middle-finger-saluting Texans, and clueless New Mexicans, I've got the mileage, if not the age.

The entrance glows under an outdoor light. Inside, the lobby is cramped, and the once-white walls are striated with grime. I scan the list of names next to the buzzer buttons.

There is no Witherspoon. Our last name is missing.

I curl a finger, rest my knuckle against the buzzer box and slide it down, stopping at each name to be sure. Gonzales, scribbled in blue ballpoint; MARSHALL in black Sharpie; Ngu in looping red ink; and a name that reminds me of G-rated swearing, SI#*%

I yank my camera bag off my shoulder and crouch, setting it on the floor. The zipper grinds open, and I unload my camera and flash, searching for the envelope that my mom handed me before I left. I recheck the address. I'm in the right place, but I notice, for the first time, that the letter was postmarked a month ago.

I taste copper. If Christian has moved, how am I supposed to find him? The envelope says 4B. Even though 4B is labeled MARSHALL, I press the button, and the buzz echoes in the tiny foyer. *Answer. Be home and answer.*

Outside, a FedEx truck roars, pauses, and roars again. Its white profile steals away, leaving only a gasp of gray exhaust. A shrunken man drags the door open and holds it for his shrunken wife. Before they even step over the threshold, they see me and stop.

I *am* quite the picture. The split lip isn't the only re-landscaping my father has done. A purple mountain is rising on my jaw, and a red canyon cuts across my forehead.

They stare at me, and I suck in my lip, hiding what I can.

At that moment, a distorted voice comes through the speaker: "Who is it?"

Can I really have this conversation over a speaker? *Remember me? The brother you left behind? Well, I've caught up.* Even in my imagination, I stop here. I leave out the rest.

"Um," I say, "FedEx."

The couple unfreezes. The man grasps his wife's elbow, tugs her outside, shoves the door closed, and helps her hobble away. Great way to start my Albuquerque tenure: scaring the locals.

The buzzer sounds. I grab the handle, turn it, and climb the steps. On the second floor, I have to stop. The red shag carpet has been accumulating odors since the 1970s and is going to take some getting used to. I block up my nose as if I am swimming and breathe through my mouth. Even worse. Now I can *taste* the miasma of hash and cat piss. At least, I hope it's cat piss. I close my mouth, wishing I didn't have to breathe as I take the steps two at a time to the fourth floor.

Gold numbers against a dark wood door. I press my palm against it, as if I can befriend the door, get it on my side. I knock and wait. I know some people go all

3

deer-in-the-headlights when they panic. Their lungs stop, their muscles freeze, even their brains silence. Me—my foot's on the gas and the map's flapping out the window. My imagination creates scenes in rapid succession:

He'll throw open the door and hug me until I can't breathe. There'll be a pizza feast laid out on a banquet table: four pies, all pepperoni and pineapple. (Okay, this part might be influenced by the fact that I haven't eaten in ten hours.) He'll wrap an arm around my shoulder and say, "I've been looking out for you, even from here."

Or maybe I'll be overwhelmed by the sweet smell of pot, and his hair will be sticking up wildly, and he'll mug me for the $3.84 I have left.

Or maybe he won't recognize me.

The door swings open, and a rush of ginger and garlic overtakes the hash/piss scent. My stomach lurches, as if it wants to go inside all on its own.

An Asian woman, maybe late twenties, is standing at the door. Her hair is pinned up, and she is wearing a little black dress. Her eyes travel me north to south and back north again. She slams the door. *Crap.*

Through the wall, I hear a voice approaching. Unmistakably Christian's tenor. It makes my scalp tingle.

"What's the problem, Mirriam?"

"That's not a FedEx guy."

I slide the envelope under the door.

"Oh God," he says.

The handle rotates, and Mirriam says, "No, don't. There's something wrong with him."

I snort. She doesn't even know my name, and she's nailed me in one shot.

"Christian?" I call through the door. My voice wavers.

On the carpet, a triangle of light widens as the door opens.

My brother. Still taller than me. A good four inches. His face has elongated and thinned. The sinew in his neck tells me he's still a runner. Incongruously, I wonder if he has made it to the Boston Marathon yet. He's only twenty-two, but crow's feet lightly scratch his skin. He wears a black suit. The knot in his tie hangs below his collarbone, and his top button is undone.

Mirriam stands behind him, a baseball bat perched on her shoulder.

"Jace." He exhales it all at once.

He doesn't look me over, doesn't stare me down, but he doesn't hug me, either. His lips curve, but I can't read his smile. He cranes his head around the door, looking for Mom.

"Just me," I say.

He begins to close the door, but then it stops, half open, while he collects some stuff off the hooks and floor. Mirriam is still in her batter's stance, watching to see what kind of pitch I'll throw. *Lady, I don't have enough juice to get it over the plate.* When he pushes the door back open, he is carrying a jacket, and a pair of black high heels dangles from his fingers. He hands the shoes to her.

"Oh," she says. "Am I . . . should I . . . ?" She slides her panty-hosed toes into her heels.

He presses his lips to her cheek. "I'll try to make it up to you. I promise."

His voice is so quiet, so mild I have to hold my breath to hear him.

"It's no problem," she says. "This seems more important."

"More immediate," he corrects her.

Ouch.

"Come over later?" she asks.

He says yes, and his gaze takes a long road to find her face; he has no idea what he's going to say.

She smiles and presses up on her tiptoes to return the kiss on his cheek. "As late as you'd like. I'll be up." Her eyes take one more appraising trip over me. "As long as you're certain."

He nods but doesn't introduce us. She sidesteps me and heads down the hall, disappearing into 4C.

Christian strings his arms through his jacket sleeves. Outside, the temperature is dropping, and my coat is in Chicago. I stare at Christian so long that he gets me a Windbreaker. When I slip my arms in, I can't reach the cuffs.

"If you're still here, we can get you a jacket of your own tomorrow." He fishes in his pocket and gets out his keys. "Do you still like breakfast for dinner? Should we go out for pancakes?"

I say yes. He tries to ask me something, doing a fish-mouth move, but can't get it out. When we reach the bottom of the stairs, he turns around and looks at me. I wait for him to unload his questions, but he says nothing, crosses the foyer, and opens the door.

When he turns back, he says, "Can I ask you something?"

"Sure," I say.

"Did he kill her?"

"Not yet."

he gives the front door an extra push for me so I can slip out. The sky is freckled with stars. A gust of wind spits dust at my jacket.

"My car's over here," Christian says.

I follow him to a mostly red Pontiac Sunbird. (The passenger-side door is white.) It is missing a wheel trim, and the rust is winning.

"We could take mine," I say, before I remember the mess—bled-on napkins, crumpled Mountain Dew cans, empty venti Starbucks cups. Lauren, my girlfriend (I mean, my ex-girlfriend) used to stick her hands on her hips while waiting for me to clean it out. It was bad enough doing it in a car, she said. She drew the line at a garbage pit disguised as a two-door Golf. I recoil from the memory of Lauren.

What was once—I don't know, maybe call it comfort? excitement? love?—something, all of those things—has bubbled up like a blister in my brain that I don't even want to touch.

Unlocking the door to his car, Christian says, "you look like you've done enough driving for one day."

I clear a couple of newspapers out of the footwell, chucking them behind me as I sit down. He closes his door and stares at me, squinting and tilting his head from one side to the other.

"What?" Is his vision sharp enough to discern the bastard that I am?

"It is. Un. Canny."

"What is?"

"The resemblance between you and Dad. I always knew it was strong," he says.

I tap my foot against the floor and wish he would turn his radio on.

"Could you, maybe, stop staring at me now?" I say.

"Right, sorry."

He looks away fast and turns the ignition key. As we pull out of the parking lot, I look at my reflection in the window, trying to distinguish my features from my dad's. His blond hair, straight nose, and quick-to-anger eyes are all replicated on me. When I was little, grown-ups marveled, "A carbon copy." I didn't mind it then. I liked it. What was my alternative? A mousy mother who quivered at her own shadow.

Maybe I should dye my hair. Black like Christian's. Get green contacts and look like my brother. I roll down my window, erasing my face, and the cool air rushes in. A parade of one-story strip malls slides by, giving off a tour of smells: BP's noxious gasoline mixes with McDonald's French fries and baked butter from a dessert place.

Christian keeps his eyes on the road, not glancing at me, not saying anything.

"So," I say, but that's all I've got. Five years to explain. Words are flowing through my brain like logs down a river. "Sorry I couldn't give you any notice."

"It doesn't matter."

"Really? 'Cause you don't seem so . . . I mean, it's good to see you."

He exhales and runs a hand through his hair. "Oh, Jace. I'm sorry. It is good to see you, too. I'm glad you're all right. Well, for the most part. You know what I mean."

I do; taking a beating isn't that remarkable in our family. It's not as if the earth shatters or time stops. You get up the next day and go to school. Maybe you work a little harder to keep up the everything's-fine-we're-perfect image, but overall, you just keep moving at the speed of your life.

He says, "I'm just . . . I was surprised is all."

With his eyes glued forward and no prodding, no questions, I can't talk. I don't even know if he wants me to start. How much has he thought about me since he disappeared one night, out of school, out of the house? He left a note in the mailbox for our dad in his meticulous handwriting. *If you try to find me, I'll testify.*

I try to think of something to say. Over the years I've collected question after question, but I can't seem to find them now. We're not ready for them, anyway, so I go for the easy ones.

"So, Mirriam's your girlfriend?" I ask. "How long have you been dating?"

"A year." He slides the knot in his tie farther down, slips the tie over his head, and puts it on his lap. "Today, actually."

"Oh." I remember Mirriam's little black dress that was cut above the knee. "You were celebrating."

"It's not a problem."

"She'll be mad?"

He shrugs and glances in the rearview mirror—that move: shrug, glance—he's about to lie. "She'll understand."

"You've been dating the girl next door for a year?" I say.

Mirriam has gotten on my bad side. Maybe it was the baseball bat.

He laughs and tells me that he moved next to her a month ago. I remember the envelope my mother handed me, stripping the letter out and holding it against her chest. Now I know why she double-checked the address.

Christian continues, "We were thinking about moving in together but . . . it felt . . . I thought this way we could each have our own space and still see each other."

"You live alone?" I ask.

When he nods again, I ask him why "Marshall" is on his buzzer.

"It's, uh, my last name now. I changed it during college."

He grins for a half second, and I get his irony. My father's a judge, which is ironic all by itself, I suppose. He idolizes Supreme Court Justice John Marshall Harlan—framed picture in the study, a shelf of biographies—the works. At dinner, he'd read us Harlan's opinions dissenting from the Warren Court while we weighed if listening was worth staying for chocolate cake.

"That's funny," I say.

His eyebrows furrow.

"I mean, the name thing. Remember the—"

"Does Mom share my letters with you?"

"Yeah." I lie because I want a part of him.

My mom has had letters, Mirriam got twelve long months, and for me—twenty minutes.

"Really?" His voice changes, suddenly remote.

Busted.

"Oh, you mean the actual letters? No, she just handed me the envelope."

He is silent. I look out the windshield.

"You never wrote me, did you?" I say.

"I didn't know what to say. You *were* only eleven."

"Sure," I say, as if that's an answer. Last time I checked, eleven-year-olds can read. And tend to grow up.

He never wanted to know a thing about me, never Googled me, or stuck a candle in a cupcake on my birthday. I stare out the window, counting the oncoming cars as they pass us.

All my logjammed words evaporate.

The place is decorated in "Aren't-you-hungry?" red. Somewhere, someone did a study and found out that red makes you feel hungry, and suddenly you can't find a restaurant without red walls or booths or chairs, or at the really cheap places, all three. As if I need anything else to stimulate my stomach. The restaurant is empty, save for a woman at a four-person table who is examining the ice in her water.

I pick up my fork and bounce it off the table. On the wall, I spot a clock that is outlined in red neon. I watch the second hand spin. In half an hour, we haven't said one important word to each other. I have discovered that he is a med student, which gives him screwy hours and means that he sees patients ("As a med student?" I asked, "That's the way it works," he said), and that he came to Albuquerque for med school because UNM has a good clinical program. But that's about it.

We've talked more to the waitress—we placed our orders and Christian asked for a bag of ice for my face—than to each other. The fifty-something waitress drops the bag on the table and puts down my hot chocolate. When it sloshes, Christian uses his napkin to clean it up. Then he starts tearing off little pieces of the napkin, which he then rolls between his thumb and forefinger, turning them into tissue-rice. Rip, roll. Rip, roll. I pick up the ice bag, hear it rattle, and press it to my cheek. I keep the pressure light and begin to freeze my face.

"Jace," he says finally, "I'm sorry that I left and couldn't take you with me."

He continues his onslaught on the napkin.

I clear my throat. "Where did you go?"

"Do you remember Paul Costacos?"

He was Christian's best friend in high school and knew everything about the animal kingdom. He had a fish tank filled with hermit crabs whose shells were painted like NFL helmets. I always liked the star for the Cowboys.

"I was at his house, and I started coughing up blood. His parents took me to the hospital, warded off the police, and never asked me any questions. That's probably why I told them everything."

I have an "Aha!" moment; he thinks he *shouldn't* ask why I'm here.

Rip, roll. I'm starting to pity that napkin. When he sees

me staring at it, he stops and continues in a straightforward voice. No emotion clouding the facts, but not like it happened to someone else. He owns this story; I can't even formulate mine. I lean forward to hear him better when he continues.

"Over the next few weeks, we planned how I was going to disappear. I lived in Hyde Park with Paul's brother. Paul's mom worked in the administration at the Lab School. She helped me transfer there to finish my senior year. His parents even took out a loan on my behalf, so I could pay for tuition. They found me a job, bussing tables in Greektown. I saved everything I could to get a plane ticket to New York and collect on my scholarship at NYU."

He has explained everything and nothing at the same time.

"If you could plan all that," I say, "why couldn't you come up with a way to swing by and tell me about it?"

"He had never hit you. I thought you'd be okay."

His napkin is shredded, and he reaches for mine. I push the ice harder against my face until it hurts just right.

The waitress brings the food. I go for the maple syrup, drench everything, and then attack. I hate the flat taste of these pancakes, but I keep going, too hungry to be picky. I don't talk. I just eat and think.

Our family was divided up into two camps: Christian and Mom, me and Dad. I know that's why Christian thought that Dad wouldn't get started on me. Maybe because I was Dad's favorite, I never had it as bad as Christian. Christian had to go to the ER for broken fingers, one by one (a bar fight was the excuse, even though he was only sixteen); repeated vomiting after a concussion (excuse: he fell down the steps); and even had some skin grafted on his arm when Dad held it on an electric burner (can't remember the excuse for that one).

Three pancakes and an entire ham steak later, my stomach quits nagging me. The blood leaves my legs and arms, rushing to my stomach. I'm slow to get up, pushing my hands into the squishy vinyl seat to haul myself out of the booth.

On our way back, the billboards begin to blur, and I close my eyes, listening to the hum of the engine and Christian's peaceful breathing. I'm half-asleep when we pull into his lot, and even when I know Christian is getting out of the car I stay put, telling myself that I'll move in just another minute. He has to prompt me out of the car. When we get to the flat face of the apartment door, I'm still unsure which side of the door he wants me on.

"So, am I staying here?" I ask.

"Do you want to?"

I nod.

"Sure. It's cheaper than a motel," he says, and grins.

I'm too off-balance to respond. He's thinking one night, and I'm thinking forever. Before I can figure out how to ask him to take me in, he says, "But Mirriam doesn't know about Dad. So, could you just . . ."

"Of course," I say. "I wouldn't."

"You can take the couch. You look exhausted."

I nod. I'm so tired that it feels like my head is detached from my body and floating above it, like a balloon.

He looks at her door. "We'll talk tomorrow, okay?"

"Sure, okay," I say.

He lets me into his apartment. I walk over the threshold, but he doesn't follow. He stares at Mirriam's door, his face taut.

"What are you going to tell her?" I say.

"I don't know. I guess I'll start with, 'I have a brother.' "

My face melts; my eyebrows and mouth droop. She doesn't even know I exist?

He runs his hand through his hair, still looking at the door. Even though I barely know Mirriam, I know that an omission this big is breakup material. Maybe that's why he's being so not-Christian-like. He used to be so protective of me; he'd take the blame for my mistakes or argue with Dad until he'd flare at Christian instead of me.

"Christian, I'm really not trying to screw things up for you."

"Yeah, I know. But if Dad is . . . Depending on how far . . . Trying might not have anything to do with it."

He closes the door behind him, and I'm in his apartment, staring at the other side of the door. The right side of it. Technically.

chapter 3

the next morning, I'm lying on Christian's couch in the limbo state between sleep and caffeinated. I'm not dreaming, exactly. I'm remembering. Exactly.

I'm eight years old and wearing a slippery yellow soccer jersey, standing under a low gray sky, looking at the two orange cones that demarcate the goal. We are losing 1–0 to the brown-jerseyed Bears. Coach Polansky has forced me into the goalie box. My dad is standing behind me, talking to me.

"See the whole field," he says. "Now he'll cross it to Jimmy. Watch out for Jimmy."

And Jimmy slams one past me. My dad chest-traps the ball down to his feet and kicks it off to the ref. Jimmy's second shot bounces off my hands but goes through. Third shot I miss entirely, guessing the wrong side. By the end of the game, I hate my coach, detest soccer, and wish a plague of prissy girls on Jimmy Tuttle. I won't come next week; I'll fake the flu, malaria—something.

The game ends, and my dad drives me to Petersen's for a banana split. When we're there and my tongue is burning from the too-cold ice cream, he says, "Wow, kiddo. You've got a real future in soccer." No sarcasm. He licks his Rocky Road. "You saw it all coming."

I stare at my pink and brown soup, pocked with maraschino cherries. "Then how did I lose?"

"Sometimes you're outmatched. You got beat, sure, but by the best player on the best team in the league. Just you wait. Jimmy'll outfox everyone this year. You'll look like a hero compared to other goalies he'll face."

A couple of months later, Jimmy Tuttle took his team to a 5–0 win in the championship match. When they were giving out those cheap gold-painted medals for participating, I even clapped for him.

Strange that my father should be the one to teach me about good sportsmanship. The other night, was he outmatched? I wonder what my dad's face looks like today.

I roll over on my side, close my eyes, and drop into a different memory.

I'm pulling into the driveway at home. The wheels bump on the cement, and the soccer ball on the passenger seat plunks into the footwell. I kill my headlights, taking the curve around the side of my house blind, and stop at the garage door.

The blue window shades are open. No trouble tonight?

Through the kitchen window at the back of my house, I see my mother from her waist up, floating. She cleans the counter, scrubbing out a spot with such diligence that I know she took a hard one. She tosses the rag into the sink, stops, goes to it, and hangs it properly. She turns her back to me, and the freezer door swings open. Out comes the reusable ice pack, and travels down, below my line of sight. I can't see what she is icing.

She picks up her cup of chamomile tea from the counter—her home cure for insomnia. Even though she has disappeared from view, I know she's tipping our honey-filled bear upside down and counting out six seconds' worth. I grab my camera bag, slide out of the car, and edge the door closed. I'd rather get in without a fuss.

I walk the brick path through the backyard. The scent of the Mock Orange blooms in the air. As I push past its cloying twigs, the bush douses me in petals. Through the window, I see the kitchen. Empty.

My mother has cleaned it perfectly, and the countertop feels smooth and slick under my fingers. The kitchen smells of banana bread. I open the breadbox and see the loaf, wrapped in blue Saran Wrap. Putting my bag down, I pull out the bread and cut off a thick slice. I'm a few bites into it when I notice a glass jar filled with Q-tips standing next to the sink. It stops me cold. My trachea clenches so tight it hurts.

He hits her, she cleans. He shoves her down and stomps on her, bootmarks imprinted in the small of her back, she scrubs the floors. He rapes her, she gets out the Q-tips to bleach the grout.

I swipe the glass jar across the counter and watch it shatter. All the white fuzzy barbells spill onto the floor. My father's tread is coming down the stairs. *Yes, come to me, asshole. I've got something for you.* The lights flash on, and I close my eyes, seeing purple inside my lids.

"What the hell, Jace?"

"What the hell, dad?" I say it with a little *d*.

"Don't backtalk, now. I've had a day."

"And Mom? Did she have a day?" I gesture to the Q-tips and glass shards.

My stomach is starting to flutter because I know what I want to do, and I have stage fright. Fist into his face. Another in his gut. After all, I've had a day. Isn't that what we're supposed to do? Hit something, hit someone. The moment our fists make contact, we feel better, right, Dad? Let it out. Punish her so she won't do it again. Right, Dad? Isn't that the way?

I could do it. I'm close enough. Right hook. Let *him* explain away a shiner. Like I've had to. *Soccer,* I've said, *Fight,* I've said, *Hockey, basketball, croquet.*

If I throw this punch, I'm out. He won't tolerate me for one second in his house, and he won't chase after me, hunt me, like he did when Christian ran. It will be over, and all I have to do is give in.

I curl my fingers into a fist and grip hard. I pull back and slam my fist into his eye.

And it *is* satisfying. A roller-coaster rush. God help me.

Even better, though, is the look of surprise on his face: his thin lips rounded into an O for a second before it tightens into an uncompromising line. And I know he never thought any of us would fight back.

He grabs my wrist, throws his first punch right into my lip, launching me against the fridge. My head strikes the stainless steel door. I'm seeing black, nothing else, when I hear the shade being pulled down. He will kill me now, I'm sure of it. He'll get the hammer from the garage or just wrap his hands around my neck.

I grasp at consciousness, trying to force my eyes to focus. Everything is a blur, but I duck fast enough, and his fist goes slamming into the chrome of the fridge. He cries out, and I see my advantage. I grab his arm and get it behind his back. My knee, my fist into his kidneys. Yes, fuck him. I want my mom to come over and take a shot too, but she stands there with her hands over her mouth. He's groaning, but I'm greedy; contact and contact and contact.

I don't see his shot coming. I don't even understand how; I'm just reeling backward, my jaw throbbing. When I fall against the stove, my head snaps back and I see grease stains no one has ever thought to clean on the underside of the hood. He's on me, and I'm taking a punch to the face. When I lift my arms to block it, I get another in the gut. *I'm getting beat, man. Do something, do anything.* His fingers dig into my shoulders, and he whips me forward. Which is when my forehead slams into the corner of the kitchen island, and I go down.

When I wake up, I'm lying on my back, looking at my parents' legs. They are sitting at the table. My father's brown pajamas with the frayed cuff, and my mother's calves poking out from under her nightgown. Her feet are bare, her ankles crossed.

My mom is pleading, please let him stay, he's your son, flesh and blood. Whatever. I know I'm out; I've done the unthinkable—I fought back. Next time, I might win.

I put my hand to my head and feel the stick of blood. I try not to groan, but the sound escapes.

"I'll go," I say. My voice is clear.

He grabs my elbow and hauls me to my feet. The ceiling lights slide down the walls and blur on the table. Where is the floor? I grab the counter and try to let my stomach catch up. I blink. He shoves something into my hands—my camera bag.

"Walter, no. He can barely stand."

He grabs my arm again and pulls me toward the front door, through the dining room—my last look at our glass table; through the living room—last look at the big couch that I liked to nap on; through the foyer, where I yank away from him so I can walk out under my own power.

"I need my keys," I say.

"Get out."

"Keys, Dad. Keys."

When he starts to reach for me again, I step over the threshold on my own. The September air immediately makes my skin break out in goose bumps.

"Mom! Need my keys!" I yell around him before he slams the door.

Forehead cuts are gushers. The blood, which flowed down the side of my head into my hair when I was on the floor, has rerouted its course, and I have to brush it off my eyebrow. I walk around the side of the house to my car.

The car door is locked.

I cross my arms, rub them, and stand, stumped, until I remember the extra set of keys in my camera bag. My mom insisted on it. And that almost undoes me, that little gesture. I want to cradle my head in my hands and sit down and bawl, but my dad has already gotten enough out of me. I dig my keys out and start the car.

The blue dashboard lights glow contentedly, as if nothing has changed, as if tomorrow I would wake up here, go back to my school, see Lauren, and shoot soccer balls with Edward. A door slams, and my mother hurries to the car. She stands on the passenger side in the circle of light under the streetlamp. I can't see a mark on her from earlier tonight. My dad's that good.

I roll down the passenger window. She leans in and hands me an envelope and my keys.

I put my keys on the seat and find a stack of bills—ones and fives—in the envelope.

"Did he give you this?" I ask.

She shakes her head. "I keep some hidden in a tampons box in our bathroom."

I nod. All this time, she's been squirreling away change, small bills that would go unmissed; she has learned from her mistake, from the last time we tried to leave and she made that large withdrawal that brought him home before we got out.

"Go. He will help you."

For a second, I think that she's referring to the Almighty, but her eyes are fixed on the envelope. I push it toward the light and see an address, but no name. I look at her, confused.

"Christian," she whispers.

I stop breathing. "Where did you get this?"

"He sent it to me," she says, and flushes. "Go to him."

"Come with me," I say. "Come on. Get in."

I reach across the seats and pull the latch so the door opens. She leans against the door, pushing it closed. Her eyes brighten with tears. She blinks them out, and they go shining down her face.

"Go," she says, "and I'll come to you."

I want to ask her when—before he takes her to Orchestra Hall, before they spend a dinner at Russian Tea Time and a weekend at the Drake, or after the next beating, when the cycle starts over again. I know my dad's fuse is only two months long, at best. So as I'm about to say "within the month," my dad comes out of the house, his bathrobe tied tight around his hips.

He slams the door, then glances over his shoulder at the light in Professor Coe's study next door. Paranoid-at-all-hours Prof Coe moves to the window and opens it. Everything slows down and changes: my dad is sauntering, not storming; his grimace upgrades into a casual smile. He bumps my mother out of the way with his hip and leans into the car.

"Come back, and I'll kill her." His tone is controlled— taut and calm. Except for his grip on the door, he could have been saying "Drive safely."

The blood runs out of my face. My breathing shallows, and I glance at my mother. Her eyes are shocked wide. This is my dad at his most dangerous. I've only seen him like this one other time, the time she tried to leave him before.

You wouldn't have the guts to kill her. You wouldn't last one day without a whipping post. You're too weak.

Now, as I lie on Christian's couch, my brain jolts all the way awake. *Oh God, did I say that?* After a lifetime of tiptoeing on ice, did I just split it wide open and leave her to drown? A statement like that, just one, and he'd take it out on her over and over again, trying to invalidate it.

I bolt upright.

No, no, I didn't say it. Just thought it. I twist the blanket Christian must have thrown over me around my hand and pull it tight. *It's okay,* I repeat in my head until I can function again. My fingers turn red, purple, blue. I unwrap the blanket.

I tilt my chin back to stretch my neck and scan Christian's apartment as I roll my head: a white ceiling; a desk with paperclips snug in their own place; a computer screen with a restless line drawing fading shapes; the mauve carpet (good taste, these landlords, eh?); compressed wood coffee table that looks light enough to juggle; the "dining room set" comprised of four metal chairs with glitter-speckled white seats, right out of a fifties diner, and a white laminate table with tri-dimpled chrome edging. Crappy place with garage-sale furniture. The couch has sunk at the back and one of the cushions is thicker than the other. This is living.

Seriously, my bedroom at home was probably bigger than this apartment.

Christian is sitting at the dining room table, stranded outside the too-small kitchen. He's wearing green doctor's scrubs and watching me. A blue teapot, a nearly empty bowl of cereal, and a mug sit on the table.

He asks if I'm hungry. Do I want tea? It's oolong.

"Yeah, I'll try it." I walk over to the table and reach for his mug.

He looks at my outstretched hand and clutches his tea to him. "I'll make you a cup."

My mom says families are no place for boundaries; we share everything: germs, money, blood, and all. Maybe someday, Christian and I will be sitting in front of a World Cup game, and our root beer bottles will get confused, and he won't care. He'll just swig and drain it.

"Nah, that's okay," I say, sitting down.

"So." He crosses his legs and takes one more sip of tea. "Where are you headed?"

He's sitting there, swirling his teacup in midair as if it were brandy, just casually talking—might as well be about the weather.

I take a big breath. "Here. I was headed here."

The tea stops its merry-go-round, and his eyes widen. My hand clenches into a fist.

"Or," I say, "maybe I could try the south of France, set up in a nice little villa, and study at the Sorbonne."

I stand up and kick the chair back into place. I walk out of the room, finding only two options: his bedroom or the bathroom. I opt for the bathroom.

I open the tap and let the water run through my fingers. I have no razor, no soap, no toothbrush. My toothbrush in Chicago is an electric Oral B, and I don't think my three and a half bucks will cover that. My teeth will rot out, and I'll have to gum my food by the time I'm nineteen.

I look at the one-person medicine cabinet in the one-person bathroom in this one-bedroom apartment. I'm okay with the couch. It's not that bad, really. I pee, wash my hands, and splash some water on my face. It's good and cold, like a much-deserved slap. The cut on my forehead burns from its introduction to water. I find one towel hanging from a single hook and dry my face with it, using just a corner.

When I return to the living room, he is putting on his coat.

"Aren't we going to get a jacket for me?" I fold my arms over my chest.

I probably look like a 1950s housewife, sulking as her husband says he's going to work late. I stick my hands up into my armpits to counter that image.

"We'll go out after I get back from work. Then we'll talk about what you'll need to do if you want to stay with me."

Thanks. Now I have something to obsess about all day long.

"Sure, okay," I say.

"I've left my cell number on the fridge, in case you

need anything. There's soup in the cupboard. I, uh, hell, I don't even know what school district we're in. Are you a senior?"

I examine my big toenail, which was blackened last week in a soccer match. Would he like me to be a senior?

"Junior."

He nods. "Listen, Jace. I'm sorry. This is going to take some getting used to, okay?"

He's almost out the door when he steps back in and pulls it closed. I exhale. He gets it now; he's going to stay, take the day off, and figure out what we need to do.

"I thought that you would have made plans. When I got out, I made—"

"He threw me out at about three in the morning. Couldn't very well go knocking on doors, now could I?" I ignore that I came knocking on his door.

"He what? He *threw* you out?"

I suddenly see my trump card. "I drove straight here."

"Oh."

"What did you think when I came here last night? That it was a vacation stop on the way to sunny California?"

Maybe if I'm nicer he'll let me stay. I try to smile with the good side of my mouth, but I'm guessing it looks like a grimace.

"God, Jace, I assumed that if you were driving cross-country, you'd have at least called or—"

"I didn't have your phone number."

He pauses and looks down. I watch him breathing.

Finally he says, "I'll be back around one, and we'll make a plan then. Don't worry, though. No matter where you end up, I'll make sure you land on your feet, okay? I promise."

26   I'm not that comforted by his promises.

chapter 4

When I knocked on Mirriam's door with a soccer ball tucked under my arm, in search of a
place to practice, she drove me out to the high school
where she teaches. (English, she told me.) The fields that
lie behind the school are decent. Two sit side by side, divided by a gully that is designed to trap escaping balls and
drain rainwater. The white paint marking the field is fresh.
No major potholes lie in wait to twist ankles, and one of the
goals still has its net up.

Mirriam lies on the grass, propped on an elbow, reading a paperback. Her purse and my camera bag are next to
her. I was too jittery to stay in the apartment, so I asked Mirriam for directions, and she ended up driving me over.

My shirt is so laden with sweat I'm certain my body is no

longer 65 percent water. I peel off my shirt, toss it in the grass, and pray for a breeze. Who ever thought that September could be so hot? Luckily, I left Chicago with my soccer gear in the car, so I've changed from jeans to shorts.

Interminable hours of driving and waiting and sitting and stressing, and now—movement. My legs in motion, my arms swinging for balance. I chip the ball in the air and pop it up for a header. My heart is pumping; my blood is flowing; everything is moving, but my brain is still fixated on what Christian said. *We'll talk about what you'll need to do if you want to stay with me.*

I place the ball inside the box to practice my penalty kicks. I take measured steps back, but I'm not focused. I'm thinking, *Like what things?* Probably won't make it easier when I tell him I'm broke. I let loose on the ball. It bounces off the crossbar, the goalie's best friend. I chase it down. What kinds of things could Christian expect? More than keeping my room clean, I suspect. Come to think of it, what room?

Nope, nope, I tell my brain. I refuse to obsess. Channel change.

An announcer's voice, scratchy from too many cigarettes, starts up. "For those of you joining us late, the score is 2–2 after two overtimes in a heated match between the U.S. and Germany. We're down to penalty kicks, Nigel."

"Yes, Dick. It's amazing soccer. Germany has scored four penalty kicks out of a possible five, missing the last try. The Americans have scored four and have one kick left."

(Bet you can guess who it's all up to now.)

The goalie has gotta be Germany's version of Paul Bunyan.

When I make the nearly impossible shot, the crowd leaps to their feet, cheering. All but Christian, who is sitting. I only hear his voice. *"You'll need to sweep, scrub, and pick tumbleweeds out of the cactus garden. Forget about college. You'll have too much to do if you want to stay with me."*

"But college was your ticket out," I call from the field.

"Well, you don't have enough to buy that ticket."

Okay. Better come up with another way to silence that brain-o-mine. I start to race the perimeter of the fields when I hear a car honk. I slow down to a jog while Mirriam gets up, brushes the grass off her butt, and shades her eyes with her hand. A green convertible is parked in the middle of the road with a commercial-worthy redhead in the passenger seat and her bulky boyfriend driving. Behind them is a cigarette-smoking blonde. The blonde is trying to find a way to hide her cigarette. Finally she tosses it out of the car.

"Are you trying to get in trouble?" Mirriam says, "Smoking *and* littering."

"Oh, I didn't—"

"Whatcha doing here on a Sunday, Ms. Ngu?" the guy shouts.

"Eric," Mirriam yells, "don't hold up traffic."

"Who's that? Who he play for?" Eric shouts again.

"Who *does* he play for?" Mirriam says.

"Hey, guy! Who you play for?"

A black-and-white cop car pulls up behind him, and its siren burps.

"See you tomorrow," Mirriam says. "We'll work on grammar, okay?"

The car jolts forward as Eric hits the gas, then jolts again as he, presumably, remembers that he shouldn't speed with a cop behind him. As he crawls the car forward, I hear one of the girls say, "He's hot."

"Eww . . . his face is all banged up."

"Who said anything about his face?"

High-pitched giggling rises over the revs, and then their voices are gone.

"Students," Mirriam says.

"I figured."

I turn my focus back to the field before brain-o-mine can start its little games again. I decide to race the perimeter of the fields. My feet churn up the ground, and I watch the horizon. Focus only on the horizon. Hor-i-zon.

Before I'm halfway around, I can't catch my breath. An elephant is sitting on my chest. I tumble over, lie on the grass, and breathe. In and out. In and out. I slow it down, counting IN one-two-three, OUT one-two-three. What is this? Late-onset asthma?

Mirriam is watching me when I poke my head up.

"Thin air," she calls out. "High altitude."

I nod, only because I can't get enough breath to do anything else. This is going to take some acclimating.

On the way back, Mirriam makes "just a quick stop" at a bookstore across the street, which, I swear to God, she *drives* us to. When we walk in, the AC blasts us, sending my sweat-drenched T-shirt into slo-mo waves. I stop and let my camera bag drop off my shoulder so the cool air can hit every inch of me.

This Barnes & Noble wannabe has a wheat-colored carpet-path that twists up to the register and branches out to different areas of the store. It's like Hollywood Boulevard, but with quotes instead of handprints. I step over Harper Lee and plant my foot on William Faulkner.

Mirriam and I break—she goes for coffee, and I head

to the Art section in search of a collection by one of my favorite photographers, Cindy Sherman. At home, I have two of her shots framed on my walls, and I already miss them.

Before I get there, a crystal chess set distracts me.

I started rescuing queens about eighteen months ago. I was downtown, had just crossed the Chicago River when I passed a gaming store. A board was set up, mid-game, facing the window, as if you could just reach in and play. The queen was exposed. Her alabaster face was stern and uncompromising, with one eyebrow arched. She looked as if she were trying to stare down the threatening knight.

When I pulled the door open, a set of bells that hung from the knob clanged against the doorframe. I picked the queen up, studying her don't-fuck-with-me mouth. I thought: *I should learn to play chess.* I thought: *I don't want to learn to play chess, I just want her.* I thought: *Yes.* I palmed her and walked out the door, past the two metal arcs that ineptly stood guard.

Alabaster, nicknamed Ally, was the start of my collection. Not counting Ally, I left six queens behind in Chicago—plastic black, sandalwood, walnut, green marble, her sister white marble, and a pewter Guinevere from a Camelot set. I kept them in a tube sock, stuffed under my mattress. I wish I had kept them in the car instead.

This queen is featureless, just a crystal orb for a head, but I recognize her by her position on the board. She's cut like a gemstone, all angles and ridges. Light bounces through her, casting mini-rainbows onto the chessboard squares. She's a beaut.

I pick her up—cold and heavy in my hand. I run my fingers over her facets and check the store for cameras.

31

The crystal queen will make a good inaugural piece for my Albuquerque collection.

No one's at the register, Mirriam's far enough away, and I can't make out any cameras. I stretch the waistband of my Hanes and slide her in. I'm not a perv or anything. I just know how to avoid getting caught. Who's gonna strip-search me for a chess piece? The queen just makes me look like God was even nicer to me.

My hand is just out of my shorts when a girl, maybe sixteen years old, appears in front of me. Her black hair is bobbed so that the ends lick at her rounded face. Her jeans have a rendition of Lady Godiva on the right thigh that takes my mind places it shouldn't go. She pushes up the sleeves of her billowy shirt as she stares at my bruised face.

"God, do I want to see the other guy?" The way she talks, as if she regrets moving her mouth, makes me think her career goal is ventriloquism.

"Car accident."

Not a great lie, but it's out of my mouth before it's gone through my brain.

"Are you okay?" she asks.

I shrug.

She gestures to the board. "Do you like it?"

I nod. "You play?"

"Nope, books are my addiction. Are you looking for anything in particular?"

"You work here?" I ask, a little disbelievingly.

She is young, and last time I tried to get a job at a book-store, I had to go through three interviews and was beat out by a PhD candidate. Or an undergraduate. Or something like that.

"Uh-huh. My dad knows the guy who owns it. D'you like

to read? Maybe you'd like this," she says as she reaches for a book. Her hand swings too far, knocking over a knight. She rights it and stares at the board. "Where's the queen?"

I lift my hands, palms open. She tilts her head, and I sense I just screwed up. I reacted as if she were accusing me.

She leans over, and I smell cinnamon and rain. She gets down and searches the floor like a blind woman, running her hands over the pale, nubby carpet. I carefully kneel to join her in her futile search. After a few minutes, she looks over her shoulder at me.

"Do you see it?" she asks.

I shake my head. "Probably just rolled off when you—"

"I didn't hear anything hit the floor, and it's heavy."

You don't say. It is pressing against my balls and sagging my briefs down. I stand up awkwardly, trying to make sure the queen lies right. The girl sits back on her heels for a moment and then, in one quick movement, is on her feet.

"Sir," she says.

Her brown eyes go distant. I've never been called "sir" before. I thought I would like it, but now I'm guessing I'm in for a whole lot of trouble.

"I'm going to have to ask you to empty your pockets."

Oh, great, now I've got Gestapo Girl on my ass. I cock my head and rely on my inherited legal knowledge.

"You can't ask me to do that. For one thing, unless you actually saw me take something and you actually know where it is, we can't even be having this conversation. It's called harassment. And second, I haven't left the store, so even if I had something, you couldn't levy a complaint."

"Who are you? Atticus Finch?"

"You're gonna compare me to a fictional character?"

Mirriam walks up, cradling a tower of books in one arm and digging through the stack of books with the other. She's gripping the rim of her coffee cup between her teeth. "I think Christian would like—" She is muttering into the lid. Then she looks up and takes in the scene. Extracting the coffee cup from her mouth, she asks Gestapo Girl, "What's the problem?"

"Nothing," I say. "I didn't steal anything."

"Jace," says Mirriam. "This would not be a good way to get started here."

"You think I'm stupid?"

"I didn't say that," she says with exaggerated patience. "But I wouldn't want this to be our first impression of you."

"Tattle if you want, but you won't earn any bonus points with my brother with false accusations."

"I don't need bonus points."

My cheeks heat up. Of course she doesn't. It's me, the one with the blood bond, who needs to "discuss what I need to do if I want to stay."

Gestapo Girl shifts her weight toward me and glowers at Mirriam.

"If you don't have anything to hide, just show her, and let's get out of here," says Mirriam.

"As long as you don't feel like your rights are being violated, sir," Gestapo says.

I tell her my name so she'll stop calling me "sir" while I pull the linings out of my pockets. Limp white cotton.

"Bag, too," Mirriam says.

I pull my camera bag off my shoulder and put it on the ground. I unzip the top, pull out my camera, and scatter my flash and filters on the author carpet. I stand up, turn the bag over, and shake it. A silver gum wrapper plunks on Ben Jonson.

"But then, where is it?" Gestapo asks.

"See?" I say to Mirriam.

"Now, wasn't that easy to clear up? No need to fight." Mirriam walks over to the counter.

"Who *is* she? Your stepmother?" Gestapo Girl asks.

"Thank God, no."

I'm about to explain when I notice she is scanning me from the top of my head down. Her eyes stop at my crotch, and she says, "Oh . . ."

Suddenly I hear my pulse in my ears. She's going to catch me, and then I'll be standing in front of Christian with Mirriam pointing an accusing finger at me while I plead stupidity. Convicted and banished.

She reaches for my elastic waist, and I back up. Jesus, what girl has that kind of, well, balls?

"Whoa, whoa," I say, hands in the air.

I turn to Mirriam, hoping for a rescue. She is unloading her books and drink on the counter. When she turns, she stares at me, hands on hips in a let's-see-just-how-big-of-an-asshole-you-are way, with a poor-Christian-to-have-his-thieving-brother-show-up-and-ruin-his-life look. I narrow my eyes at her, glaring. Gestapo has caught my expression, pauses, and follows my gaze toward Mirriam.

Mirriam calls from the counter, "Are you kids done yet? I'd like to go."

Gestapo turns back to me—my hands still frozen in the air, my telepathic brain pleading for God, Krishna, Zeus, something to intervene. She drops her hands to her sides, as if they were never on the attack, screws up her face, and mouths *blah, blah, blah*. She has recognized the common enemy—bossy, bitchy grown-ups.

I exhale and tug my shorts up higher on my hips.

"Maybe the queen found a better place to rule." Her full lips open and close as she fights a smile. "Let me just recommend this book to you. You know, for next time."

She grabs that book from the shelf behind me and hands it to me. The cover picture is someone's fingers pushing over a chain of dominos. *The Book Thief.*

I should probably go all indignant, but I laugh. What's the use in pretending? She's not going to bust me.

I say, "I'm without my books. Just moved. If it's all the same to you . . . ?"

"Dakota."

"If it's all the same to you, Dakota, I'll start with *Flowers for Algernon*." I reach for it, remember I'm broke, and turn the gesture into a point.

"I just thought you might relate." She quick-wrinkles her nose and replaces *The Book Thief.*

"I relate better to Algernon."

"The lab mouse they did all those experiments on?"

I glance at Mirriam, press my index finger to my lips, and whisper in my best Elmer Fudd voice, "Be vewy, vewy quiet. I'm being tested."

Mirriam is leaning on the counter, the toe of her shoe bouncing against the floor. She lets out a big sigh.

"Oh, sorry to keep you waiting," Dakota calls over to Mirriam. "We're short-handed—looking for help." She leans over to me, and I get that cinnamon-rain scent again, while she whispers, "Be sure to come back, okay? I'd hate to break up a chess set as gorgeous as this one."

Oh, yeah? Everything breaks up. It's called entropy.

Dakota walks over to the counter and starts scanning the bar codes of Mirriam's books. I watch her moving, lifting the books, bending them for their bar codes, and sliding them across the flat screen, her eyes on her work.

I begin reloading my bag. I'm not sure if she's actually pretty, or if I just think that now that she's saved my hide. When I pick up my camera, I figure I can decide later. I take off the cap, line up the shot, and adjust the aperture. The shot looks boring, so I wait until I can see her eyes flash or her head turn—something. She reaches down for a bag, and when she comes up, her hair swings, her lips puckered while talking, and I click.

chapter 5

after we get back and I've showered, I walk into Christian's bedroom, hoping he won't mind if I borrow some clean clothes. My jeans are covered in the dust of four states, my shorts in the sweat of an impromptu World Cup final.

A pile of *New England Journal of Medicine*s is stacked inside a wooden cube that doubles as a night table. His walls are empty: no framed pictures, no postcards stuck in the mirror's edge, nothing. His dresser is decorated with only the practical: an empty money clip, a change jar that's heavy on the silver, and a pocketknife. Who lives like this?

I find jeans and a black T-shirt with hot air balloons that says DUKE CITY MARATHON on it. The jeans are too big. I transfer my belt to Christian's jeans and roll up the cuffs.

My dirty clothes lie on his carpet like roadkill. Looking for the hamper, I open the closet. Something bangs against the inside of his door. I turn—his diplomas are framed and hung.

I stop. It's the first thing of him I've recognized: his pride twisted up with his modesty. Yes, he puts them up, but where no one can see. He probably stares at them every morning for a second, marking the distance between here and Chicago, but I'll bet no one knows they're here.

When he was in ninth grade, a girl he was trying to impress came over and laughed at his room, at how all his awards were framed and hung on his walls—his boyhood immortalized. He boxed all the awards and stashed the box in his closet. But some mornings, I would hear him slide the cardboard across the floor, and I knew he was looking at them.

Now I toss my clothes in his hamper and pull his high school diploma off the hook. I slide my thumb along the glass that protects his printed name: Christian Emerson Witherspoon. The University of Chicago, Laboratory School. On the one from NYU: Christian Emerson Marshall.

He was supposed to go to Northwestern or the University of Chicago, stay in the city. NYU was his third choice. I pulled the bratty little brother routine, hiding the letter for a couple of days before I let him see it. But when I gave it to him, he just chucked it on his desk; he'd already been accepted to Northwestern.

"An acceptance, right?" he asked when I picked it back up and handed it to him.

"Yes," I said, looking up at him.

"Good to have a backup, I guess," he said, and I knew

he was going to stay in Chicago, that he'd be around for another four years. At the time, I thought it was because of me. I never considered where he might go after he graduated from college.

Now I look at the NYU diploma and glance at the date.

Twenty-eight months ago. More than two years. Two years. What was I doing the day he graduated? It was the summer before I started high school, before I even met Lauren, but after my dad started in on me. The blister in my brain wobbles threateningly.

I want to prop the diploma on my fingertips like a waiter with a tray and then whip it over, slamming the glass against the dresser's corner. Shatter it. Anger coils in my chest, and I hold it there, refusing to let it strike. No smashing of sentimental objects. Too much like my father. Carefully, I rehang the frame.

When I hear Christian's voice, I jump and whirl around. But he isn't in the apartment; he's in Mirriam's place, and the walls are thin.

I'm tempted to stay and press my ear to the wall, but I figure I shouldn't add eavesdropping to my steadily growing list of crimes, bastard that I am. I start to back out of the closet, hoping a board won't creak, when I hear Mirriam say, "You'll have to think about it. I mean, he'll need to transfer into a school, and I'm just saying I can help you guys look into them."

"I can't make any plans right now. I don't even know if he's staying."

That stops me. I push through a row of shirts, step over to the wall, and lean against it. Cold plaster against one shoulder. I'm sandwiched between dress pants and a blue long-sleeved shirt. I push the sleeve out of my face.

"Wait, what? Isn't he?" There is a pause. "He's your brother, Christian. Family."

"And that means something different to me than it does to you."

There's another pause, and I picture her putting her hands on her hips like she did in the bookstore. Even without seeing her, I know that they're having a silence-off. I press my shoulder deeper against the wall and wait.

Wait.

Wait.

Finally, Christian caves. "You have a great family. You're always around for each other."

"So, tell me about it, about yours."

I hear the bedsprings squeak. When Mirriam speaks again, her voice is coming from farther down, so I know she's the one who sat.

"Tell me something, anything, about him."

Christian's voice is closer to me now. "He was a typical little brother. He was pesky and tagged along and . . . Okay, I remember something. One Halloween . . ."

Family legend time. I dressed up as a knight, and he bought me a sword with his own money since my mother wouldn't hear of such a violent instrument in the hands of her son. Ironic? Why, yes.

He tells her about our neighborhood's haunted house and the witch who lived there (really just a lonely widow, as we discovered later). For Halloween, she put cobwebs all over her gate, had howling ghosts that lurked in trees, and a mechanical skeleton in a coffin beside her door. But she gave out Mr. Goodbars, and not the fun-sized rip-off, but the real deal. We used to tell this one together to our family friends, each of us adding a part.

41

"Anyway," Christian continues, "it was creepy, so I went with him. One year . . ."

I was six, and you were eleven, I add my lines silently.

". . . Paul, a friend of mine, had dressed up as a skeleton. He must have done something to the widow's skeleton and climbed inside the coffin. So when we came to the door, this skeleton sits up and grabs my arm, its whole hand around my wrist. Paul starts to pull hard, so hard that I start falling in . . ."

And he's yelling, "Your turn in the box, mortal!"

". . . I'm freaked out, not just startled. Jace, who is beyond terrified, leaps *toward* the coffin . . ."

With my sword blazing.

". . . Plastic sword blazing," he echoes, and I bask in my newfound telepathy. "Starts beating this skeleton's hold on me, screaming 'Die, die, die!' "

My hand covers my mouth, and I start whisper-laughing. I hear him laughing with me. Plaster wall or not, we're together. Mirriam's laugh is high and strange, foreign to our duo.

All three of us ran when the widow/witch came out screaming and swearing about her skeleton. Christian had grabbed my hand and pulled me with him. There was a time when he wouldn't leave me behind.

"He obviously adored you," Mirriam says.

I pick up the blue sleeve and run my fingers along the cuff, thinking about that October. He was already a runner, training for Boston one day, and I couldn't keep up with him. So I would take out my bike and pedal along beside him, mile after mile, morning after morning.

Christian mumbles something that I recognize, even though I've caught only a few words. My mom used to say it to him when she wanted him to set a good example for me: *Every kid wants to be like their older brother.*

"What? Christian?" she asks. She waits. "Christian?"

"Yeah."

"Where'd you just go?"

"No, it's nothing. I was just remembering the skeleton." His voice is quiet, and without a breath, he rushes on, louder now. "What do you think of him?"

That pattern of speaking, it's a verbal tell. When someone would ask us how our mom was after she'd taken a good one from my dad, he would do that. His voice would get soft and hurried, sounding dismissive. "She's good," he would say, and then he would rush to another subject, always something spectacular like, "Did you know that [somebody or other's] comet will be showing up soon?"

Mirriam says, "I'm scared for him. I think if you don't let him stay, he will head into some real trouble."

"What are you talking about?"

After she snitches about the bookstore, she says, "He is going to need your help."

Silence.

She continues, "It isn't like you to . . . Why not let him stay?"

Silence.

So she says, "Did your father start hitting him before or after you left?"

Did he tell you that?

"Did he tell you that?"

"Don't you think I've seen enough abused kids to figure it out? He shows up here looking like that and suddenly needs to live with you?"

"Whatever happened to bring him here is his business. Even if he had told me, I'd keep it to myself."

Damn straight. Fraternal loyalty, lady.

"Okay, well," Mirriam says, "what are you going to do? Hide out here from now on?"

I hear the bedsprings whine a second time; he is sitting down next to her. "I know he's my brother, that I'm responsible for him. I just don't know how to live with him and not . . ."

"Not what?"

"I left. All right? I left. If I were to dig all that back up, it would be an ugly sight," he says.

"I'm sure. Why'd you leave?"

Here we go. I push hard against the wall, digging my shoulder in. I'm a student of Fightology.

"I've told you why. I didn't get along with my dad," Christian says.

"How about you tell me the whole story this time? You left because your father used to beat you, right?"

Fightology Lesson #1: Start with a loaded question.

After a pause, Mirriam says, "You know, this is what I'm talking about. Maybe *that's* something that should have come up."

"What difference does it make now? Or do you think that's all that defines me? Not New York, not running, not med school."

I start tugging on the blue sleeve.

"But that's exactly what I mean, Christian. Choosing med school looks different to me now. Telling me you wanted your own space so we should move next to each other looks different to me now, too."

"See, *that's* why I didn't say anything. Now you think

that taking it from my dad is everything, as if it's all I'm about," Christian says, his voice escalating.

Fightology Lesson #2: Don't be the first to yell or you risk being at fault.

"Not *all* that you're about, but important, essential even," Mirriam says, hurried and louder.

"It's not that important," he shouts. "It's not. I doubt you'll understand this—"

"Now I'm too simple to under—"

"It's only as important as I let it be. I don't think about it anymore. It's over and done with."

"Right, keep telling yourself that while you kick your own brother to the curb."

Fightology Lesson #3: Fights have their own rhythm. Words accelerate until they start to run over each other—faster, louder. I'm expecting Christian to start swearing, name-calling. I'm waiting, but instead I get a silence. What the hell is this silence about?

"All right. Maybe I should have said something about it." When Christian speaks, his voice is quiet.

"You shouldn't have lied."

I tug harder on the blue sleeve, and a white thread hangs off. I begin pulling it.

"I didn't lie about it. I just didn't mention it."

"Let's dispense with those semantics right now, okay? You've been *actively* covering it up. You've worked at it. An omission is an 'oops, I forgot'; a lie is making someone believe something false. I have to be honest with you. I'm not sure that I can be with someone who lies to me."

There's a long pause. The bed squeaks again, and Christian's voice sounds closer to me when he says, "Okay."

"So, wait, you're willing to let us go just like that?" she asks.

"You're the one deciding, Mirriam. I will not stand here and persuade you. I'd never try to get a woman to change her mind about leaving me."

I hold my breath. It's the first thing we have in common. Undeniably in common.

"You won't even . . . I'm not going to get . . . I don't even get an apology?" Mirriam says.

Oh, okay, I get it. It was just a pause, a glitch in the fight; they're back at it now.

"I'm sorry that it hurts you that I didn't tell you—" Christian says.

"Thanks. That was genuine." In spite of myself, I admire her sarcasm.

"But I met you when you were getting out of social work. And I remember you said—the first night we slept together, we were in bed—and you said, 'I'm not sure I can handle all that sorrow 24/7.' "

"I said that?" There's a quick pause. "But those kids were hopeless, no future. They were broken."

"That's right. I'm not, and I wasn't going to be lumped in with them, with something you had to get away from."

Mirriam sighs and says, "See, now there's a reason I can understand."

I turn my back to the wall and lean against it.

"Are you all right?" Christian asks her.

"I'm all right; I'm just . . . I know it's hard for you to talk . . . I know that kids protect themselves and shell up and . . . the worse it was, the less they talk . . . I'm hurt. I thought we were closer."

"If it helps, this is the most I've said about it since I left Chicago."

"Oh, honey. You know you can't just keep it bottled up. You have to talk about it."

"Not now, okay? No more arguing?" he says, his voice worn out.

"Not now."

I wonder if I'm a broken kid. Was Christian ever broken? My mother would say, *No, too strong,* and would sneak a satisfied smile at her folded hands.

What about me, Mom? I would ask.

And the smile would leave her.

She would be right.

I hear a shuffle of feet against the floor as Christian walks toward Mirriam. In my imagination, he is kneeling beside her, putting his head on her lap. She might stroke his hair and then, with her hands on his cheeks, lift his head and kiss him.

Through the wall, I hear Mirriam moan.

O-kay, if I stay in this closet any longer, I'm going to require therapy. That is, more therapy.

Is that what a fight is like for normal couples? Is this what people are supposed to do to make up? I remember Lauren and I making up after our first and second breakups. It was probably as loud as our fights. We were so driven about it. In our hurry, our teeth clanged against each other, and I backed her against a wall. I pressed hard against her while her teeth drew blood from my shoulder. Come to think of it, I'm not sure we weren't still fighting.

I push myself off the wall, shove through the clothes

and out of the closet. The pink shag brushes my feet as I walk to the living room.

The apartment suddenly seems cramped. There's nowhere to move. I try walking a loop from the couch to the desk to the kitchen and back again, but they are only about six steps apart.

In Chicago, I knew everything. I could look at the sky and know how warmly to dress; I knew where every street led, and where every fight would end. I could look at my father and know when to keep my mouth shut, when to piss him off so I could take the hits for my mother, and when only his wife–punching bag would do. I understood when a fight was coming, how fast it was going, where it was going, everything. Fights have a rhythm; they do. I swear it. And they don't end up like that. Not where I'm from.

What am I doing here? I can't even breathe right in this too-thin air.

Should I drive nineteen hours straight back and apologize until he opens the door?

My brain jumps to the night I left. My father said, *If you come back, I'll kill her.*

I look at the phone on Christian's desk. *Can't go back, can't go back.* But I can talk to my mom. I can hear something I know, something I recognize. He never said I couldn't call, and it's not like he's looking for me.

I pick up the phone, turn it on, and dial my home number. Out the window, I stare at a swimming pool in the courtyard. I haven't seen or heard anybody use it, even though it's Sunday. Maybe it's because of the green patches of growth on the bottom.

Ring. Ring. Ring.

Maybe she's not home. I glance at my watch. 2:08 here, 3:08 in Chicago on a Sunday. Where is she?

Ring, says the phone.

Thu-dump, says my blood.

Do I leave a message?

Ring.

It's not like my father would call me back and invite me home.

What could I say on the machine? "When, when, when?" That would do the trick if I wanted him to break her arm. Or worse.

Ring. Click. "You've reached Judge Witherspoon and his family. Leave a message so one of us can get back to you," comes my father's mechanized voice.

I hang up as I hear the beep.

I go to Christian's computer and wiggle the mouse. Before his homepage is even open, my fingers go on autopilot, calling up my e-mail. Where the hell is my mom?

New Mail! it tells me. I click on it and find four e-mails. Two are junk. The other two: one from Edward, RE: Monday after school by the fields. The other from Lauren, RE: Shithead.

Nice.

Should I open Lauren's and reply? I hesitate. That blister is still too sore. I don't want to read it, don't want to think about our fights, making up. None of it.

Maybe I don't have to. Look at how Christian did it. He never looked back. That's what I need to do. Forget about Lauren, forget about Starbucks, forget the whole thing. If you leave a blister alone, it disappears eventually; its fluid gets reabsorbed, and no mark is left. I'm here now. That's all that matters. Yes, a new life. Out with the old. I trash both the e-mails, hit Compose, and start writing to my mom.

I made it here okay. He looks good,
different, older. Come see? When? Can't
keep tabs on you from here. Reply ASAP
or I'll drive back and get you.
JW

I read it over and over again. I hadn't known I was going to write that I'd get her. I wonder if Christian would come with me. We're older now. We could protect her together. We could get her out.

I don't send the e-mail. How can I drive back if I don't have any money for gas? How do I know what Christian wants? Hell, I don't even know if he wants me here.

I lean back in his office chair and realize that it swivels. I press my toes into the carpet and push off. Three-quarters of the way around. Push and whirl. The screen saver appears, and I watch a line zooming around in unpredictable patterns.

Why didn't I drag her into the car? Why didn't I grab her wrist and yank her through the damn window? Why didn't she get in on her own? She could have.

I push and whirl, thinking about that. I spin and spin until my stomach rises, and I flush hot. Too dizzy. I push away from the computer and put my head in my hands until the floor stops spinning.

I thought she stayed because we had nowhere to go, but the night I left I was sitting in my car, my speedometer's needle pointing to zero. While I was wondering who would take me in, she came out and handed me an envelope. Christian's address.

In the missing letter, had he begged her to come? Had he

told her she couldn't, that he wouldn't help her? No, when I arrived, he looked down the hall for her. Has he been waiting for her, year after year?

I look at my e-mail again.

When?

If I send it, she might refuse to come. She might admit that she'll never leave him. I delete my threat to come get her, replace it with:

I need to hear from you ASAP, or I'll send the police over to the house, report you missing, whatever it takes.

That ought to do it.

chapter 6

i'm practicing why-Christian-should-let-me-stay arguments. The "I'm so desperate" plea seems less than persuasive. I'm going to have to rely on familial affection. There's got to be some of that, right? Christian taught me how to ride my bike when I was four, how to read when I was six, how to throw a punch when I was seven. It can't just vanish. It hasn't for me. I'm still hoping for that reception where he's as happy to see me as I was to see him.

When Christian walks in, he looks me over and chuckles. I remember my too-big clothes and say, "I had to borrow some clothes, okay?"

"I can see that," he says, and tosses a brown paper bag at me.

It has a bagel with cream cheese, that is marred by long green stringy things.

"So finish eating, and we'll go shopping."

I take a breath and then fess up straight and fast. "I don't have any money."

"Right."

His eyes glaze over while his brain goes into problem-solving mode. I bite into the bagel and wish I could extract the spinach from the cream cheese while I watch him thinking. He inhales sharply. Ding! Solution found.

He walks to his desk and takes out a green American Express card from a drawer. He peels the sticker off the back of the card, gets a pen, and signs his name on the white strip. He doesn't hesitate. Christian Marshall.

Jace Marshall. That's going to be weird. Whether I stay or not, I'm now Jace Marshall. Leave all that Witherspoon crap behind.

"Well, clothes first, job next, okay?"

"Sure, okay," I say, but I don't move, not even as he gets his jacket and his keys.

Listen, I want to say, *I've just been killing myself in this desert, sweating out every drop of liquid in my body, trying not to think about this conversation. Can we just get it over with?* But I can't demand more. That's the problem of living off charity. Or rather, driving the charitable into debt.

"What?" he asks.

"Nothing."

He snaps the card down on the coffee table, sits on the couch, and lifts an eyebrow.

"I just want to know if I'm staying here," I say. "You know, so I know what to buy."

"You can stay if you'd like—"

"If I'd like?"

"As long as we can agree to some ground rules. If they don't sound good, we'll plan out your next move, okay?" Christian says, his voice calm.

I sit down on the two-person couch and face him. Stand for court, sit for negotiations.

"Rule One: You don't ask me questions, and I won't ask you, either."

"Sure, okay," I say.

He looks at me for a moment, chin tilting, eyes narrowing. "Really?"

"Yeah."

" 'Cause whenever you say, 'Sure, okay,' I'm not so sure."

What would you like me to say? Give me a script. "Well, no problem, then."

"Rule Two: You can't call Mom from my phone. I mean, from this phone."

I swallow, remember our caller ID at home, and consider confessing. I seriously doubt that would help my case.

"He's not looking for you anymore," I say. "He gave up a long time ago."

"Or maybe he just lost track of me. When the statute of limitations expired from the last time he hit me, he tracked me down in New York. That was when I changed my last name and studied in Spain for a semester."

"What happened when he found you in New York?" I ask Christian.

His jaw muscle jumps. "Rule Number One violation."

I suddenly get how my very presence threatens all he has done to escape, staying with the Costacoses, living family-less in New York, crossing the Atlantic and back. And

how that has made him shut down any familial affection,

how he probably had to freeze it out just to get by. The familial loyalty argument dries up in my mouth.

"Well, he won't be looking for me," I say.

"I wouldn't count on it."

"No, he won't. It's not like you. I mean, *you* left *him.* That's not going to go over well, right? But he wanted me to go."

He goes still, and I can hear the question he won't ask: What did you do? But according to Rule Number One, he can't ask, and I'm not volunteering. If I told him that I hit my father, and hit him first, would Christian clap me on the shoulder or consider me too violent, too much of a risk, and kick me out?

He sits back and closes his eyes, and now I understand why he was so cold. He thought Dad was right behind me, and after five years of running, I had screwed that all up for him.

"Well," he says, "if you're right, that's huge. But I still don't want him to know where I am. So no phone calls to Mom. And don't give her the phone number."

"What if she needs to call?"

I feel like he's handing me a shovel—dig that grave. Her tombstone will read:

HERE LIES
JENNIFER WITHERSPOON
BATTERED WIFE AND ABANDONED MOTHER

"Go," she said, without touching my hand. *"And I'll come to you."*

I look into Christian's blue eyes. He's leaning forward, his hands together, watching me. This is a deal-breaker.

"Sure, okay." *The shovel cuts into the earth, the first gap for her grave, and I pitch the dirt aside. Swoosh.*

"Most of the money I send to Mom—" Christian starts.

"Whoa, whoa. You send her money?"

"At least stick by the rules for the length of this conversation."

"Sorry," I say.

"I send it to her so she can leave him . . ."

I stop listening. She had access to his address, to his money, and she stayed there? I don't get it. Why didn't she just get in the car with me?

"What?" I say, tuning back in.

"I send her cash so Dad can't track it from the account. I send it from a post office box without my address. And I use a phony name for her, so it will look like it's just the wrong address. Anyway, if you have to write to her, we can make that work."

"You send her cash?"

Christian nods.

I swallow, wondering if she emptied her stash for me or just gave me a month's worth. "Wait a minute. How did she get . . . She gave me a letter with your address on it."

"The one you slipped under the door? Yeah, I risked sending her one letter. I put in some phony letter, but used our code name, which, by the way, is Henry Higgins." He gets a private smile on his face, and I'm sure that that name is some joke that I'm not in on.

"I wanted her to have my address when I moved, so she would know where to come if she leaves him."

"E-mail?"

"Jace, come on."

I pick up the Amex card and press my finger hard against the edges.

"No e-mail." My stomach is hollowing out. "Except . . ."

He raises his eyebrows and stares at me. It isn't a bad way to test the water, to see if I can tell him about the phone call.

"Except that I . . . already did."

"Jace! Damn it."

I push the credit card as hard as I can into my finger and watch my skin whiten as it cuts off the blood flow.

He takes a deep breath. "I'm going to need you to start thinking before you act, okay? I'm not ready to raise a teenager. I can't be a better version of a father to you."

"I don't need a father." *I need you.*

But that won't matter one bit if I tell him I called. That has never mattered. He'll be just as fast—faster even—than my dad to throw me out on my ass. Why did I ever think any differently?

"He'll help you," my mom promised.

Yeah, right.

My fingers curl into a fist. I start to picture myself throttling Christian. *My hand will wrap around his throat; I can feel his skin bulging between my fingers. I'm going to hit him.* Control slips from me. My fist flies, but I choose the table rather than Christian's face. He jumps.

"Shit," Christian says. He runs a hand through his hair once and then twice. "I'm sorry. You didn't know that you couldn't contact her."

"For Christ's sake, don't apologize to me. I should apologize to your table." I bite hard, crushing my teeth together.

Why are people always doing that? Apologizing when I lose my temper.

"My table will survive." He pauses. "You have to not do that, okay? It's too weird. You looked just like Dad."

Now it's like he punched me. I have no air. Can't even

talk for a second. I place the credit card down with great care on the table. Inhale slowly. Exhale slowly.

Finally, I spit out, "Just tell me. What am I supposed to do?"

"Yeah, all right. E-mail is probably okay."

"He doesn't know she has an account," I say. "When I got one through school, I gave it to her, let her use the address as if it were hers."

"Good, then you won't need to call."

Do I tell him? Is that going to be my mantra if I live here? *Do I tell him? Do I tell him?* So far, I haven't mentioned that Mom is on her way; I haven't told him about the night I left, about Starbucks, and now this.

I decide not to worry about the phone call. I'll bet it would come up as a private number anyway, given how paranoid he is.

The rest of the rules are easy: don't do anything to get social services involved; stay in school. And then he says that from years of roommates, he has learned that roommates must contribute in at least two of three ways: emotional support, financial support, and keeping house.

I'm thinking, *No problem, I can clean, learn to cook. That ought to cover me,* when he says, "So you can help out around the house, and we'll find you a job."

And the door, the physical wooden door that I wedged my way through last night, sure, he opened that for me. But everything else is closed.

He puts his hand out. "Agreed?"

"Sure, okay," I say.

He looks at me hard.

"I mean," I say, "no problem."

I shake his hand. I should be grateful that I have a place to stay. Instead, I feel like I've lost my brother all over again.

chapter 7

Welcome to my new life. Part One.

It's more complicated than you'd think to establish new residency. My parents made it look easy the few times we moved. Even though I remember the move right after Christian bailed the best, I still didn't realize that they had found new schools and had gotten transcripts, transfer agreements, course accreditations, birth certificates, and given their pound of flesh. Two pounds, if you're under eighteen and can't sign anything without a legal guardian or parent. And that's just for school. Never mind car registry, plates, and insurance (which costs far too much when you're a male teenager, good-student discount and all).

It took me three days just to gather all the paperwork I needed, much less figure out what to do about it. While I'm 59 sitting here surrounded by papers all demanding a signature, wondering if I can lie my way around the forms, I hear the bolt slide, and Christian walks in. I want to ask him if Miriam can use her English-teacher privileges to cut through the red tape at the new school, but I can't read his mood yet. He glances at the littered papers, says nothing, and heads into his room. I hear him in the bedroom, putting his keys on the dresser, changing into his running clothes.

When he comes back, he's geared to the nines in sunglasses, a baseball cap, a chafe-free, meshy shirt, and tighter-than-I-ever-needed-to-see leggings. He pulls a piece of blank paper from the printer's tray and rests it on the desk. He scribbles on it, crosses it out, scribbles again, and a third time. He shows me the page.

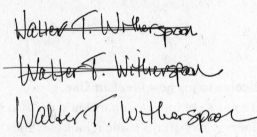

My father's signature.

"I'm out of practice. How's that one?" Christian asks.

"Use the first one."

"Really?" He frowns at it. "Muscle memory, I suppose."

He replicates that one on the practice page again before he begins signing. I stand up, hovering over him as I hand him page after page. When he's done, he returns the stack.

"Forgery is punishable by up to five years," I say.

"Me? Wasn't it you?" He claps a cupped hand next to his mouth and whispers loudly. "Take the heat, Toad."

I grin dopily, like a six-year-old with a new bike, since he resurrected my family nickname.

He continues, "You're underage, remember? Slap on the wrist."

The next morning, I'm armed with the papers, sitting in the parking lot of my new school, people-watching: three guys who apparently get their fix at Abercrombie & Fitch, a couple of duuudes who wear their hair long and remind me of Shaggy from *Scooby-Doo*, and a pride of girls with that redhead, who is a half-step ahead of her pack.

First days usually suck; everyone is trying to classify you.

Former classification: Cool kid. Jock. Smart. My status was enhanced notably when I started dating Lauren. By the end of freshman year, she had taken me from the seats in the middle of the school bus, the wannabe seats, all the way to the farthest-back seat, the one where you can stare out the back window.

New status: ?

I've switched schools before, but this time it will be different; this time I have an actual clean slate. So who will I be, remade? I ponder that for a second and then come up with an answer: I will be a bastard no longer.

I don't have any idea how to do that, but at least I have a goal.

The Land of Enchantment Charter School, a.k.a. LECS, is a three-story adobe building that blends into the brown buildings all around it, save for the four sets of doors in the entrance. The steps up to the doors are flanked by foot-threatening cacti. Inside, I find the office and go through the whole red-tape thing. They inform me that I'll have a buddy. Not a mentor, not a guide—a buddy. For a second, I wonder if I registered for the third grade by mistake. But

61

when I meet my buddy, I'm sure I'm in high school after all. It's the redhead from the convertible. Her name is Caitlyn, and her tank top is tight, and her hair is pulled back in a ponytail that is like something out of the fifties: all the hair gathered into a single bounce.

She turns around and gestures at her ass. She wears a pair of sweats that have WELCOME written on the butt. Well, that's direct.

"I just wanted to make you feel, well . . . welcome," she says, and laughs. "Are you gonna try out for the soccer team?"

"What are you? A cheerleader?"

She bats my arm as if we've been friends for years. "Nope, no cheerleaders here at LECS. We're all too serious for such things," she says, turning her face into a mock frown.

All right, so after two years in high school, there are some things you can tell right away. She has a pack; that I already saw. She's into soccer players. LECS is too small for a football team, so the soccer jocks rule the school here. Socially, this place will be a breeze as long as I stick by the girl with the following.

While we walk to the classroom, she tells me that LECS is a small Montessori school. Only 120 people, divided into four classes, all multi-age settings. Instead of group learning, individual lessons are taught by subject teachers who go from classroom to classroom, student to student.

"Weird, but cool," she says.

She's right. The classroom is weird. It's more like someone's house: there's a kitchen on one side where a girl is at the stove, grilling toast, while a younger guy washes some dishes. Against the far wall is a workshop with hammers, a table saw, a bucksaw, and rows of other equipment. Through an arch, I can see another room with only two computers.

Caitlyn tells me that this is the way you work here—independently. No blackboard or pre-ordained desks. I could drop and kiss the floor. No more lectures, no more passing notes and getting busted, no more "Back to reality, Mr. Witherspoon."

When the teacher, Mr. Ortiz, asks her to introduce me, she takes me around, her hand on my triceps, taking possession. But the kids all blur together. I notice only that there is no Dakota in this classroom, and I notice Eric, who says, "Didn't I see you shooting a soccer ball at the fields here last Sunday?"

"Yep."

I look him over. His jeans strain across his thighs (only soccer players and maybe gymnasts have this problem, buying jeans wide enough to accommodate our quads), his hair is cut clean and simple, and I can just picture him on the field. He'd be decent.

"You play?" I ask.

His mouth twists, and he crosses his arms. "I'm the captain."

Okay, then. Captain. Don't get into a pissing war with me. I don't want to brag, but I will if I have to.

"Where'd you used to play?" he says, pressing me. When I tell him, he says, "Are they good?"

I remember my bastard-no-longer pledge and don't tell him that we took third in State for the last three years, that I was bumped into first-string varsity this year, and that my nickname on the team is "Bullet." *Better than you, you piss-ass, pathetic wuss.* I just nod.

"You gonna try out?" he asks.

"I'll see what I can do."

After school the LECS coach, Coach Davis, is standing on the fields. He doubles as the history teacher. Or rather, he's the history teacher who doubles as a soccer-coach-wannabe, judging from the team's 0–2 record.

"My varsity team is pretty tight right now. And we're looking for a leader on the JV team, so let's just see what you can do, okay?" he says.

"Okay, sir."

Cardinal rule of sports: don't piss off the coach. Not unless you like running extra laps and sitting on a cold bench.

He smiles at the "sir" and says, "It's not the army. We're here to have fun, remember?"

To have fun? No. To complete, to battle, to win. Got it? Sir.

"Okay," I say.

He claps me on the back. "What are you waiting for, son?"

What kid has ever liked to be called "son"? I bite back my sarcastic remark and take off running. The team rounds the corner of the track. I sprint to catch up, and by the second length, that elephant is already resuming his comfy seat on my chest. Cannot, will not stop breathing.

After drills, we split into two teams, and he puts me in my usual spot, right forward.

The right midfielder, whose name I don't remember, passes to me—or it's supposed to be to me—but it hops to the sweeper. He cocks his leg. I turn on the speed, pull the ball from under his foot, and take off down the center. I look for anyone in the triangular patterns that all soccer players form to pass and move the ball, but there's no one.

Not even anyone running square. I face off against Eric, who is subbing for the goalie. O Captain, my Captain.

I feign a hard kick, presenting to the left. When he bites down on it, dropping to the post, I tap it right and wink. The bastard-no-longer pledge can wait.

The second string team beats the first string 3–2 and, bang, I'm on varsity.

chapter 8

Welcome to my new life. Part Two.

I yank on the door and walk into the air-conditioned cool of the bookstore, looking for Dakota, queen in my pocket.

At the chessboard, the queen has been replaced. I pick up the new one. Even though I'd love to start my Albuquerque collection with a set of twins, I put her back in her spot.

I am heading over to customer service when I spot Dakota crouching in the Sci-Fi/Fantasy section, pulling books from a cardboard box. She inspects the spines before placing them on the shelf. Her skirt pools around her, hiding her legs.

When I approach, she turns her head and stands, her

skirt rising like a curtain, revealing smooth skin. Her ventriloquist's mouth refuses a big smile, but the corners lift for half a second.

"Sir?"

"Call me Jace."

"Not until I have that queen in my hand."

"Hmmm." I tilt my head as if I'm considering her offer. "Nope. I'm not that easy."

"You're here to bargain?" she asks, her voice going high in disbelief.

"You bet."

"A Get Out of Jail Free card wasn't enough? You've got some balls."

I remember her hand reaching for my belt and glance down. "We're two of a kind."

Her mouth tugs into a half smile. "Your face looks better."

"Thanks."

The mountain has receded, and the red canyon in my forehead has faded to a scar. I appear normal.

We small talk: You don't go to LECS? No, she says; she's at La Cueva, and I learn that she lives across town, in a nicer neighborhood, but she drives here after school because she wanted to work in a bookstore—"better than a pizza joint"—and could get a job here.

"Where's your chaperone?" she asks.

"You think we need one?"

She lifts her eyebrows and puts her hand back out. "So, what's your offer for getting my queen back?"

"I was hoping you'd help me with something, seeing as how you know you can trust me." I pluck the queen from my pocket, close her in my hand for one last moment, and then let her roll down my palm. Dakota catches her.

I say, "You said you were looking for help?"

"You want a job here?"

"Yeah."

She smoothes out her skirt and seems to think about it for a second. I can see the "no" forming on her lips. But I jump in, King of Persuasion.

"I didn't have to come back, and it won't happen again, I swear. Besides, you need the help, and I have retail experience. Last summer, I worked at a shoe store, and before that—"

"You didn't have to steal her in the first place."

"I know," I pause. "But that was just a second, you know, an impulse. I've had some time to think about it, to decide, and then I came back. Come on, you can take credit for my moral rehabilitation."

Her lips tense up again in her not-a-smile smile. "Do you know anything about books?"

I nod.

"Okay . . . who wrote *A Tree Grows in Brooklyn*?" she asks.

"Betty Smith. Something harder."

"Name three Hispanic authors."

"Isabel Allende, Sandra Cisneros, and Pam Muñoz Ryan. I said, harder."

"Favorite Shakespearean line?" she says.

" 'I am in blood stepped in so far that, should I wade no more, returning were as tedious as go o'er.' " The phrase that kept playing through my brain on my nineteen-hour trip.

"*Macbeth.*" She pats my shoulder as she walks by me. "Let's go get you a job."

chapter 9

Christian and I finally went shopping, and now I'm surrounded by bags: two white plastic ones from the secondhand clothing store, another from Walgreens, and two adorned with red circles from Target. Underwear, toothbrush, sweaters, undershirts, T-shirts, long-sleeved shirts, jeans, and a jacket.

Christian bought linens "for the house": a couple of towels and bedding for the couch, which, I've discovered, pulls out. He even got me a backpack that he told me was a "belated birthday gift," a.k.a. guilt gift. I averted my eyes whenever the cashiers totaled. I pretended to be fascinated with a chili ristra, which, as it turns out, is a string of dried red chilies, but I saw enough to know his Amex bill won't be pretty. I can't imagine how I'm going to repay him.

Christian comes in from the bedroom and says, "I've cleared out the bottom two drawers of my dresser. Do you need any closet space?"

I say no, and we agree to keep my bathroom stuff on the bottom shelf of the medicine cabinet.

"Do you want soup for dinner?"

What I want is a stuffed pizza from Edwardo's. "Sure, okay."

I gather the bags, stringing their handholds up my wrist, and step down the hallway. Laden, I'm too wide to fit through the doorframe. I turn sideways and crab-step through. Gravity pulls the bags off my arms, and I begin to organize: socks, underwear, undershirts on the left, T-shirts and long-sleeved shirts on the right. Jeans and sweaters in the bottom drawer. Everything lies down neat and simple. As if it belongs here. I smooth out the wrinkles on a folded sweater.

When I walk back to the kitchen, I see that Christian's cooking skills have not improved. The tomato soup is boiling over. Bubbles slide over the top and sizzle on the stove beneath while he sits on the couch with a textbook on his lap. I turn the heat off, pick up the spoon that has dripped tomato soup on the counter, and stir. I open his fridge and stare at its emptiness.

Milk and yogurt. One of the bottom bins is dark through the glass. I open it and find mushrooms, tomatoes, mushrooms, yellow asparagus, and more mushrooms.

"I thought I might steam some mushrooms," he says.

I get that I'm a beggar, but mushrooms? Soft and sticky and a flavor that makes me want to transfer the entire contents of the bin to the trash can. I mean, they *are* a fungus. Really, I want a pizza.

"Sure, okay," I say.

"Or not," he says, and I realize that I've given away my disgust for mushrooms.

I search the cabinets for something worth eating. Wheat Thins, whole-wheat pasta, brown rice, and an entire cabinet of tuna. There are cookies, but they're low-fat and from Nature's Choice; low-fat dessert is an oxymoron. His spices: salt, pepper, and—let's get crazy—onion powder. He has no taste buds and is out to kill mine.

At home, the cabinets always had some junk food: a bag of Fritos or a box of ice cream sandwiches. A stash my mom and I shared that was supposedly all for me. I wonder what she's doing for frozen pizza now.

My dad hated my affinity for junk food and said that Mom was ruining my tastes when she bought it. Too low-class for him, an echo of her factory-town past—another dig about how she married into money and away from food chosen by coupon, how she was the only one in her family to go to college, while he was third-generation Yale. I close the cabinet slowly.

"Is the soup ready?" Christian calls.

I tell him it needs to cool and check my e-mail. One from my mom. I open it, curse his download speed while I'm waiting, and read.

I skim for my answer:

glad you made it . . . miss you . . . tell him
I love him . . .

I find what I'm looking for:

Thanksgiving.

I go back and read the sentence:

```
I will come at Thanksgiving. I should
have the money by then.
```

She's on her way; she's getting out. I delete the e-mail, call up his calendar, and count. Just shy of eleven weeks. Seventy-six days.

I walk into the kitchen, glance at the finally-cool-enough-to-be-simmering soup, and watch the steam rising. I have no idea how to tell Christian she's coming. One family member descending was almost too much to handle. I remember how my clothes look in his drawers and decide the news can wait.

I look into the dining room/living room/office/my bedroom. Where will she sleep? He looks up at me as I stand in the doorway, my eyes roving for more space.

"Soup?" he asks.

He tells me where the bowls are, and I put them on the table. Christian stands up and gets a yellow highlighter from inside his desk.

"Christian?"

"Just one second," he says as he marks a passage in the book, the highlighter squeaking against the page.

"Mom wrote back," I say.

The highlighter goes quiet.

"She sends her love," I say.

"Right."

"Right?" No *"Tell her I love her, too"*? Not even a *"How is she"*? They used to be so tight that my dad would half-joke, calling Christian "Oedipus" just to watch them both

squirm. Of course I didn't get it at the time, but reading that play subsequently freaked me out.

"She seems all right," I say.

"Oh."

"How well do you guys get along these days?"

"Rule violation," he says.

"Exception."

We used to recite legal tidbits to each other all the time. I was shocked when I found out that most nine-year-olds don't know that *res ipsa loquitur* is Latin for "the thing speaks for itself" and is a legal term that shifts the burden of proof to the defense. Now I slide into our familiar legalese.

"Need-to-know exception. I need to know so I can figure out what to say."

"We get along fine. She doesn't write me back."

I am too thrown to respond. Whenever my dad was out, she started with the, "Remember the time Christian won that marathon?" "I wonder what he's doing today?" *Do you think he still runs, still eats, still breathes?* Until I was ready to ask her if she had noticed that I was still playing soccer, eating, and breathing.

I place the spoons out slowly.

"I asked her not to," Christian continues.

"How come?"

"Tell her I'm fine, all right?"

He goes back to the couch, closes the book, and puts it on the corner of his desk. He is putting the highlighter away when we hear a knock. I have a crazy panic moment, thinking that Mom is on the other side of that door. But it's just Mirriam, bringing over dinner.

After they kiss hello, I take the bowl from Christian and put it down. Real food. Chicken, snow peas, and bamboo shoots, too. I might drool.

In a few minutes, we have places set and food served. Christian chooses the soup; Mirriam and I don't. I heap rice on my plate and ladle her concoction on top of that. I wish for chopsticks. Eating Chinese food with a fork feels like I don't know better.

When I take a bite, flavors explode on my tongue.

"This," I say with my mouth half full, "is great."

Mirriam smiles, takes a bite, and then says, "So, Jace, tell me about Christian. I haven't met anyone else from his—excuse me, I mean from *your*—family. I want the dirt." She smiles big. Suspiciously big.

Christian's elbows press tight against his waist. He stares at me, wide-eyed. I put down my fork, wipe my face with my napkin, and begin.

"Let's see, there was the time when he . . . Wait, no, that was me. Um . . . How about when you . . . ? Hmmm . . . Me, me, and me." I shake my head. "The most remarkable thing about Christian is that he has no embarrassing stories. Isn't that embarrassing enough?"

Christian's elbows release. This guy is so closed off, I'll need a crowbar.

He gives Mirriam a quick victory-look and then glances at me and does one of those small "thanks" nods. I return a "you're welcome" nod. Mirriam scowls, slumps back in her seat, and jabs at her food.

"Wait, wait," I say. "There was the time when you forgot the blender top."

He smiles, so I tell her about how we tried covering up blueberry splatters on the ceiling with leftover white paint.

But it was the wrong shade, so we had to paint the whole ceiling before my parents got home. They couldn't figure out why our house reeked of fumes.

We do the "and how was your day?" thing; I bring them up to speed on my first days: No, so far, I haven't found a niche. Yes, the classes seem all right. My favorite subject is English, which makes Mirriam smile, and I'm just grateful I didn't get her assigned to me. Then we get off of me, and I ask Christian, "How're your marathon times? Still aiming for Boston?"

"They're okay."

"He's being modest," Mirriam says. "He made the last one in under three hours."

"Boston, here you come."

"We'll see," Christian says.

"Why not?"

He shrugs and glances away. Warning: Lie impending. "Money."

"Christian told me that you're looking for a job?" says Mirriam.

"Got one."

I tell them about the bookstore gig.

"That's great, Jace. Congratu—" Christian says.

"Christian," Mirriam interrupts. "I'm not sure he should do that. I mean, he does have homework, and LECS is a demanding school."

"I'll be all right," I say.

"I mean . . . It's not the . . . If he has to quit something, maybe it should be this job. Soccer is a great way to stay—"

Christian drops his spoon loudly into his bowl.

Mirriam corrects herself, "To meet people. It just . . . It seems like a lot of pressure. And what happens if it gets to be too much? If he has to make money . . . It can just invite trouble."

"So far, it seems fine," I say. "The homework isn't hard, actually. Easier than my old school."

A smile plays on Christian's face until he takes another sip of soup to hide it.

"But the grading might be harder," Mirriam says. "And you might want to try to get good grades."

"He gets good grades," Christian says. "I mean, don't you?"

"Yeah."

"Good enough for college?" Mirriam asks.

"Coll-ege?" I say, as if the word is unfamiliar to me. Christian shakes his head at me, so I modify my tone. "I'm applying to Stanford next year."

She stirs her food. "That's a good school. He'll need excellent grades. For students to succeed at LECS, they need to spend about three hours a night on homework and more on weekends."

"Really, I've got it covered," I say.

I'm in the same room or hadn't you noticed?

Mirriam starts to object, but I go on, "If my grades fall, Christian and I will decide what to do, okay?" *My life, lady. And by the way, there's the door.* "Until then, I don't have any reason to quit soccer or my job. Besides, the season's so short. We've only got a couple of months left."

Mirriam sits back, her eyes narrowed.

There's a pause, and I dig into the garlic chicken.

"Jace," Mirriam asks, "do you play chess?"

I stop, fork in midair. I don't know whether my cheeks are suddenly so hot from embarrassment or anger. Now I get why Christian was glaring at her earlier. I've been dubbed: Kid-At-Risk. I'll start stealing for profit or peddling drugs if I'm required to bring in cash.

"Mirriam," Christian says, a warning in his voice.

"What? He seemed interested in the chessboard, that's all."

After a kid at my school lost it and beat his teammate with a lacrosse stick, the school required all students to attend an anger-management workshop. What did the anger-management guru, a blond-haired twenty-something with horse teeth, say? Count to ten and visualize. One, two, three . . . my dad would have the table overturned by now. Four, five, six . . . twisting an arm behind her back. Just a split lip and I would erase my embarrassment right out of the world. Seven, eight, nine . . . Counting is not working, and I have a feeling these are the wrong visualizations. Something else. Breathe, right. Didn't horse-teeth lady say "breathe"?

Mirriam continues, "And anyway, Christian, you wanted to know about his interest in chess too, didn't you? I mean, you said—"

I stand up so fast that the chair flips over. Suddenly the guru appears before me, screaming, "And walk away. WALK AWAY!"

Right. Walk away.

"Thanks for the food, Mirriam. It was really good," I say. "For the record, I've never played chess in my life."

My plate is shaking as I scrape my leftovers back into the bowl and walk into the kitchen. I don't want to go back out there, but there's nothing to do in here but shake and breathe. I feel both of them staring at my back. I glance around for something, anything, to do. I will . . . wash dishes. Yes.

I turn on the faucet, and water pours loudly into the metal basin. Their voices start squabbling behind me, but I can't make out the words. I don't really want to hear them; it's enough that I walked away. *Don't break the plate.* I rinse it clean and put it in the dish rack. I clean the soup pot and my fork, and then there's nothing else.

Damn my lack of bedroom, my lack of door.

I settle on an urgent need for coffee.

When I turn off the water, I hear Mirriam say, "He's already stealing for the fun of it—" and goes silent as she registers the quiet.

I dry my hands on my jeans and return. "I could do with a coffee. Anybody want some?"

They both shake their heads. They don't say anything as I right my chair, get out my car keys, and put on my new jacket; I escape before the explosion.

When I'm in the car, I remember that I don't have any money for coffee. I drive the one route I know, to the school and back again, so I won't get lost.

I slip in the apartment building's security door as someone is walking out, and I had left Christian's door unlocked.

Christian is lying on the couch with his feet up, a book unfolded on his chest. No Mirriam. He watches me through eyes dragging against sleep.

"Hi," I say. "Didn't mean to wake you."

He closes the book and gets up. He stumbles to the bookcase and back and then, as if the couch cushions are heavy, slowly pulls them off. He must have been in a deep sleep. I'm surprised he doesn't zombie off to bed. I yank the foldout's handle, and the bed lets out a long, metallic moan. He gets the sheets from the table and hands me a corner. Together, we unfold it and tuck it in under the mattress. This isn't roommate behavior. It's brother behavior.

"I'm sorry about Mirriam. About tonight. I shouldn't have dragged you into our problems."

Oh, I see. It's guilt behavior.

"Mirriam did the dragging. Other than cooking, what do you see in her? Is it an older-woman thing?"

"Jace," he says, with a quiet reprimand in his voice.

"What? So far, I've seen her pry and fight."

"Fair enough. She has not been at her best, but that's my fault. I put her in a situation where she felt like she had to pry, and she's not good at that sort of thing." He shrugs.

"So?"

"She is a fighter."

"Yeah, I got that," I say.

"Not like that. She just doesn't put up with any nonsense. And you have to admit that she's pretty smart."

I grab the top sheet off the table and hand him the corners. "Hmmm," I say, not convinced.

He continues, "So, where did you go? There's a Satellite coffee half a mile away. Did you go there?"

We spread out the sheet. He leans over and starts brushing away the wrinkles. He brushes more and more until it's smooth. And then he keeps on going. Brush, brush. I watch him, my head tilted, trying to figure out this sudden need for a lake-smooth surface on a bed I'm about to crawl into.

"Did you think I wasn't coming back?"

He grabs the blanket from the table, and it spills open. I pick the ends up off the floor, and still he doesn't say anything. His face is pale, and his jaw is tight. While we are putting the blanket, folded, on the foot end of the bed I'm thinking, *He was sleeping out here, waiting to see if I would come back, waiting to hear the buzzer. Maybe he was hoping I'd come back. Maybe he was hoping I wouldn't.*

Finally he says, "We didn't give you much incentive to stay."

I'm too confused to answer. Does he want a brother, after all? I have a sneaking suspicion that I'll wake up in the middle of the night, knowing how to respond.

He sits down on the bed. "I had forgotten about painting the ceiling together."

He looks at the wall, but it seems like he's looking beyond it, looking back. Maybe he's seeing us again. Me up on the ladder, him on the counters.

"In spite of Dad and everything, we had some good times," I say, sitting down next to him.

He looks me over, and I sit still and tall. After he makes his assessment, he pats my leg in a you're-a-good-kid gesture. He gets up and walks to his bedroom.

"Good night," he calls over his shoulder.

I kick off my shoes, realize that we forgot to buy pj's, and strip off my jeans and shirt. I crawl under the covers. Much better than a lumpy couch—a lumpy mattress.

When I'm lying there, I realize what I should have said to his "we didn't give you much incentive to stay."

"You're the incentive."

during my lunch period, I'm at a computer in the media center, trying to adjust my pictures in Photoshop, when I hear the door swing open. Mirriam is *click-clacking* over to me in her low, all-day-long teacher heels. She looks up and down the row of computers, as if she's registering the total emptiness before she sits next to me. I glance at the seeds that fleck my sandwich.

"What are you doing?" she asks, twisting a blue coffee cup in her hand.

I recognize it from the morning tea ritual she and Christian have going: whoever has the blue cups makes the tea that morning and brings it over. Part of their whole so-together-in-our-separate-apartments thing.

"Just compositing an image."

She smiles. "Do you eat here every day?"

I shrug. "Like you said, I haven't got a lot of time, and no one disturbs me here."

"Except me," comes a voice.

We both turn. Caitlyn walks in from the other side and asks if she's interrupting.

"No, no. I have to go, anyway," Mirriam says, and goes *clickity-clacking* out. Before leaving the media center, she glances back, a little smile on her face, now that I'm less pathetic.

I, Mr. Chatty, can't think of anything to say.

"You shoot pictures?" She opens a tub of hummus and unwraps a pita. She leans over to see what I'm working on. "Who's that? Girlfriend?"

"Coworker," I say.

"Good. Where do you work?" she asks, and then Mr. Chatty takes over.

Blather, blather, "bookstore." Blather, blather, "Dakota." I hardly care what I'm saying. I'm talking to another kid. Someone who is listening to me.

When the bell rings and the other kids file in, Eric spots us. He sets his jaw and drags Caitlyn off to work on some Bio thing they're doing together. He keeps looking over at me the rest of the afternoon. At some point, I'm gonna get it.

There should have been a loudspeaker announcement at practice: Today the part of Coach Davis will be played by Eric Beise. Since the coach has a teachers' meeting on Wednesdays, Eric runs warmup and drills.

We huddle up at Eric's command, but Eric is looking beyond the circle, at the edge of the field behind me. I follow his gaze over to Caitlyn. Next to her stands her second,

Heather, a girl who tries to mimic Caitlyn's ponytail, but instead of bouncing up in a neat, organized curl, Heather's hair rebels into frizz. Caitlyn is talking, and Heather is nodding.

When Caitlyn sees me watching her, she yells out, "I never knew soccer shorts could be so hot!"

I grin back.

When it's time to run the fields, Tom, the right forward I just busted to the bench, falls in line in front of me. He has to be at least half a foot taller than I am, so I can't see the line over him. The elephant on my chest has started to lose weight, but I'm still at the back of the line, waiting for the beast to sit down and cut off my oxygen.

"Last to first," Eric screams from the front of the line. A collective groan floats up and then is peppered with complaints. "Ah, Eric. Come on, man." "Why do you want to start us off with that?"

I have no idea what they're talking about, so I keep quiet, checking my steps.

"Last to first," he shouts again. "Marshall. Move it."

I step out of line a little to see around Tom the Giant so I can learn the drill from Marshall, whoever he is.

"Marshall, damn it." No one reacts. "MARSHALL!"

Oh, right. That's me. "What?" I say finally.

"Last to first. Go." Eric veers off the front of the line and waits for me to catch up. "Too good for drills?"

Tom says, "Eric, lay off, man. He doesn't know the drill. Follow me, Jace."

He peels off the line and sprints, his long legs chewing up the field. I swing my arms faster, and my legs automatically keep pace. (A trick Christian taught me way back when.) I don't even notice that I'm getting out of breath or

83

tired until we get to the front of the line and Tom veers in at the lead. He stretches his hand out and motions me to pass him. I want air. I inhale fast, exhale faster. I push harder against the ground and overtake him. In the lead, I get to watch the mountains commanding the earth, obliterating the horizon. But that lasts only about half a second before the whole team passes me, one by one, and I'm in the back again.

I get it now. Last to first.

Once more around the field, but when we're huddled up, I see Eric cheating out to the side so that Caitlyn can see him. He stretches his arms up and peeks around them. I look over at the girls. When Heather pulls out a box of Virginia Slims, Caitlyn's mouth turns down. Heather slides a cigarette out. Caitlyn slaps Heather's hand, and the white rod falls on the grass. Caitlyn's voice rises, and I can make out what they're saying: "God, Heather. You know I'm, like, trying to quit."

"Oh, yeah, I forgot," Heather says, and I see her sneak a smile as she replaces the lighter in her purse.

"Hey, Marshall," says Eric. "Soccer now. Perverted gawking later. Try to keep up."

The team laughs, and I go hot. His eyes flick back to Caitlyn. This has nothing to do with soccer and everything to do with Caitlyn's attention. I remember how I thought they were dating when I first saw them in the convertible.

"Whatever you say, O Captain, my Captain."

"You've got some mouth, you know? Want me to fix it for you?" He steps toward me.

Okay, so I get that you don't disagree with coaches. Other players are a different story.

I laugh long and loud, sure to draw Caitlyn's eye. I

check. Both she and Heather have gone still, in eyewitness mode.

"Don't make an ass of yourself. Not when she's watching," I say.

Tom grabs my arm. "Hey man, leave it alone, okay? You don't know what you're talking about."

We both ignore him, staring at each other, and Eric says, "Somebody's gotta put you in your place."

I set my teeth against each other and grind them together. I yank my arm free. My place, if he must know, is on top of him, pinning him under my knees, wailing on him.

Tom grabs my arm again. I shake him off, turn, place both hands on Tom's chest, and shove. He doesn't move his feet for balance; he just begins to go down. His eyes widen and before I know it, I've reached out for his jersey and caught it.

God, what is wrong with me, going after bystanders?

Tom pushes my hand off. "You're on your own," he says.

"Sorry," I start to say, but Eric pushes my back, and I whirl to face him.

I stare at Eric. He's probably a good twenty pounds heavier than I am, but a little shorter. I've got the reach and, let's face it, the experience. His eyes scan me, sizing me up.

"Eric!" a high-pitched voice calls out.

Caitlyn is walking onto the field. She passes by me without a glance, her ponytail bouncing. And I think, *See, there you go, just when you have a girl painted in black and white, she goes and does something unpredictable and, you know, decent.* She breaks up a fight by simply stepping on a field, undoes the rivalry she started by not looking at me as she passes by.

"Eric," her voice changes, softer than I've heard it before, as if this conversation isn't happening with a circle of guys around them listening to every cadence, as if her words are just for him. "Heather is . . . Well, she's a bitch. Can you take me home after practice?"

"Um, sure." He keeps his eyes on me, lifting his eyebrows, which makes me want to land one on him.

"Good." She kisses her finger and puts it on his chest. Her red nail flashes. "You're such a good friend." She barely hits the f-word, glancing off it before picking her way to the sidelines.

I'm surprised she didn't dig her nails into his chest and pry out his heart. But no, that would have been too direct. Just a little bit of flesh at a time. Makes the fun last longer.

When she passes by me, she winks. Worst part is, I wait until Eric can see me, and then I wink back. I'm not doing very well on my bastard-no-more pledge.

Truth is, I just miss Lauren.

after working an extra shift at the bookstore, where Dakota wasn't, I pull into the parking lot at Christian's and turn off the headlights. As I'm clicking them off, I realize that it's eleven-thirty, and I didn't call. Crap. My boss asked me to come in on my night off, and I said yes without thinking about Christian.

I clench the steering wheel. Gotta face the music.

I walk into the foyer and hit the buzzer, wishing I had a key and could slink in. The landlord is out of town for a week, and Christian couldn't get an extra. Damn landlord. Doesn't he appreciate the importance of his job? I mean, people rely on him.

Christian's voice comes through, "Jace?"

He sounds out of breath. I. Am. Screwed.

I trudge up the stairs. For two flights, I wonder just how pissed he's going to be, and my throat is tight with anticipation. On the third flight, I remember his damn ground rules. And by the time I've reached the fourth, I'm spoiling for the fight.

I push open Christian's door. He is sitting at his computer, the chair turned to face the doorway as I enter. His legs are crossed, and his hands are crossed. Crap.

Fightology Lesson #4: Holding it in is the ammunition-building phase of a fight.

Now who resembles my dad?

Mirriam is standing behind him with her hand resting on his shoulder. Her fingers work at his muscles, the end of a back rub.

"Where have you been?" he asks, his voice quiet.

"Work."

"You don't work late on Monday nights," Mirriam says, smirking; she thinks she's caught me in a lie.

She puts a hand on her hip, and I glare at her.

Christian swivels toward her. "Thanks, hon," he says. "I've got it from here."

She lifts her eyebrows, her forehead erupting into waves. "Okay. But tell him what a problem this is. You know, because I wanted to call the police. He needs to—"

"Mirriam," he says, without even a hint of the irritation I'm feeling. "Thanks for waiting with me."

She sighs and kisses him on the cheek. She looks me over and shakes her head before she goes. I swallow down the bitter invective that threatens to leap through my teeth. When she leaves, she takes the heat out of the room, and I'm back to the cold, knotted-stomach phase.

"I'm sorry, Christian; I didn't mean to make you worry,

but, I didn't know the phone number here; I forgot it, which is funny considering how many times I wrote it down on all those forms, but I couldn't remember it, and then—" I can't believe I'm doing this. I sound like a regular kid. I'm not standing silently without an explanation, knowing anything I say can and will be used against me when his temper flares.

"Slow down, Jace. Where were you?"

"I was at the bookstore. I picked up another shift."

"Really?" His voice goes distant. "Another shift."

"Really."

"And when you forgot the number, you didn't think to look it up?" He still doesn't believe me.

"Where do you think I was? Out scoring drugs? Does Mirriam think I'm at risk for that, too? Or are you worried I stole some TVs and got held up trying to hawk them?"

"Hey, don't get pissy with me. You're four hours late."

"You didn't mention a curfew in your 'ground rules.' " I gesture the quotes with my fingers.

He jumps to his feet, and I don't move back, but my breathing is fast. As he lifts his hands, I watch to see if they're fisting. I relax my muscles so it won't sting as much if he belts me. But he puts both hands in the air, palms facing me.

"You know what? You don't want to call? Fine. Come and go as you please." He walks to the bedroom. "Your key's on the table," he says, just before he shuts the door.

I listen to the door latch.

The silence settles.

I walk to the table and see a key next to a plate of cold food. He made dinner. Granted, it looks unappetizing— runners' food, fish on top of broccoli and mushrooms. But it also looks like a lot of work compared to a Swanson frozen dinner.

I blew that all to hell. Stupid, stupid. I shove the chair away from the table and plop into it. But *he* was the one who said that we were going to be roommates, that I had to contribute with money and labor only. So what does he expect from me?

I choose to ignore how he has waited up for me. I poke at the cold fish. I couldn't eat it now, anyway. Hunger has drained from my stomach.

I hear the click of the door to his bedroom and turn around in my seat.

He walks past me without a look, gets a thick textbook from his desk, and starts back to his room.

"Christian," I say as he's passing.

"What?" He stops but doesn't face me, his gaze glued to the textbook.

"Thanks for the key."

"You're welcome."

He takes a step, but I stop him with, "No, I mean it. And I'll call you from now on if I'm going to be late."

He sighs, tugs a chair out, and sits opposite me. "I'm not like Dad. You know that, right?"

I swallow and wonder if I flinched when he lifted his hands.

He continues, "You don't have to mouth off to me to bring it on faster or to direct the anger toward you. There's no Mom here to protect."

"I know. Sorry."

"It's okay; I understand it, I do. But you're out now, and you'll be okay, I promise. Just try to relax, okay? It'll take time to adjust, to stop shadowboxing."

It's weird when someone gets you, understands what you would never say, not even to yourself. It's so weird that it makes my throat tighten up again. When I speak, my voice comes out small.

"How long did it take you? To stop shadowboxing?"

"There wasn't a specific date. It was more incremental than that. When you pummeled the table the other day, I didn't anticipate it. So we can assume it's less than five years."

I nod. "Christian? Thanks."

He stands and grabs his book. "You might want to apologize to Mirriam, too."

"Really?" I grimace.

He turns the book face up and examines the cover again. "I'd like it if you could try to get along with her."

Great. To fit in his life, I've gotta make nice with Witchy Girlfriend? What's next?

"I'll try, but I'm not promising anything," I say.

"Fair enough. Are you going to be working four nights a week, then?"

"No, someone was sick."

"Good." He pauses. "I mean, I didn't mean that it's good that someone was sick."

"Yeah, I know what you meant."

I pick up the house key and gesture to my backpack, which is propped against the couch. He leans over and tosses it to me. I get my keys, pry the ring open, and jolt the new key along between the two metal circles until it snaps into place. It will be easy to spot, the gold one.

"The landlord came back early?" I ask.

"Mirriam gave it to you. She wanted to apologize for the other night."

I sigh, press my palms against the table, and stand up. As I head toward the door, Christian claps me on the back.

"Don't take any shit, okay?" he says.

"Right."

Two minutes later, I'm standing in Mirriam's kitchen with my eyes stinging from the onions she is cutting. Her stove is crowded with a fat covered pot, a deep saucepan, and a shallow frying pan. The burners are turned on, and everything seems busy. I'm waiting for the hand-on-hips posture or the lecture-tone, but she just says, "Did you and Christian work that out?"

I nod and thank her for the key.

"Sure. It's your house now. I owe you an apology for tonight, too. I'm just protective of Christian."

She thinks he needs protection from me? She thinks I'm that bad? Hell, she's probably right.

She continues, "He's just so closed off about what happened that I know he was badly abused."

I don't say anything, but I wonder how he explained away the skin graft. Maybe it's not noticeable now.

She puts the knife down and wipes her palms on her apron. She starts toward the fridge, and I swing the door open for her. She ducks in, grabs, and emerges with tomatoes and some kind of green herb in hand. I eye them suspiciously.

"I guess you don't like tomatoes?"

"Depends. Not raw or anything, no."

Holding the tomato in her hand, she begins cutting down toward her palm. She turns the tomato over a couple of times, still cutting. Finally, she throws the tomato cubes into a pan and they sizzle.

"What do you like?"

"To eat?"

She nods.

I still don't answer. I'm wondering what I'm supposed to say. Do I admit that I have two speeds when it comes to food—gourmet and junk—that I'm a closet Twinkie fiend and that Ho Hos are my friends? Or do I stick with the beggars/choosers model?

She opens a cupboard, and I see a bag of chips. My stomach roars back to life.

"You can have some," she says.

"Really?" I unclip it and dig in. "You're making dinner *now*?" I ask, looking at the time.

She says she didn't get anything earlier and doesn't mention that I'm the reason for that. She just goes on, busying herself with pasta and pans. I can barely keep track of what she's doing. One minute she's at the stove, the next she's preparing ingredients. I remember watching my mother cook. It was one of the few times I could get her to notice me. She would look at me even while she stirred and sliced. It's only sixty-five days until she comes, and then maybe she'll make us her shepherd's pie.

"My mom likes to cook, too."

"Is that why Christian can't cook to save his life?" she asks.

I laugh. "He has no taste buds."

"Here," she says, handing me a knife. "Would you cut up the basil?"

"Okay," I say and pull off a leaf.

I try to get a comfortable grip on the knife. Truth is, I've never really cooked anything. Mirriam comes over to me. "Let me show you this trick."

She plucks a bunch of leaves and layers them one on top of the other, with the biggest leaf on bottom. Then she rolls it up tight. "Now try."

When I cut through, I end up with long strips of green unfurling.

"There you go. You're a natural," she says, and I know that I'm not, but she's a teacher, and that's what they say.

"Listen, Jace. Don't mess it up with Christian, okay? It might not seem like it, but he's trying really hard."

I probably shouldn't say anything to her, but I finally have someone who knows him.

"I never know what he's going to do. One second he's distant, the next . . ."

"I don't think he knows, either. Be patient with him. He's trying to figure out family, and the only two modes he has is the protective big brother and the . . ." She looks like she's trying to find the words.

"High-alert orange?"

She smiles. "I was going to say, protective of himself. He'll probably flip between them a lot, you know. He hasn't . . . I mean, neither of you have had such a good experience with family yet."

"Yes, we have."

"I know about your dad, that he hit you."

"That doesn't mean you know a thing about our family."

She grips the cheese and concentrates on the grating. Then she stops. "Maybe you're right. What's your dad like?"

"He's considered one of the best judges in Chicago. And he isn't corrupt or anything."

"Is that the standard?" she says.

"You ever been to Chicago?"

She smiles and shakes her head. "No, but I've heard stories about the corruption."

"I remember this once, he went to bat for me against an algebra teacher, Mr. Phillips, that . . ."

"That what?"

"Nothing." I stir the tomatoes. "If I tell you, it will only add to your 'at-risk' diagnosis of me."

"I'm not that bad, am I?"

I listen to the tomatoes sizzle.

"Okay, I promise I won't judge you."

I'm skeptical, but I do notice that she hasn't asked me where I was or lectured me or anything. And Christian *did* ask me to try to get along with her.

So I tell her about this teacher, Phillips, who claimed that I cheated on a test because I got an A and everyone else got around a D. My dad demanded that Phillips devise a new, commensurate test. I got another A.

"But here's the thing: my dad never asked me if I cheated on the test; he knew I wouldn't. A lot of fathers would assume the teacher was telling the truth."

I want to tell her about the post–soccer game chats we'd have, but it's not a story per se. It's just a thing we would do. We would go into his study, and my mom would bring us lemonade—two glasses that she would chill in the freezer for a frosty look. She would lay a towel over the leather chair that seemed to sit there just for me and close the door on her way out. My dad and I would talk about scoring percentages, and he would tease me about how loud Lauren squealed when I scored. Or we would talk about Lauren being fickle. He knew she had cheated on me a couple of times. My mother never even knew we'd broken up. She thought we had been dating for eighteen months straight. She never really bothered to ask; she was too worried all the time about what made him happy, what made him mad.

"Is that done?" Mirriam asks.

"What?"

She goes through a quick chef-thing, measuring spices in her hand, pouring a little of this into the deep pan and some of that into the shallow pan and sniffing while asking me for the salt, the pepper—no, the red pepper. When she's satisfied, she mixes everything in the pasta. She fills a pasta bowl and says, "Would you taste some for me?"

I get a fork and a soup spoon. I sit down, put the fork into the pasta, rest it against the spoon, and twirl. I shove it in my mouth and close my eyes for a second. Nutty pasta and, what do you know, I like these tomatoes. When I open my eyes, she's staring at me with a little grin on her face.

"What?"

She gestures to the spoon, and I stop twirling the pasta.

"You're just a little more sophisticated than a lot of the teenagers I know," she says.

I put the bite in my mouth. "A big-city thing."

"Sure, your parents must have made an effort to take advantage of it."

"My dad did. My mom—not so much. He took me to fancy restaurants. And we would spend one Sunday a month at the Art Institute, looking at the new exhibits and the photography." I sound like a victim. "I'm not defending what he's done or anything. I just don't want you to think of him like that."

"Like what?"

"He doesn't have horns or anything."

"Jace." Her voice has gone soft and sympathetic.

Pity. *Just what I need.*

"It's all right to miss him," she says.

"Yeah, right. What's to miss? The name-calling, the heavy hitting?"

"I mean the times when he wasn't mad."

I pick at the basil with my fork and squeeze my teeth together. It's not really all right, is it? I mean, who would miss that bastard? Shouldn't I hate him, just simple, pure hatred? Shouldn't I write him a thank-you note for getting me out of there, for not wanting me around anymore?

Dear Dad,
*   You're not the father I wanted,*
either. Thanks for kicking me out.
*   Your ex-son,*
*   Jace Witherspoon*

"It isn't your fault," she says.

You think? Yeah, lady, I'm well aware. An unwanted image flashes: skin bulging through fingers as the grip around her neck tightens.

"Do you think that people can change? I sort of do," I say. *Or at least, I hope so.*

"You can't change him. Only he can make that decision."

"I know that. But"—I pause and steady my voice so it comes out casual, not as if her answer will control how fast my heart is beating—"people can change. Don't you think?"

She stands up and begins to pile the pans and bowls we sullied in the sink.

"Maybe," she says, but she means no.

I lose my appetite again and push the food away. She puts a dish down and stops, as if she's just thought of something else.

"Well, maybe sometimes. If they work hard enough."

Like if they change cities, change their name, and declare a bastard-no-longer pledge? Is that enough? I want to ask. Instead, I thank her for the dinner and go.

chapter 12

"**h**ey, **Dakota.** Have you got a minute?"

I've looked at her work schedule and know that she gets off now.

We walk out from behind the counter and head toward the café in the back. Her hair goes from blue-black to black as we step from the fluorescents into the low-light spot-light look. After we get our drinks, we find a two-person table and sit down, setting our cups on the mosaic tabletop.

"What's the occasion . . . sir?" she asks.

"Mouth off at me now, and you won't get your present."

"My what?" She sips her drink, and I notice a tawny kiss mark on her straw.

I unzip my backpack and hand her the little bag. I lean on my elbows toward her to get a good view of her reaction.

"What's this?"

She pulls the bow's tail until the small green ribbon uncurls and the handles spring apart. She pulls out a rolled-up picture, and I get a little-gasp-and-a-wide-eyed response as she looks at it. I Photoshopped the picture I took of her that first day and added another image, from the art fair: a bolt of raw silk that curtained one of the booths. A breeze had made it swing when I snapped the shot. I cropped her face and enlarged it. Her lips are puckered, and I shopped in breath toward the material, making it look as if she's blowing the curtain. It's one of my better ones.

"How did you do this?" she asks.

"I just wanted to thank you for getting me this job."

She brushes her hair behind her ear. "I don't know what to say."

I grin at her. "See, right there. That makes it all worth it."

She almost laughs and then says, "Oh, you're all charms and flattery, aren't you?"

She gives my hand a squeeze, and I know this is my moment to ask her out. But I end up pulling a Christian fish-mouth. Open and close.

Before she goes, she says thanks again and kisses my cheek. I inhale her smell, close my eyes, and keep my bastard mouth shut. The last thing I should do is date a girl I like.

When I get home, the temptations haven't stopped. Three unopened e-mails from Lauren lurk in my inbox. Bold print. Waiting.

RE: Where the hell are you, coward?
RE: I hate you. Call me.
RE: You owe me, bastard.

I should delete them, like I did with the first one, and fling Lauren's e-mails into oblivion. Instead, I gaze at her RE: lines.

Just a click and I could read the words that she wrote, considered, rewrote, and then sent. She is careful in e-mails, preferring phone or face-to-face. Edward says she avoids e-mail trails. Gives her deniability. I try distracting myself by counting the days till Thanksgiving, but it only takes about three seconds to confirm what I already know—sixty-two days.

I begin to bargain with myself: If I promise not to ask Dakota out, can I read Lauren's e-mails? If I don't reply to them ever, can I ask Dakota out?

I force my chair back, the wheels protesting over the thick carpet. I walk into the kitchen and open the fridge door. Cold air trickles out. There's nothing to eat, unless you consider mushrooms edible. I peek at the screen though the kitchen doorway. Her RE: lines are like the goddamn Greek sirens.

I could silence them if only I had a distraction, but Christian's at work; I already tried calling Dakota; there's no television in this place (God help me); and I can't afford to download any music or movies. Hell, I can't even drive aimlessly since Christian's car died (big surprise) and I let him use mine.

I listen to the white noise of rain pattering on the roof while my gaze lingers on the last RE: line.

You owe me, bastard.

I do owe her, but *what* do I owe her? An answer, or as much distance as I can put between us?

Maybe Mirriam is home. I walk down the hall and knock, but after waiting a century, I know she's not. I start walking the steps. Downstairs, turn around, climb back upstairs.

Lauren would not endorse my bastard-no-longer pledge. She would laugh and say, "But without your edge, you're not nearly so hot," and kiss me, stealing away any resolve.

Up: step, step, step.

Lauren's probably hanging with Edward. *They're watching a movie in her den with her enormous screen and surround sound, and she's leaning against him while he holds her homemade cheesy popcorn.*

Unwanted images flash through my head: Q-tips trapped in glass on the counter, stumbling on high heels, skin bulging between fingers as the grip tightened.

When I return to the apartment, I hit the Send/Receive button again and *ding*, an e-mail pops up. From Lauren.

RE: Warrant for your arrest?

I read it over and over before I press the Off button, and the screen goes black, erased. I pace over to the window. When my face is reflected, I turn off the lights, and then return to my spot. A bolt of lightning startles the room alive, and I start counting: one, two, three. *Don't think about that last night in Chicago at Starbucks.* Thunder breaks, and the window trembles under my fingers. *Don't think about Lauren.*

I press my fingers against the cold glass and trace the path of a raindrop. *Don't think.*

I close my eyes and try to stop the memory, as if I could scrabble away from it; try to find my brain's Record Over button—anything. But somewhere in my gray matter, a Play button is pressed and the memory rolls. . . .

We were sitting at a Starbucks table, a venti decaf standing next to my *Complete Works of Shakespeare.* The dark outside had turned the windows into pseudo-mirrors. I studied the picture reflected in the window, thinking about how it would translate in a photograph: a barista in the background, scrubbing a spot off the counter; in the foreground, I sat surrounded by my friends—Edward leaning back in his seat, his scuffed sneaker saving Lauren's empty chair, which was waiting between us; Marisa perched across from me, sipping her herbal tea with the lid off, leaving the steam to curl into specters. I was wondering whether my own double-lined reflection would look artistic or just blurry when Marisa caught my attention. She flipped her long black bangs out of her eyes, leaned forward onto her bony elbows, and looked at me through thickly mascaraed lashes.

"I'm ready," she said.

Is she honestly flirting with me? I thought. Lauren returned to the table with another cup of coffee, and I grabbed her hand and pulled her down on my lap. Had to draw the boundaries.

Marisa straightened up off her elbows and sat back. Lauren tore open two yellow packages of Splenda. The grains cascaded into her coffee, chasing both sugars already in the cup.

Edward looked from the cup to her face. "Lauren, you do realize that's the equivalent of like six sugars?"

"Sugar, chocolate, and coffee—my healthy addictions," she said, reciting a hard and fast rule she'd created in response to her mother, the recovering alcoholic who is not so consistent about the recovery part.

"What's healthy about that?" Edward asked.

Lauren tensed up. I felt her butt muscles stiffen against my quads. She had kept her mom's problem pretty quiet. It was something I only learned about, during this, our third on-off stint.

"What's healthy about it is not to ask," I said.

Her butt softened, and she kissed the top of my head. "I'm adding you to the short list."

I squeezed her hand.

"Oh God," said Marisa. "Enough of the lovey-dovey. Quiz me, Jace."

I tried to let go of Lauren's hand, but she squeezed tight.

I thought about a good quote. " 'I am in blood stepped in so far that, should I wade no more, returning were as tedious as go o'er.' "

"*Hamlet,*" Marisa said. She leaned back and crossed her arms over her chest.

"*Macbeth.*"

"*Hamlet.*" Marisa sat up again.

I shook my head and stirred Lauren's coffee for her.

"Not a chance, Marisa," Lauren said. "Jace is the hottest nerd we know. He's always right."

I glanced at her and smiled vaguely. We both knew Lauren wasn't book smart, but she was smart in a different way. She knew people, when to play and when to soften; she saw flaws and strengths that were barely perceptible to every-one else and could spout off unpredictable, totally sexy flashes of insights into relationships. She was the only person I would defer to since I had learned she was right most of the time, and I was the only person she would defer to. Which made for some pretty funny conversations.

"He's not right this time," Marisa said. "Remember, I *played* Ophelia."

"You played one scene, and it was like a hundred years ago," Lauren said.

I glanced at Edward, and he rolled his eyes. We had both seen them spat before. Their warmups were lame, their finishes exhausting.

"Warped sense of time. Try two years ago," Marisa said.

"What . . . ever."

I began flicking the onion-skin pages loudly, searching for *Macbeth*.

Lauren bounced in my lap. "Go, Jace, go."

"Lauren, you should lay off the caffeine," Marisa said.

"Caffeine doesn't affect me."

She had always claimed that nothing could alter her sleeping schedule, but after the night her parents were gone and I got to stay, I knew better. That girl never slept. Whenever I had woken up (which was often, stuffed on that twin bed), I had seen her eyes reflecting the street-lamps. Cat-night eyes.

I glanced up at her and was about to say as much when she leaned down and kissed me. Warmth spread deep into my torso.

In the reflection, I saw Edward glare at her, his chin stuck out in a deep sulk, until she lifted herself off me and took her former seat.

Odd.

I put my finger back in the book, found the quote, and pushed the book around to Marisa. "And it's in . . . ?"

"Macbeth." She slumped back and glanced at Edward for his usual consolation.

But he ignored her, watching Lauren instead.

Odder.

Lauren let out a delighted shriek, leaned over, and stuck her mouth on mine again. This time I kept my eyes open and watched Edward, thinking *Not him; no way; they don't even like each other,* but he winced when our lips made contact.

When Lauren drew back, she turned away from me. I'm sure she thought I couldn't see her, but in the glass, I watched her mouth at Edward, *Sorry.*

Fightology Lesson #5: Anger comes in all forms: a slow burn; relentless, constant flames; or a hot flash, popping here and there. It can lie in wait, and you think you've forgiven, you think you've doused it with trust, but give it a sudden burst of oxygen and—backdraft.

I grabbed Lauren's arm and hauled her out of the seat.

"Ooooh," she said, clambering to keep up, "Was the kiss that good?"

I yanked her out the door. The September air streaked into my lungs, its cold burning my throat. Lauren wrenched her arm free and waved at Marisa through the window.

"Can we do this somewhere else?" she muttered through clenched teeth and a forced smile.

She grabbed my hand and led me around the corner. She glanced up and down the street. Empty. Then she looked at me, her face schooled into blankness.

She shrugged a shoulder. "What?"

"Is that all you have to say? Not an 'I'm sorry'? Not a denial? You were better at this last time. Scratch that—the last two times."

A car appeared from around the corner, and its headlights swung over her. When the lights caught her eyes, it turned them golden. Cat-night eyes.

After the car passed us, she lifted her eyebrows and said, "I don't know what you're talking about. You're too suspicious. Where's your trust?"

"In bed with Edward."

She looked down into her chest and chuckled to herself—a private joke.

Backdraft.

Now in Christian's apartment, I close my eyes and try to will the memory to stop, as if I could prevent the blister in my brain from bursting, now that I have pricked it.

I try to imagine that I didn't call her a bitch, that she didn't say, *What, I should let you flirt with Marisa nonstop?* I try to imagine that my father's litany of names didn't spew from my mouth like a song I've listened to too much; I try to imagine that she didn't scream back, *Shut up! Stop acting like what we have is so special. It's not as if we've found the real deal. It's not like this is true love.*

But I can't imagine it any other way. For once, my imagination, my fail-safe, has failed. I stop fighting the memory and let it transport me, like Dorothy's tornado. . . .

I'm back in the street, rolling my fingers into a fist and slamming it into her face. My knuckles bang against her cheekbone. Lauren falls backward from the impact, and I hear her head *thunk* against the brick wall. A grunt pops from her throat. Her high heels can't find a hold, and she is on her way down. My hand clamps around her neck, and her body weight hangs in my grip until she manages to scuttle her feet under her. She claws at my wrist.

I squeeze.

I'm watching her skin bulging between my fingers when my brain catches up.

Cold lightning strikes down my spine.

Oh God, what am I doing?

I freeze, and I feel her nails digging into my skin. I let her go. She crashes to the cement in a heap of ragged breaths.

I go down with her, putting one palm on the cold pavement and the other on her back.

"Lauren, Lauren. Oh God." The words rush out. Someone has opened a tap, and shame pools onto the cement around us. "You've got to know I didn't mean to hurt you. I'd never hurt you."

But I just have.

She drags in breath. She pushes up, her weight on her hands, her back curved, her hair shielding her face. I fully expect her to toss her head and slap me or to lean over and bite a piece out of me, but instead I watch her shoulders jerk up and down as she sobs. This isn't Lauren's MO— Lauren Elizabeth Silver does not cry.

I smooth her hair, urging it back in place. "Oh God. Please forgi—"

I hear myself. I hear those words in my voice, and I flash on our future:

At her door, I will leave a basket brimming with a pound of coffee, her favorite raw sugar, and chocolate. I'll attach a note: **107**

Missing a fix? I'm missing you. *I will surprise her in chemistry, giving her my lab results so she can get that A her father keeps begging her for. Every day, I'll tape a KitKat to her locker until she decides not to throw it away; she'll rip open the crinkling wrapper and give in to her habit. After school, I'll wait at her car with the photo I took last year of her at the lake. In it, she is laughing as the surf crashes against the cement blocks. It's a shot she has always wanted. When she accepts it, I'll promise never to hurt her again, and she'll promise she will leave me if I do.*

But then she won't. Not when I demand that she never speak to Edward again, not when I go ahead and flirt hard and deep with Marisa in front of her face, just to test her. Not even when I cut off her hair as punishment for talking to Edward when they run into each other at the lockers—the scissors will rasp against her hair, and she'll end up thanking me for not plunging them into her back. She won't leave me, not after the next backdraft and the next and the next.

It's as if it has already happened. It *has* already happened—just not to us.

I am jolted out of the land of imagined futures when Lauren falls toward me, wrapping her arms around my neck, her forearm resting against my spine, her face against my shoulder. I start to pull back, but she hangs on. I want to gently lift her arms off me, to square her shoulders against me. But I can't touch her.

"Jace," she whispers. She takes in a big breath, and when she lets it out, I feel the rush of wind against my ear. "I shouldn't have. Not with Edward."

I pull out of her grasp. I turn, sitting down on the cement. My back presses against the cold bricks. Bits of uneven mortar prick my skin through my shirt. I lean my elbows against my knees and fold my arms into a bridge, resting my forehead on it.

"I'm sorry."

But she's the one who says it.

I want to shred my own skin, yank every thread of DNA out, and give it to her as an offering. But would that be enough? Is there any way I can fix this? I shouldn't even apologize, since that will shove the burden of forgiveness onto her. Who the hell am I to ask for her forgiveness? Who the hell am I to twist her into someone who could forgive the unforgivable? I know exactly who I can turn her into.

"Please," she says, and touches my arm.

I look up.

She has one hand clamped over her face. "Please take me home. I don't want to get on the train. I took the train in."

Her face contorts, and tears squeeze out of her closed eyes.

I stand up and offer her my hand. I drive her home in total silence except for her sobbing. The lights of Chicago tick by us.

Standing in Christian's apartment, I can hear the thunder cracking the sky open and the onslaught of rain. The window has fogged completely, making the air inside the tiny apartment feel even closer. Car or no car, I can't stay in this place one second longer. I hurry out the door and race down the steps.

Outside, the rain drenches me. Thick drops penetrate my cotton shirt and soak my skin. I walk to the edge of the pool and watch the water undulate under the force of the storm.

The rain mutates into hail, and little balls of ice race

past me. Some slam against my face and skull. The hail graduates from gumball-sized balls to full-fledged icy golf balls. I watch them ricochet off the cement and plummet into the pool. The wind kicks up, sending my hair over my eyes. Hail hammers my shoulders, arms, hands. One crashes into my neck, bouncing off my vertebrae. The cold makes me flinch.

I stand there, taking it, until the hail peters out and finally stops. The pool settles and slowly stills. I half hope I have bruises to show from this ersatz beating, but I doubt it. What do I owe Lauren?

I head back inside, climb the stairs, walk over to the computer, and flip the monitor back on. It buzzes and clicks before it shows me the white screen. I open Lauren's last e-mail. RE: Warrant for your arrest?

> Marisa thinks I should just let it go
> since you're not around. Edward, and
> I'm sorry to mention him to you, Edward
> thinks I should swear out a warrant for
> your arrest. Me, I just want to talk to
> you. Please call me.

No haughty edge, no bitchy comments, one hundred percent vulnerability. I've already ruined her.

My soaked hand drips water on the desk. I try to dry my hands off on my jeans, but they're too wet. I use the couch. Then I violate my self-imposed no-contact order, bend my fingers to the keys, and type.

> The instant you sign your name on the
> complaint, I will love you more than I
> ever have. Show some self-respect,
> girl.

I grab the mouse and push my cursor over to the Send button, where it hovers. I read the message over and stare at the word *love*. Shouldn't there be an unbreachable chasm between love and hitting someone?

I never even asked her if she was all right. I never spoke to her again.

When she left, she said, "We'll talk tomorrow."

I said nothing and stared straight ahead.

The cursor blinks. I press Delete and, character by character, my message disappears. Before I can think myself out of it, I type in two words and send the message.

```
Do it.
```

When Christian comes home that night, I can feel him watching me while I'm flat on my back on the pull-out; I'm sure it looks like I'm staring at white pimples on the textured ceiling. He takes off his shoes, watching me. He goes into the bedroom, and his keys clatter against the bureau. When he comes back, he resumes the vigil.

"Hey," he says.

" "

Even from the corner of my eye, I see him edging closer and examining me.

His eyes stop at my shoes, still on. "Are you all right?"

" "

"Do you want to talk?"

" "

Yeah, can't you tell?

He kneels at the foot of my bed, unties my shoes, and pulls them off my feet.

"Thanks," I finally manage to get out.

He sits next to me for half a second before jumping back up. "It's wet. You're wet."

There's a long pause while I muster up a response. "Sorry."

"I just meant . . . Why don't you take the bed tonight?"

"No."

I want to tell him that he shouldn't have to sleep in the swamp I've created, but that's all that comes out. Right now, anything else just feels like an effort.

"I'm all right," I say.

"You're a liar."

I roll over and push my face into the mattress while the tears tide in.

He sits back on the bed and puts his hand on my shoulder. He stays with me until I'm done. It takes a long time, but he never complains, never tries to slow me with questions or banal comforts; he never takes his hand off.

it's lunch period, and I coaxed Tom to come shoot with me to try to make up for the other week. We're just dribbling, having fun with ridiculous moves, when Caitlyn, Eric, and Heather show up. Caitlyn waves, and Eric comes up to us. He joins us, passing the ball, chipping it into the air. His lobs are slightly off the mark and have too much spin on them for a friendly shot, making them hard to handle; he's trying to make me look bad in front of our guests. He shoots one at me that I bumble a little. He laughs, but I get it off to Tom, just not with as much control as I'd like. Tom shanks it completely. It ends up in Caitlyn's hands.

Caitlyn and Heather both snicker.

"Great shot," says Heather.

"Oh, come on," says Caitlyn. "He's just trying to include us, aren't you, Tommy? Now that you've been demoted to second string, you're looking for someone at your level?"

Eric and Heather laugh. Maybe it's because I'm the one who dragged Tom out here, or maybe it's because I'm the one who replaced him, but I'm trying to figure out how not to pop Caitlyn in the mouth. She looks over at me and sees my cold expression.

"Oh, Tom," she says, "I'm just teasing you. Just flirting a little."

Lauren and Caitlyn are so similar. Both erupt with the same catty remarks and cover with a smile. I used to be Eric, laughing at all her jokes. Now, Tom isn't the stupidest guy or anything, but it takes someone pretty nimble to keep up with Caitlyn. Practice with Lauren has trained me well.

"Tom can't flirt at your level," I say, and Tom's chin hangs even lower. "He needs more than a high school girl who thinks that a WELCOME sign on her ass is an effective come-hither."

Tom grins at me, and I lift my eyebrows back. After a pause, Eric and Heather crack up. Caitlyn saunters over to me, lifting her sunglasses up. She stops in front of me and rolls her shoulders back. Stretched tighter, her T-shirt buckles into little ripples between her breasts.

"Oh, so you're still thinking about my pants?" she says. "Thinking of a way to get in them?"

She has probably seen me watching her a little too often since I started here. Sure, she's hot and popular, but there's something else: if you try to give her any shit, you can be pretty sure she's going to fling it back in your face.

And that's something I can't resist: unflappable, unbreakable women.

"Is it keeping you up at night? Keeping your lonely hands busy?" Caitlyn says.

In some relationships, there's a moment where you've gotta decide whether you're going to dig deep into trench warfare or flip the switch and become something else, something hotter.

"Whether or not I get in your pants, if I hang out with you, I'm getting fucked, aren't I?"

She doesn't get embarrassed, doesn't hesitate; she just flings it back at me.

"Take me out, Jace," she says. "Let's see what happens."

"Hey," Eric calls. "Are we going to stand around and chat?"

Eric's face is blanched white, and he's holding his breath. I toss the ball to him before Caitlyn and I walk off the field together.

The movie-popcorn smell is thick in Caitlyn's car when we drive up into the mountains and find a place to park. Caitlyn has her mom's SUV, and I'm guessing the seats fold down. She puts the car in park and turns the engine off, letting the battery run the radio. I think about Lauren and how I had to climb over the gear shift, couldn't get over it fast enough for her.

Caitlyn unclicks her seat belt and leans in. She kisses me, her lips slippery with too much lip gloss. I taste an unfamiliar peachy flavor that makes me pull back. I catch sight of her red hair, and everything's wrong.

Where are the cat-night eyes? Where's that voice of

Lauren's that can go from a warm purr to cold steel in a fraction of a second? Where are the stories she would tell me about her mother's drinking? I want to hear again about the time her mother went on a bender and forgot an eight-year-old Lauren in a grocery store; how Lauren stayed in canned goods, reading labels; how she still hates Bush Beans cans. And I want her to pull a jar of body chocolate out of her purse, like she did that night, and we both escaped into each other's skin.

But I'm here staring at Caitlyn and feeling like a jerk. No one wants to be a replacement. No one deserves it, not even Caitlyn.

She leans in farther and starts nibbling on my ear. "I just want to be clear about something . . . What I said about, you know . . . about going all the way . . . It was for show. I just don't want you to expect anything—well, everything."

Going all the way? Who says that, except for a . . . virgin. Oh. My. God.

Caitlyn's like a Lauren knock-off. Lauren wasn't popular because she worked at it, made bitchy statements that she couldn't live up to; she was popular because she got off on power, on twisting the knife. And I loved that about her, how she would go for what she wanted without permission, how she would never back down, never take any shit. Until me. Caitlyn would fold the second I raised my voice.

Even if Caitlyn was as tough as Lauren, even if she was a girl I could date without breaking or without her breaking me, taking her out isn't going to make me forget about Lauren.

"You know what," I say, pulling all the way back, "let's

just . . . not hook up. You don't really want to be up here with me, anyway. This is more about Eric than me."

Her mouth pops open in surprise; I've divined her master plan. She hides her face in her hands, but even in the dark, I see her neck going red.

"It's okay," I say. "I'm thinking about someone else, too. Don't be embarrassed."

She drops her hands into her lap. "So, you don't want to even . . . kiss or anything?"

"We could just hang out. That will keep Eric's interest, all right?"

"On one condition," she says. "Tell me who I'm a substitute for?"

"An ex," I say. "Something that is over."

"For something that's over, you can't seem to end it," she says, and giggles.

I wonder how rude it would be to hike home.

chapter 14

"**l ike this?**" I ask Mirriam, as I whip the egg whites.

I have the bowl tucked under my arm and resting against my hip, the way Samantha does it in reruns of *Bewitched*.

"Sure, you can do it like that," she says.

"No, really, how?"

"Put it down." She takes the whisk and mixes a different way—more up and down than circular. Then she turns the bowl around on the counter with her other hand. "This might be faster."

She asks me about school, and I tell her that Tom seems okay, that he's actually teaching me to play chess, which makes us both laugh.

I glance at the clock. "We won't be done before Christian gets here."

"That's okay." She takes over, mixing everything together and then pouring the pancakes on the skillet. "Why don't you get started on your homework?"

I tell her I wouldn't leave her to finish all the work, but I have a paper due. When she asks on what, I give her a quick rundown: "interdisciplinary" paper, combining history with Tim O'Brien's *The Things They Carried*. She talks about the benefits of an interdisciplinary education, and I think about the benefits of an A.

While she goes on, she grabs a measuring cup and drops measured batter onto the skillet. I watch her doing it without thinking.

"Mirriam?"

"Yeah?"

"I was thinking about Thanksgiving dinner." I hesitate. "Christian said you and your family are close. Are you going out to see them? Or . . ."

"My parents are abroad this year, and we're doing a big reunion for Christmas, so I'll be around. Why?"

"I kind of want to make it a big deal because Christian and I are together again for the holidays. So I was wondering if you could teach me how to cook a turkey."

"Well, sure, Jace." She smiles like a teacher does when you turn in your assignment early, all mushy-eyed and proud.

I frown and walk to the computer. Except for moments when Mirriam goes into her teacher-mode or, even worse, her must-rescue-the-broken-kid mode, she's okay. In fact, she has been making me feel more at home than Christian sometimes.

Before I start my paper, I do my daily Mom e-mail check, hoping I won't see a reply from Lauren. I sigh in relief. Only one from Mom. I open it up and read it. In the four and a half weeks since I've been here, her e-mails have been getting progressively shorter.

They went from this:

Things are good here. I'm still saving up the money you boys are sending me. What does Christian say about me coming out? Tell him to write me. What's your new school like? How's the soccer team?

To:

I can't wait to see you both. What is the news on Christian these days? Is he seeing anyone? Looking forward to Thanksgiving.

To:

I'm fine. Don't worry.

She used to get quieter when my dad was gearing up for a big one. She never spoke that much anyway, but when she sensed my father's stress, our dialogue would turn into me monologuing, just to fill the room, just to see if I could eke a smile out of her.

I look at her last e-mail: *Don't worry*. I know time is running out. His fuse must be burning up a little more each day. I tell myself her reticence is just due to the natural half-life of e-mails. After all, my e-mails have been getting shorter, too. No more long descriptions about the people

I'm meeting and how everything is great out here and how Christian and I have hit it off since day one. I lie because I don't want her to worry either.

The door behind me clicks, the bolt sliding out of the way.

"Hi, Christian," I say, not taking my eyes from the screen, as if I could will her words to multiply.

Mirriam comes out of the kitchen, and they kiss their hellos while I consider writing my mom the longest e-mail ever, just to test my half-life theory.

"Are you okay, love?" she asks.

I turn and look. She still has her arms around him, and his face is tight and pale.

"Yeah," he says, his voice unusually low. He clears his throat.

"Are you on ER rotation? Bad day?"

He pulls back from her, but her arms just stretch longer. He glances at me.

"Nothing I haven't seen before."

"Mirriam," I say, "the food."

"Oh, right." She lets go of him and races into the kitchen.

He takes off his jacket and hangs it. Then he walks over to me. I want to ask him what happened, but I feel him reading the screen, her four-word reply.

"Everything okay?" I ask.

"Is that Mom's e-mail? Short."

I resist glaring at him.

"How often are you guys e-mailing?" he asks.

"Every day. I want to hear from her every day."

His jaw clenches, and his voice hardens with scorn. "You're still keeping tabs on her?"

"Yes. You have a problem with that?"

He shakes his head. "It's your life. Waste it how you want. Are we having pancakes?"

I click the window closed and slam my palm against the monitor button to turn it off. I stare at the dark screen and breathe. In, hold, out. *Manage your anger, don't let it manage you,* the blond woman with the horse teeth said.

"Maybe you should just tell me what I did," I say.

He walks into the kitchen, brings out plates, and puts them down gently. Even the plates don't get rough treatment.

He turns to me. "It's not you. I treated a girl today. She was tight-lipped and practiced in stonewalling."

Mirriam walks in with a platter of pancakes. She slows down and listens.

"I called the police, a social worker, but her mom took her home," he says.

"I'm sorry, love." She grabs his hand. He doesn't close his fingers around hers.

Christian says nothing. Mirriam says nothing. I say nothing. I would suggest lighting a candle, but it would sound flip, and I don't mean it that way.

"Is she going to be all right?" Mirriam asks finally. "I mean, physically."

"She ought to be."

"Then you've done all you can," Mirriam says.

Christian grunts. "Sure, okay," he says, picking up my phrase.

We sit down in silence, and Mirriam fills our plates with pancakes from the platter. Christian is only at the table for a couple of minutes. He stares at the pancakes and pokes one with his fork, leaving four dents. He says he's sorry we went to the trouble, but he isn't hungry. He has a lot of work to do and should study.

"Christian?" I say. "Do you want company? I have a paper to write."

"No thanks."

Mirriam glances at me before she gives it her best shot.

"Christian," she says, and gives a half laugh. "Remember how you keep telling me that I need to develop professional distance? It's okay if you can't rescue everyone either."

He just shakes his head.

"Maybe one is enough," I say.

He looks at me, confused.

"I mean, you know." I touch my chest and shrug.

For the first time since he came home, he looks me in the eye.

"Yeah?" he asks, his voice rough.

I contemplate life on the street. "Yeah."

He gives me a little nod, and I can practically see his shoulders slide down. Somehow, his eyes look less hollowed out. He leans over and kisses Mirriam on the top of her head.

She grips his hand, and he says, "Thanks, guys."

He swallows audibly, and then his voice is lighter when he asks her, "Did Toad—Jace—tell you about this tradition?"

"Wait . . . Toad?" she asks.

"Nickname," I say. "For family only."

"How did you get it?"

I shrug and look at Christian. "Do you remember?"

He shakes his head.

"Me neither."

"So," he says, "tell her about the pancakes."

He walks into the kitchen while I begin talking about how he taught me to flip pancakes. He comes back with the syrup and goes around the table, letting the sweetness drizzle down.

chapter 15

i'm on a break at work, sitting in the café with *Joy of Cooking* in front of me while I suck a smoothie through an extra-wide straw.

After looking at the ingredients for Stroganoff, I decide to try something easier. I've only mastered fried eggs and pasta so far. How about a good hamburger or macaroni and cheese? What will my mom think when she comes out here (forty-six days away) and discovers that I can cook? After flipping to the index and back again, I notice that legs are standing beside my table. I look up and see Christian. He's wearing his scrubs, carrying a paperback, and has his murse (man's purse) slung over his shoulder.

"Hey, what are you doing here?"

"I thought I'd bring you something to eat. You went off 125

without breakfast, right?" He hands me a banana and puts a granola bar on the table.

"Thanks." I bend back the banana stem until it breaks and start to peel it. "It's like a breakfast break."

"Sure."

He stands there, and I watch him for a minute. As the silence gets more awkward, I clue in that the banana is just an excuse. I put it down and look at him.

Finally he says, "Oh, and here. You got this." He digs in his murse and hands me a letter.

I immediately recognize the handwriting. Mom.

"Thanks," I say, and put it down.

He watches it lying on the table. I'm dying to open it, but before I share, I should probably tell Christian that she is coming.

"It's kind of interesting, really," he says.

"What is?" I ask through a banana-filled mouth.

"That she sent you a letter."

"What kind of cheese do you like? I mean, for mac and cheese?"

He picks up the envelope and flaps it against the table. "It's thick."

I tap the recipe. "I once had it with Gruyère. It was great."

"What was?"

"Mac and cheese," I say.

He stares at me uncomprehendingly. I lift the book so he can see the cover.

"Oh," he says. "Okay, I'm heading to the hospital."

"Thanks for the food." I take another bite.

He starts to go and turns back. "But she hasn't written to you before, has she?"

I put the banana down. "I'm sure she's fine."

"Yeah, me too. Are you guys still e-mailing?" he asks.

He knows that we are. The apartment is pretty small for secrets. Or for those kinds of secrets, anyway. The letter is sealed; he hasn't read it. And I don't think she's e-mailing him. But maybe she sent her own letter to Christian about coming, and he's giving me the chance to tell him.

"I'll bet her left hand is hurting, that's all. It's probably hard for her to type."

"Does it . . . It still hurts her?"

"Sometimes. She's keeping in touch; I'm sure she's fine," I say, trying to sound confident.

Out of the corner of my eye, I see Dakota coming in. She waves, and I return it. Christian looks at her and then back at me.

"Is that the girl who got you the job?" He looks her over and smiles. "She's pretty."

I probably shouldn't care that my brother approves, but still, it matters to me.

I glance at Dakota. She's talking to Douglas, the cashier, ordering something. Christian is back to staring at the envelope. I grab its corner and slide it toward me.

"Okay, so see you later," he says, and leaves, and I'm thinking *that was weird. And kind of cool.* First of all, while Christian is no longer recoiling from contact, he doesn't tend to initiate it. Second, I was going to see him in two hours. *Very odd. Maybe he does know. Maybe this was my opportunity to tell him about Mom coming.*

I start to open the letter, but before I have it out of the envelope, Dakota comes over. I shove it in my bag.

"Hey, Jace."

I slide over, and she sits beside me on the bench so that 127 we're right next to each other. She puts her water on the table and rips off the top of the straw's wrapper.

"Was that your brother?" she asks.

"Yeah," I say, trying to remember if I've mentioned Christian.

"I knew it. You guys look alike."

"Funny."

"Well, I don't mean your coloring or your features or anything."

"Thanks. That's much clearer." I take the lid off my smoothie and tilt the cup to suck it down more efficiently.

"Shut up," she says. "You move the same way, you talk the same way, and you have the exact same voice, only you're a lot louder."

I stop sucking, my mouth full. Two things my brain processes: 1) she sees a similarity between my brother and me, and 2) she has noticed the way I move. These are two good things.

She raises an eyebrow. "Are you going to swallow that?"

I do. "Thanks. I mean, whatever. Thanks." I pause. "You overheard us talking?"

"No, he was looking for you earlier, and I told him you were on break." She grabs her hula hoop–sized earring and tugs on it. "So, I'm probably going to regret this, but I was wondering if you . . . Have you ever had Indian fry bread?"

I shake my head.

" 'Cause out by Jemez, I know a place that . . . You know, if you wanted to."

I smile, flattered by her sudden case of inarticulation. But then an image flashes: *Lauren collapsing on the street, her legs splayed, her shoulders jolting when she cries.*

"Well," I say slowly. "Not like a date or anything, right?"

"Well, no. No. Nothing like that. I mean, do you want it to be a date?"

"I'm still kind of seeing someone else."

Can't exactly extract Lauren from my head. Ever since the blister popped, it's sort of oozing everywhere.

"Oh," she says.

"Then sure. I'd love to. When do you have off?" I ask, even though I know when; I've been trying to match my schedule to hers.

Why am I doing that, when I've just blown a chance to date her? *I'm seeing someone else?* Where did I get that?

We set a time, and she walks out of the café, but as she turns the corner, she checks to make sure I'm watching her.

When she has disappeared from eyeshot, I pull the envelope out of my backpack. I stare at it for a second. Every day I click on my mom's e-mail and rush-read. Then I reread it. This time the clean white envelope waits for me, and I hesitate. Christian is right. Why is she writing me?

I tap the envelope, making sure the letter has slid down before I tear off the end and let the papers fall onto my fingers.

Jace,

I wanted to assure you that I'm coming, and this changes nothing, but we'll need to talk when I get there. I'm so sorry. Destroy your copy, so that you can say you didn't know about it.

Love you,
Mom

Okay. I have no idea what she's talking about.

I fan out the papers. It's a photocopy of a warrant for my arrest. Lauren's well-rehearsed signature is scrawled on the bottom of the complaint.

Good for you, Lauren. Good for you.

my breath frosts the way-too-early-morning air. I can't believe Christian convinced me to hike this early. We get off something called a tram, which is like a small subway car that hangs from a cable. The cables are strung on these enormous towers, and the tram rides them up, up, perilously up the sheer cliffs of the mountains. I'm glad when my feet hit the deck.

We climb along the crest, and I'm getting amazing views. I have never been at the top of a mountain before. The land is dry and ragged. I had always assumed it would be like a hill, smooth and graduated, but it's more like a huge dome that's been sliced in half. There are jagged outcroppings and deep fissures.

It's so early that beneath us everything just looks dark, 131 and since I don't have a tripod and don't want to use a flash, I keep my camera tucked away. I'm wondering why we had to get up so early.

Once the sky begins to lighten, Christian points, and I follow his gaze and startle. Hot air balloons dot the sky. Red, yellow, and blue. Striped and solid. Untethered, they hang as if weightless.

"The Balloon Fiesta," he explains. "Mirriam and I came out here last year. Isn't this a great way to see it?"

We scramble up to the edge. I pull out my camera and try to shoot, but in the finder, the view loses something. I keep trying until I realize that I'm boring the heck out of my brother. We sit, dangle our feet in the endless drop, and watch the sky fill with little dots.

When I was little, it used to irritate me that my mother would anchor all birthday party balloons to my wrist. I would work at the ribbon until I could get them free just to watch them float up into the ether, on to something new.

"How do they work?"

He explains about mixing air with propane and heating it up for liftoff, about the gondolas where the pilots sit, and it's like we're back to the days when he knew more about everything than I did.

He takes off his pack and sets it down. I unzip it and dig out the trail mix that is our breakfast. He pulls a thermos out, unscrews the top, and pours. The brown liquid sloshes into the metal cup.

"Tea?" I ask.

"No. On a morning like this? Hot chocolate."

I inhale the scent.

He raises it to his lips and drinks. I pop some of the trail

mix into my mouth and chew. It doesn't taste nearly as

cardboard-crunch like as usual. Maybe I'm starting to appreciate tasteless food.

I stare at the horizon. There must be hundreds of balloons pinned against the sky. Suddenly the motionless picture is broken as one balloon, shaped like a cactus, falls under the orange-and-yellow-striped orb next to it. It sinks below the ridge, out of sight.

"You came here with Mirriam last year?"

He mumbles a yeah and seems suddenly fascinated by the rock we're sitting on.

"You guys doing okay?" I ask. "You and Mirriam, I mean."

"Well." He leans down and brushes some gravel over the ledge. It drops out of sight, like it never existed.

"You've seen us. We don't usually fight. I mean, remember the night you showed up? She just went to her apartment, no questions asked. That's what I'm used to. That level of faith."

I wait, knowing another question will make him quiet, but quiet will make him talk.

"Now she wants me to . . . talk to her," he says.

"About Chicago? Before you left."

"How am I supposed to do that? How can I sum all that up? 'It was awful. It's done.' "

"She doesn't like that informative and emotional answer?"

"Smart-ass," he says, and bumps me with his elbow. "She says the fact that I don't want to talk means that I should."

"That's kind of twisted."

He sips the hot chocolate. "Maybe she's right."

He looks out again, and he's not watching the balloons. I wait, letting the silence erode his barriers.

He continues, "I don't know. I think she has a right to know, don't you? It's not technically a lie, a lie of omission. But whatever it was, it's the cold opposite of intimacy."

I can just about hear the fight he had with Mirriam; I recognize her words coming out of his mouth. I remember that when I eavesdropped, he promised her he'd talk about it another time. I'm guessing he hasn't.

He picks up a piece of gravel and throws it. He collects a handful of pebbles and starts tossing them over the edge one by one.

"Why don't you tell her about the time with the hammer?" I ask.

His mouth turns down.

"Okay, what about the time he cut her hair off when that guy at the Historical Society told her he liked it?"

"He what?"

"Oh, yeah. That was after you left."

He looks down at the rock floor and then tosses another pebble over.

I try again. "Well, what about when he—"

"Jace."

"What?"

He stands up, and this time looks after the pebble as he drops it.

"She's easy to talk to, actually," I say. "She's not as judgmental as I expected."

He snorts. I collect my own handful of gravel, scooping out the broken bits from a divot in the rock floor. I stand up next to him and watch the balloons.

"How many are there?" I ask.

"Hundreds."

I take a breath and then go ahead and test the ground rules.

"Why don't you tell her about what happened when he found you in New York?"

He glances at me. "Did anyone ever tell you subtlety isn't your forte?" He pulls his shirt out from the grip of the pants waistband and lifts it. His skin knitted into a slim ridge on his back. "I told her I got mugged."

"But that scar is . . . perfect," I say, looking at the smooth line.

"Surgery. I had left, and you know how he is. How well do you think he would deal with that? He told me he'd kill me, and he certainly did try. I don't know which blow broke my ribs. One of them punctured a lung, so the ER docs had to operate."

I am quiet and watch the sun creeping up the mountain's face, pushing the morning blue before it.

"He was waiting for me when I walked in. My roommate let him into the dorm. He was just sitting on that ratty old couch, you know the pull-out you're sleeping on? He said one of his law clerks had a cousin running in the New York Marathon, and so she looked up the results. Her cousin and I crossed the finish line one after the other."

I start putting two and two together: he won't run in Boston because my dad might find him. We all knew Christian wanted to run that marathon. When I think about it, my dad watches it on TV every year. I always thought of it as a homage to Christian, not as a way to find him.

He continues, "He knew I had been accepted at NYU, but the scholarship letter came after I left the house, so he never thought I could afford it. He found my dorm through the school records. Remember, I was only seventeen when I went to college, still a minor. Anyway, he told me I was coming home and didn't I know I was breaking Mom's heart and how she worried and a bunch of other crap. He didn't mention you, and I . . . didn't ask. I'm really sorry about that, Jace. I mean it."

I look down at the rock and suddenly want to become a part of it—smooth and simple, just melt into the earth. I should probably tell him it's okay, that I get why he couldn't take me to college with him.

"I had asked the Costacoses to keep an eye on you, but when you guys moved and he hadn't hit you . . . And I didn't tell them about Mom, so they were just trying to make sure that he didn't start in on you . . . Guess they weren't good at judging that sort—"

"I managed."

"Did you?" He throws the whole handful of rocks, and I watch his chest expand and contract fast. He presses his elbows to his sides.

"What do you think happened after you left?" I ask.

"I know exactly what happened, Toad. Hell, I taught you how to do it, didn't I?"

"Do what?"

"How to provoke him so that he'd let it out on us, rather than her."

I wonder if he's remembering the same night I am, the first night my dad hit him.

"Every kid wants to be just like his older brother, right?" he says. "How many times did Mom tell me that? And still, I showed you. Why did I think that you wouldn't step up, step right into my place?"

"What else could you have done?" I ask, hoping for an answer that makes sense.

"I could have killed the bastard."

I watch his breath float in the air, coming in fast puffs. I feel like I'm talking someone down off a roof. I tread carefully. "You'd be in jail."

"Yeah, and Mom would be out, and you would be out, and I wouldn't spend half the time hating her and the other half hating you because you still get to e-mail her."

I clench my teeth together to keep from asking why he doesn't contact her again. I look down and try to dig my shoe into the stone.

"She talks about you all the time, Christian. She wants to know how you're doing."

"Then she can leave him," he says.

I lift my head and look at him as I get it. "You gave her an ultimatum? You told her you didn't want to hear from her unless she left him?"

"I used to write all these lies. I'd make up these desperate situations to try to make her come out for me."

"And she still wouldn't?" I thought she'd do anything for Christian, her golden child.

He raises his palms and mocks looking around for her. "You'd think I'd give up, stop sending the money. She used to tell me she would leave him and then . . . nothing. If she was going to, she would have by now."

"Christian," I say, taking a deep breath, "she's going to be out here in thirty-nine days. She promised me. Thanksgiving."

"She *promised* you?"

I nod.

Christian's face rushes through emotions so fast it looks like a train is passing, windows flashing, over his features. He sits down slowly. I walk over to him and sit with my legs dangling in free space. We stare out at the balloons, silent, while he adjusts his whole guilt-inspired world.

"He'll come after her," he says.

"If he can find her. He won't think to look for her out here. If she can just get out cleanly, she'll disappear."

He nods.

The sun has scaled the cliff, and I watch the blue rock beneath me turn white as the sunlight finally finds us. The slanted rays carry heat to my legs.

Eventually he says, "I suppose Mirriam's going to get to see my family for herself."

"It won't be enough to get you guys on the right track."

He shakes his head. "I know. I'll tell her about New York. It wasn't that hard to talk about it."

"Let me know if you need to practice another story. I know them all now."

"God, you *are* a smart-ass."

I grin, and he swats at the air between us.

"Thirty-nine days, huh?" he says. "You've been counting?"

"I don't know the hours or the minutes."

He smiles. "That's only because you don't know what time she's leaving."

"Now who's the smart-ass?" I say. I look down and see something moving beneath us. "Christian, is that a bear?"

"Yup."

Christian holds me by the elbow as I lean forward, my torso over the edge, and watch the dark shape lope along, nose to the ground, searching.

"You're not in Chicago anymore, Toto. Come on." He pulls me back from the edge, and we return to our spot on the broad, flat rock.

He grabs the thermos, pours more hot chocolate into the cup, and hands it to me. No hesitation. No this is my cup and that's yours. I hold the warm metal in my hands, tip the cup, and let the chocolate wash into my mouth.

chapter 17

another soccer game lost. Our record: 0–5. We so need a new goalie. After said ass-whipping, I'm munching my corn-chip dinner and trying to gussy up my *Hamlet* paper in the twenty-minute window I have post-shower and pre-bookstore. I'm typing in "The undiscover'd country . . . [that] puzzles the will / And makes us rather bear those ills we have / Than fly to others that we know not of?" when the e-mail account dings at me. New mail! I open it, assuming it's my mom's check-in, only to find that Lauren has replied. Which means that right now, she is at her computer, too. *Kismet,* says a sly part of my brain. *An opportunity,* adds Señor Sly. *Apologize, help her forgive you, tell her about your new life. It's not like you could hurt her again. Thirteen HUNDRED miles of distance. She's sitting in* *her rose-colored room on her perpetually unmade bed, cross-legged with her laptop on her knees, waiting to hear from you.* I call up the memory of her body hitting the sidewalk, which shuts up Señor Sly. I click on the RE: Warrant for your arrest? line.

Above my *Do it,* she has written:

```
Done.
```

It took her days to write this one word, days in which her complaint was processed and served, days in which my mom copied it and sent it to me. Did she know that tipping me off was a surefire way to help me duck a summons?

I click on the dictionary icon to find the textbook definition for *ambivalence:* having mixed or contradictory feelings about something. Am-biv-a-lent *adj.* Am-biv-a-lent-ly *adv.* Example: Jace feels ambivalently about the warrant for his arrest. Jace knows that this warrant is proof positive that Lauren will return to her normal self, that he hasn't broken her. Therefore, Jace can uncoil the knot in his back. However, Jace is also happy that he is in New Mexico, where he won't be found, much less arrested. Finally, Jace suspects it's a bad sign that he is referring to himself in the third person.

The door clicks, and I shut down the e-mail before I turn around. Caitlyn is making her way over to me.

I glance at the clock. "What are you doing here?"

"Looking for you," she says.

She tells me everyone (a.k.a. her pride plus the soccer guys) is going out for pizza, and do I want to come? And oh, Eric's not going to be there.

"Would you have tracked me down if he was?"

"Of course," she says, but I'm not as certain as she is until she says, "He might ask me out if he sees me with you."

"Caitlyn," I say, "you could just ask him out, instead of acting all weird about it. You asked me out."

"But *you* hadn't broken up with me already."

"Oh."

I had assumed she was the puppet-master, but she's just trying to refertilize her burned-up ego.

"So, you see?" she says, and takes a chip and then starts to laugh. "You look so surprised."

"Well, yeah. You've got him on a string."

"He bailed when I said those three little words. If he wants me back, he's gotta answer 'em." She pauses and looks at my computer screen. "Anyway, come out with us."

I would like to blow this off and hang out with her and her friends. I've been eating lunch with them, and Heather even burned me a few CDs to save me from a twenty-two-year-old brother's music collection.

I shrug and remember how often I would hang with Edward and our soccer team. Now this team is going to eat and joke around and talk about nothing. I could do with a little nothing.

"I can't."

"The paper isn't due for—"

"No, I have to work."

"That's what sick days are for," she says. "Don't you feel sick?"

Dakota isn't scheduled to work, and I can finish the paper when I get back to the apartment.

I smile up at her, and we head out the door. I use her cell phone to call work and tell Robyn I'm not feeling well, and for one night, I actually get to feel like life is a little normal again, like there's a place where I fit.

When Eric comes in, Caitlyn's mouth drops before she can cover. He made it, after all. *Great*. Caitlyn scootches toward me to make room. But when Eric goes to sit next to her, she goes, "Oh, could you get me a coke." When he comes back with it, she has her elbow on the table and is turned toward me, using universal body language to block him out. I go ahead and flirt back while Eric is slumped on her other side, eating cold pizza. I'm being a bastard again, but this time, it's community service.

A few days later, I'm sitting on a stool in the middle of Dakota's kitchen with my shirt off. My shoulders and neck are wrapped in airless, moist, blue plastic wrap, and newspapers lie on the floor under me.

"You're sure you want to dye your hair?" Dakota asks for the third time.

"You're sure you can do it?"

"I did Douglas's."

"Really? You're good."

She sketches a bow.

"Do you think it'll look good?" I ask.

She shrugs. "I like how it looks now."

I think of my dad's blond hair and my own. "Go to it, Van Gogh."

She asks me where the box of hair dye is, and when I tell her, she gets it out of my bag.

Dakota and I have started hanging together outside of work. After the Saturday shift, we head out to someplace desert-beautiful. (She seems to know them all.) Turns out she loves to draw; she drew the pix of Lady Godiva   143 on her jeans. So she brings her art stuff, and I bring my camera. She hangs and draws. I wander and shoot. Though she has dropped me off and come up to the apartment once or twice, this is the first time I've been to her house. It is a sprawling one-story and has the no-molding-around-the-windows-and-doors, remember-the-Spanish look.

She brings in the box and a print of mine that was in my backpack.

"I like this one," she says. "I liked it more when it wasn't Photoshopped."

I sigh. We've been disagreeing on that since day one. She says nature photography shouldn't be Photoshopped because it misrepresents our world. I argue that as soon as I choose what to take a picture of, I'm already making decisions about what to represent and what to leave out; every photo, nature or not, is manufactured.

There's nothing quite like Photoshop. Once I took a silver-processing film class. Hated it. On the computer, I can change whatever I see after the fact. Taking the images isn't the fun part; it's fixing them. I composite images, erase imperfections, arrange colors. It's a little like playing God.

She goes on, "But I guess you like it more Photoshopped. Satisfies the control freak within."

"I am not a control freak. I just want it to be right."

"Yeah, but right according to you. Control freak."

I can't think of a comeback, so I lean backward as if I'm in a salon, my neck craning over the metal and my head hanging in the sink. She sits me back up, picks up the bottle of dye, and starts dragging the nozzle along my scalp—a light scratching as she changes my look. It smells sharp, like hydrochloric acid. I don't want to distract her, so I keep quiet, but when I feel the bottle moving more swiftly, with more confidence, I say, "Hey, Douglas said that that old woman came back, the one with the attitude and earrings?"

Some woman with a deep, loud voice and a Slavic accent came into the store the other day and put up a big fuss when Dakota couldn't find a book on the shelves that was in the system. She started telling Dakota something about finding a boyfriend—a young, pretty girl like yourself doesn't have a head for this kind of thing—and Dakota just stood there, taking it. When I stepped in, the woman went all soft and sweet with me.

"Yeah," she says.

"Did she give you a hard time?"

"She's just a crackpot with retro views on the world."

"You shouldn't let her kick you around. Just tell her to shut up," I say.

"I didn't *let* her, and I want to keep my job—you know, the job my father got me."

"Oh, Robyn doesn't care about that."

She shakes her head. "Yes, she does. She told me when I started working."

"Well, she doesn't anymore. She called you the 'model bookstore service representative' when I interviewed with her. Besides, if Robyn tries to give you a hard time, I'll back you up."

She puts the bottle down. I glance at her from the corner of my eye, careful not to move my head.

"That's gracious of you, but I can fight my own battles," she says.

"Well, obviously not."

"Hey. I appreciate it that you stepped up for me the other day, but don't tell me how to live my life."

I suddenly wonder what would happen if I pissed her off and she left my hair half my dad, half my brother. I'm not going for the yin-yang look. "Okay. Sorry. Just trying to help."

She picks up the dye and continues. "Didn't you . . . Did you . . . Hasn't anyone ever kicked you around?"

"Not really."

Lies come so easily that I answer without thinking. Then I wonder who I am protecting. Who was I ever protecting? I used to lie because that's how it was done. *Because that's how it's done* isn't so persuasive anymore. Hell, I used to stand up and take my mother's beating for her because that's how it was done.

"No . . . Yeah." My hands start to shake. "My dad."

"That's different," she says. "Parents are never happy. If it's not the way you dress, it's your grades. If it's not your grades, it's your friends. Are you cold?"

"Shirtless." I wonder if I will ever stop lying.

"Wait a minute. Where *is* your dad? I haven't seen either of your parents in that little apartment of yours."

"He's in Chicago."

When she asks, I tell her no, he's not traveling on business; he lives there still.

The bottle slows again. "So, are your parents getting a divorce? Is that why you moved out here?"

"No, they're still together."

"She moved here from Chicago, but she doesn't want a divorce?"

I sense that the lies are about to unravel. I want them unraveled. Why not pull the string? I think of the tight-lipped victim Christian was talking about the other night. I think of how I accuse Christian of not talking, but no one in my new life has even heard about Lauren. If I want to change, is this the way?

"It's just my brother and me here. My mom is supposed to come out in"—I realize how neurotic I'll sound if I say *thirty-four days*—"at Thanksgiving. She hasn't left him. Yet."

"She sent you out here to live with your brother?" she asks.

I'm silent. And so is she. It's like the world is on pause for a second. I want to turn and look at her, but I don't want to move my head, either.

"Jace," she says finally. "Remember the day we met?"

"Yeah."

"You said you got in a car accident."

"Yeah," I say.

"But was that . . . Just now, did you mean literally? That your father *literally* kicked you around?"

I tell myself that I'll be able to handle whatever reaction she throws at me. She might put the bottle down, fold her arms, and ask me the questions I've been asking myself.

"How could you leave your mother behind to take it without you? Why aren't you banging down the door, calling the police, testifying against him?" she'd ask.

I'd say, "Do you understand the court system? No prosecutor would bring a he-said, she-said case against a judge in Chicago. And even if we pretend that there is a gutsy TV-hero attorney, no judge would ever let another judge get convicted."

She'll try to tell me about the effectiveness of the justice system and how I should trust the courts, but I've seen the system fail too many times, been weaned on my dad's stories about its limited protection, been told about how the law can be twisted, evidence ruled **147**

inadmissible. Too many ways to go wrong. Too many ways my fa-
ther could walk free.

"*When he gets out, she's dead,*" *I'll say.* "*An order of protection
is just a piece of paper.*"

Whatever she throws at me, I'll be able to handle.

I watch my hands shake. I tell myself that this will be the
hardest time to say it, that it will get easier, that my face
won't burn and my throat won't close, that lies are verbose,
and the truth takes one word.

"No." I laugh a little to cover. "No, of course not. My
dad isn't a monster, or anything."

I suddenly get who I'm protecting. As soon as I call my
father out, Dakota won't understand anything else about
him. And I know the same thing is true for me—if I tell anyone about Lauren, they're never going to see anything but
my fists.

"Really?" she says.

I cover: my father has high standards, he won't accept
anything less than perfect; that one time when I missed a
score in a soccer game, he kept after me for three weeks;
that's what I meant when I said he kicks me around. That
my mom hasn't filed for divorce *yet,* but she's leaving him.
Once Dakota looks like she believes me, I say, "Come on,
let's see your work."

"Not yet," she says. "It needs to sit for a little while."

She puts a plastic bag on my hair, and I take off the
sweaty Saran Wrap. I put on my shirt and button it up before we go into the den, where her parents and her little sister, Missy, are watching some Saturday movie. When they
laugh, they all sound the same. Dakota in surround sound.
I rest my back against the cushions, and Missy ends up
148 with her head on my lap while she watches. When Dakota

notices, she doesn't apologize for this sudden familiarity, and I don't want her to.

It's loud here, sure, but there's a stillness underneath, a promise that tomorrow will look the same as today.

After half an hour or so, Dakota tells me we need to rinse my hair, and when we're done, she leads me to a bathroom to inspect the look in a mirror. She did a great job. It's dark and contrasts with my blue eyes. No doubt about it: I look more like Christian than ever, but in truth, still not much.

Dakota is looking down and pulling at her cuticles.

"What do you think?" I ask. "Do you like it?"

"No."

"You don't like it?"

"No."

"Well, don't sugarcoat it on my account."

"I believe in unadulterated honesty," she says.

"Does that make you a lot of friends?"

She laughs and then says yes, it does. And I think about the lie I just told her.

"gin," **Christian says,** and lays out his cards.

He's like a freaking gin rummy genius. I've been trying to convince him to play chess, since Tom and I have had a couple of games now. I even bought a five-dollar chessboard that Tom found at a garage sale. But Christian isn't up for that right now. He seems to be up for winning. I have a full fan of cards in my hands because I hoard my cards. I hate giving up a possible three of a kind or a sequence. I frown.

"Want a turkey sandwich?" I ask.

"Sure, okay," he says. "Want to play again?"

"Deal."

I walk into the kitchen and get out our multigrain
bread and the leftovers from the turkey that Mirriam and I

made yesterday. She has never made a turkey dinner before so we decided to practice. Our second attempt is defrosting on the counter. While I'm making our sandwiches, I call to the other room.

"Hey, are you really good at gin, or do I just suck at it?"

"Is there a polite way to answer that question?"

"Yes."

I plate the sandwiches and am bringing them out to him. He watches me.

"Your hair looks pretty good," he says.

It has been startling me whenever I look in the mirror, but it's better than the alternative.

He is taking a bite when the phone rings. He gets up and answers while I look at the cards he has dealt me.

"Hello?"

I start sorting my cards. Ace, four of hearts, two of diamonds, jack of clubs . . . a crappy hand.

"What? Who are you looking for?"

His voice gets hard, and his decibels finally go up to a regular level. He turns toward me, his lips pinch together, and he tilts his head. Somehow, I'm about to get it.

He continues, "You have the wrong number. There is no Witherspoon here."

The blood drains from my face. Could Edward or Lauren have gotten the number? No, that's too much to hope for. This is blowback from the phone call I made to my parents' house the day I got here.

When Christian turns, I hear my dad's voice leaking from the cell phone. I jump to my feet.

"Who is this?" says my dad.

Christian clicks off the phone and places it very slowly

on the coffee table. He grips the edge of his desk and squeezes his eyes shut.

"You son of a bitch."

"I didn't know."

His eyes spring open, and his grip tightens. "You what? You're going to claim now that—"

"I called before you asked me not to."

He deliberately releases his grip on the desk. His jaw is clenched so tight that his mouth barely opens when he says, "Sit."

He points at the couch.

Like the dog I am, I obey. This is just the excuse he needs to throw me out on my ass.

"Explain." This time, I don't think his teeth separated.

"I just wanted to tell Mom I got here, but the machine picked up."

"That's not what I meant." His voice is escalating. He stops, and when he speaks again, his voice is back in its normal register. "Why didn't you tell me when you found out that I didn't want you to call? If you had told me, I could have changed the phone number."

"It's not like he has the address."

"Jace, it's called reverse directory. He can get it."

"But he won't. I mean, he thinks he had the wrong number. And it's . . . Isn't it listed as Marshall?"

"I'm sure he recognized my voice. I have a life now. I have a career, I have a girlfriend. I can't just pick up and . . . Where is Mom going to go now?"

I freeze. I've cut off her escape route.

He closes his eyes again and pushes his hair back, and I watch his chest expand, hold and release. I wonder if he's counting to ten. When he opens his eyes again, he doesn't look murderous. "Let's talk about this later, okay?" he says. "I'm going out for a run."

He walks into his bedroom and closes the door gently. I can't believe that I've screwed this up, too. How many people can I wreck?

The phone rings again. The door pops open, and he rushes out.

"Just let me," I say.

"Are you kidding?"

Ring.

"He'll think it was me before." Dakota said that our voices sound alike; that was how she recognized Christian as my brother. "Trust me."

"You *are* kidding."

He reaches for the phone to get it before the voicemail reveals everything, but I grab it first.

"Dad?" I say.

Christian's eyes widen in alarm. I cover the mouthpiece with my hand and whisper, "We sound alike."

"Jace?" His high voice comes through the receiver. "I thought it was you. You goddamn liar. What the hell, 'there is no Witherspoon here'?"

"I panicked. I'm sorry."

"You panicked. Why would you panic? It's just me."

Gee, I wonder.

"It's a long story," I say, urging my brain to work faster.

"Start talking. And this time, the truth. No more lies out of your little mouth, you got it?" He has that "or else" sound to his voice, but "or else" what? He's gonna reach over thirteen hundred miles and whop me one?

"I thought . . . There's a warrant out for my arrest," I say, and watch Christian's eyebrows come together while he shakes his head.

"I'll start packing," Christian whispers.

I wave him away and turn my back to him, praying that he can't hear our father the way I did. I have no idea how I'm going to explain the warrant to Christian now. Christian only backs up a couple of feet.

"Oh, yes," my dad says. He has an Oh-yeah,-and-I-meant-to-yell-at-you-about-that tone going. "A sheriff brought that to my attention, thank God, not in open court. It was humiliating, Jace. Humiliating."

"I'm sorry, Dad. I wasn't thinking about your reputation at the time. You know how it is." Why not go for the dig?

"You can't go around doing that, Jace. She isn't your wife."

"Marriage vows make it okay?"

"Don't mouth off at me. Try saying 'thank you' instead."

"What for?"

I'm about to say *For all your valuable lessons?* But Christian takes a step toward me, and I remember what kind of game I'm playing. I wave him back again, walk into the corner between the desk and the couch, and stick my finger in my ear.

"For getting rid of the warrant," he says, his voice smug.

"What? How did you do that?"

"I talked to Lauren."

I can't tell what's worse: the cold lightning that has just shot down my spine or that I'm so nauseated that I turn, push Christian out of the way, and walk to the bathroom, preparing to puke in the toilet.

"What did you say to her?" I try to keep my voice calm, but it's shaking.

"I reminded her how serious a battery charge is. I reminded her that this could affect you forever, keep you out of college, ruin your future. I used to be a lawyer, remember? I can be very persuasive," he says.

Oh God. Oh my God.

"We talked about love and second chances."

I pull the phone away from my ear and stare at the ceiling. Bile slides back down my esophagus, burning as it goes. Christian hovers in the doorway, and I hear my father saying, "Hello? Jace?"

It's okay, I mouth to Christian. Full voice, I say into the phone, "I'm here, Dad. Why'd you do that?"

"For you."

And you've got a bridge to sell me, too, right?

"I shouldn't have, probably," he says, "but it's easier to make the charges go away than to answer to them in open court."

Oh, right. His reputation. Gotta protect that.

"If you want a thank-you, come out here and beat it out of me," I say.

"Jace!" Christian whisper-screams.

My dad breaks into a bunch of screaming, and all I catch is "ungrateful little shit."

I imagine Lauren opening the door and seeing this older version of me in a black robe. *She invites him in, and they sit at her kitchen table, and he reminds her of all her mistakes.*

Christian touches my arm. "Stop it. Get off the phone."

"Are you listening to me?" I hear my dad shout.

"Of course I am. I'm sorry. You're right." I swallow and try to force the two words he wants me to say out of my   155 mouth, but the best I can do is walk a verbal line. "You're right. I should say thank you."

"You're welcome." There's a pause. "I don't recognize this area code on my caller ID. Where are you?"

"What?" I stall for time while I shift my brain back into lying gear.

"Where are you?"

"I'm in Taos, New Mexico." I test to see if he knows I'm lying. If he does, he'll call me on it and then ream me out.

"What are you doing there?"

I breathe; he doesn't have the address yet.

I nod at Christian. Christian's shoulders lower a notch.

"I ran out of money. I was trying for California."

Another notch. Christian signals the "hang-up" motion.

"Why'd you call last month?" he asks. "Did you talk to your mother?"

"No, I haven't spoken to her. No one was home. Why are you calling me now?"

"Do you have money?"

What's this? Concern? "I'm bussing tables."

"Who are you staying with?"

"I'm sharing a room with a waiter."

"C. Marshall?"

I hold my breath. He has figured us out. He's playing me. "Who?"

"On the caller ID, it came up as C. Marshall."

"Oh, right. No, that's just because the phone is in his mom's name. Charlotte Marshall. She's a pediatrician."

Christian slices through the air at his neck, and I stop talking about Dr. Charlotte Marshall. "Why'd you call, Dad?"

"Well . . . ," he says, and I hear him searching for a legitimate reason. My dad is not schooled in the spontaneous save-your-ass kind of lying; he prepares in advance. "Because your mother is sick with worry."

"She's what?"

"Well . . . she just wanted to make sure you were all right. I'll tell her," he says, and hangs up.

I stare at the phone in my hand. That was so weird.

"Did he believe you?" Christian says.

"Yeah," I reply, thinking about why he would lie to me. He didn't call about the warrant; it had nothing to do with that.

"Jace, it's not just about me, you know. I'm worried about you and Mom, too."

About Mom, too echoes in my ears while my brain puts two and two together.

Why did he lie about my mom? I just got an e-mail from her this morning. Things were fine; they had gone out last night for a movie. So she was okay, then. She couldn't have run. Not yet.

Oh God.

I bolt to the computer. I call up the e-mail.

```
Mom,
He is suspicious. Get out, now!
Jace
```

I flush hot, and my stomach flips again. He'll kill her. Asking her to come out here, I've killed her.

Christian is reading over my shoulder. He catches my hand before I hit Send.

"He doesn't know. He's just policing her contacts. It's all right. He used to do that at the end of every month—go through the caller ID for numbers he didn't recognize. That's all it is."

I stare at him, trying to process what he's saying.

"Calm down, Jace, and think. If he knew, he wouldn't be calling here, and she'd be dead. See, it's November third, okay? Beginning of the month."

"But she can't come out here now," I say.

"He believed you about Taos, right?"

I nod absently, thinking about where she can go now. He takes me by the shoulders and shakes me gently so that I'm back in the apartment with him.

"Jace, are you sure?"

"You think he'd tolerate a lie?"

"I'll make us untraceable now, all right?"

He takes over the computer while I walk into the bathroom, feeling my stomach turning over and over.

I lean over the toilet. I could have gotten my mother killed. All it would have taken was for me not to have answered the phone the second time. That's it. He would have demanded to know who was calling her from New Mexico. Was she seeing someone else? Was she making plans to leave? We all know what would happen if she tried to leave.

I kneel over the toilet as my stomach again threatens to empty. I watch sweat drip from my forehead into the toilet water, making a ripple. The tile feels so cool on my knees that, when the nausea recedes, I lie down and press my face against it, trying to find a pattern in the black-and-white hexagon tiles.

"Jace," Christian calls. "You all right?"

No, I'm screwed up beyond belief. I say, "Yeah. I'll be out in a minute."

"We're all set, okay?" he says. "We have a new number. It's not listed, and no address is attached to it on the Internet or via Information."

"How did you do that so fast?"

"I told them the truth."

"You what?"

"I've been known to do that occasionally," he says.

I laugh, and my face bounces lightly against the floor. I just want to stay here for another minute, but I know he's already worried, so I get up and flush the toilet for good measure.

When I come out, he's waiting for me.

"That was some quick thinking. What was all that stuff about a warrant?"

"Um . . . I . . . It's nothing . . . Just a bunch of unpaid moving violations, speeding tickets or something," I say lamely, and then use his lie-distraction technique. "I'm sorry I didn't tell you about the phone call. I should have fessed up."

His features tighten up all over again. "Don't do that again. I have the right to know."

For about half a second I consider telling him about Lauren. But there is no way he'd stand for that.

"Okay," I say.

He runs his hand through his hair again, and his face is wiped clean of the tight jaw and the narrow eyes.

"How do you do that?" I ask.

"Do what?"

"That, that—calm thing?"

"You think I'm calm?"

159

"I can't do that. When I get mad, I explode."

"I don't know, Jace. Probably all the practice you've given me over the years. A blessing of being the oldest." He grins.

How can he smile now? I try to imitate it and feel my muscles twitching.

"Are you all right?" he asks.

"Yeah."

"Yeah? Okay, then, I'm going for a run."

I say okay, but I wanted a real answer. How *does* he do that calm thing?

When he leaves, I return to the bathroom, pull off my shirt, and lie down, pressing my spine against the cold floor to suppress any leftover nausea. I think about my dad sitting at Lauren's kitchen table, making excuses for me, making apologies, and telling her to forgive me.

We talked about love and second chances.

Second chances. Who deserves one of those, anyway?

chapter 19

What is it about New Mexico and cliffs? I am standing at the top of another one, looking over the edge. Thank God I don't have a real fear of heights. Just a healthy one. I scoot my feet farther from the edge. Beside me, Dakota is watching the waterfall that is crashing beneath us, churning up a sulfuric smell that I can't figure out.

Dakota offers me the last bite of the Indian fry bread we've been munching on, but I let her take it.

A few feet from us on the ledge, two boys are shouting and pushing each other.

I hear the ubiquitous "Chicken . . . *bok, bok, bok*" call.

"If I do it, then you do, too," says the chubby guy.

"On three?"

They approach the edge of the cliff, count to three, and jump. I grab my camera and start shooting as their figures plummet through the air and splash into the water below. I hold my breath until they both emerge.

"What the hell?" I say.

"Wanna try it?"

"Are you nuts?" I look at the water racing past. "Why is this called a dam?"

"Don't change the subject."

"Soda dam? I mean you wouldn't think—"

"I'm doing it," she says, and starts climbing up to the natural bridge over the waterfall, leaving her painting stuff on the rock.

"My camera?" I say.

She looks around. It's just us and the kids.

"Leave it there."

I watch her hips in her tight jeans, muscles working for the climb. I put down the camera and follow her.

"From here?" I ask.

"Listen, the key is that there's only one spot where it's deep enough, so you've gotta know where it is. If you miss, you might not come up, got it? So let me lead, okay?"

I take a breath, and I can hear my heartbeat over the roar of the water. "Wait a minute. Why would I want to jump off a roof?"

"I think it's higher than that," she says.

I back off.

"Aww, come on. Haven't you ever jumped off a high-dive?" she asks.

"Once, but that was only because when I tried to climb back down the ladder, a couple of kids started throwing things at me."

She looks over the cliff and starts the countdown. "One."

"They threw watermelons . . . or something."

She rolls her eyes at me. "Two."

"Has anyone ever died doing this?"

"Three."

I'm holding her hand, safe on the cliff top, when she leaps, and her hand rips out of mine. She falls, her body straight and tight. Her head disappears under the water below. I wait. She does not rise. I search the churning water, but I don't see her.

The water is racing past. Maybe she hit her head, and she's sinking. Maybe she's down there drowning while I stand up here watching.

I throw myself over the cliff, but my stomach stays up there. The sound of the air. The pull of gravity. The cliff face blurs before me as I fall.

Oh God, this is why they say you should look before you leap. They say a lot of things. Carpe diem. Even platitudes contradict each other. Man, this has to be the longest fall ever if I have the time to think all this.

I look down and see the water rushing at me. And then I'm under it. The world goes *glub,* and my jeans have been pushed up over my calf into the bend of my knee, to say nothing of what just happened to my butt and my underwear. The water is warm. I open my eyes and endure the stinging, looking for Dakota under the water. I pop up for a breath.

"Jace!"

Dakota is in the shallow part of the pool, climbing out. All right, I'm an idiot, and she's a witch—a safe, breathing witch who I want to kiss.

I swim to her, and she offers me her arm. I take it and crawl onto the bank.

She is laughing. Her wet hair looks even blacker. It is pressed against her head, dripping onto the rock below. Her clothes are stuck to her skin, and I can see the curves of her body without even trying. My imagination didn't do her justice.

"Isn't it a rush?" she says.

"You scared the shit out me."

"I did?"

"You didn't come up for air," I say.

"Yes I did, but you were already on your way down. I thought you were jumping with me." She pats me on the back. "Thanks for trying to rescue me. Want to go again?"

"No!"

She laughs again. "I'm sorry. Really, I am." She shifts her weight onto one leg, and the curve of her hip pops into exaggerated relief.

"It was worth it to see you like this."

She puts her arm around me, leans in, and kisses me. Her wet lips slide over mine, and I can taste the warm river. My hand skates along her hip to the small of her back. A vibration purrs in her throat.

Lauren's throat is small enough for me to strangle her with one hand.

I gently pull away from Dakota. "I can't. I can't do this."

"I'm so sorry." She stares at her shoes, and her wet hair falls forward, obscuring her face.

"It's just that . . . ," I say.

"You're with someone else."

I don't want to lie anymore; it's just getting so damn confusing. I don't want to hurt her feelings either. Just how am I supposed to be a good guy here? What would Christian do?

"No, I'm not. I lied about that."

She stares at my face for half a second, her mouth falling completely open, before she turns and starts hiking away, leaving sloshy footprints on the rocks.

"Wait, Dakota. Wait." I run to catch up with her and walk with her, even though she will not look at me. "I was dating someone in Chicago—Lauren. And we're over, but . . ."

"You're still hung up on her?"

"More like stunned by our explosive breakup. More like unable to see myself with anyone right now."

Or ever again. I stop walking. How am I ever going to date anyone? Dating someone I didn't like, namely Caitlyn, didn't work. And if I can't date someone I *do* like . . .

My. Life. Is. Over.

"Why did you lie about it?" she says, stopping when she gets to our stuff.

"It was easier to say there was someone else than that I'm just a wimp who's still dealing with . . . I wanted you to think better of me. I'm sorry, but I'm telling you the truth now." I puppy-dog-eye her. "I'm working on it. Honesty lessons."

"You're an interesting guy, Jace. You steal, you're sorry for it, you bring the loot back, and you charm your way into a job. Then you lie, but you admit it, apologize, and charm your way back into this friendship. You could charm your way out of hell, couldn't you?"

What was that phrase my mom used to describe my dad? *Could charm the trident away from the devil*—something like that.

She continues, "I see a pattern forming. You might just turn yourself around, Jace, sir."

I grip my hands together to keep them from going around her, and I bite my lip to keep from kissing her. I'm not going to be able to keep this up. I release my hands, but she grabs our stuff and hands me my camera.

"I have emergency towels in the car," she says, "and I'm freezing out here."

I clasp my hands back together and follow her.

mirriam calls from the kitchen, "Can you peel these potatoes?"

We've only been working on turkeys so far, so I ask why we're doing potatoes, too. She explains that putting together a dinner like this requires that she work out the timing. I realize that she's nervous to meet my mom, which reminds me . . .

"Hey, did you and Christian talk?"

"I'm thinking of getting a cat," she says, scrubbing a dish.

She stops, dries her hands, leans over, and gathers her long hair into a ponytail and then curls it around itself, tying it into a knot. When she comes up, she reminds me of the night we first met, her black hair tied back.

"What?"

"A cat. You know, purr, purr."

I can't figure out the connection between a cat and my question, so I figure she didn't hear me over the rushing water, and I let it go.

"Yeah, I know what a cat is. Ever had one?"

"No."

"They're not that much work. Lauren just adores her cat, Kali."

"Who's Lauren?"

I freeze for a millisecond, my potato peeler on pause, and then hope she hasn't noticed. "No one."

"Girlfriend?"

I nod.

"Still together?" she asks.

I shake my head.

"Hmmm. You talk about as much as your brother does, you know that?"

"What do you want me to say? I liked her cat. So, you know, get a cat. They're . . . furry."

"Keeping my ear to the ground, I heard you've been talking about a girl from work," Mirriam says.

"It's a damn small school."

She nods and smiles. "Gossip heaven."

I remind her of Dakota and their meeting. She says she's embarrassed about how she acted when they met and that she hopes they can get along, that it won't be awkward.

"Where would it be awkward? It's not like I'm having her over for Thanksgiving. It'll just be a family affair."

Mirriam's lips curve into a crescent, but she doesn't look happy. She glances at the clock and asks when I think

Christian will be back. When I tell her fifteen minutes, she picks up the pace of her cooking.

"You're acting funny," I say.

"I'm . . . not . . . I am? I'm just worried about the time. I have a parent-teacher conference . . . phone call tonight. Is Lauren the only girl you've dated?" she asks.

"No, but Lauren was the only one I fell in love with."

She smiles again, and my lips tighten.

"You think I'm sixteen, so I don't know what love is, right?"

She shakes her head, sad smile on again. "Sometimes I wonder if that's the only time we really get to love someone completely. Without fear. After that first big breakup, we keep ourselves a little more protected, a little more hidden."

She's staring off.

"What are we talking about now? You?"

"No, Lauren. What's she like?"

I think for a minute. How to describe Lauren?

"She has a backbone of iron; she can be a little bitchy, you know, just because she knows what she wants, and she's not afraid to get it."

"Oooh," she says, as if a lightbulb has popped on over her head.

"What?"

"I just understand why you would like her, a girl like that."

"Why?"

"Well, she's not your mom."

I slam the potato peeler on the counter. It doesn't help that I know Mirriam's right. I never noticed it before, but now, thanks to Amateur Psychologist, I see it, too. Every moment I spent with Lauren is cheapened by need.

"This isn't let's-analyze-Jace hour, all right? I mean, I'm just telling you something, and you go and find a way to make it all . . . psychological. Lauren and I weren't like that; we weren't all desperation and dysfunction," I say.

"Okay."

"We were good for each other." *Her head is hitting the bricks, and her heels are scrabbling for purchase.* "Sometimes."

"Why'd you break up?" Mirriam asks.

"Why are we talking about this?" I pick up the potato peeler again and jerk it over the skin of a Yukon Gold.

"Just making conversation."

"Really? Why don't you tell me about your ex-boyfriends? Why did you break up with them?" I say.

"All right, all right. I get the point. But I don't feel like I should apologize for worrying about you. You have to admit that you're coming from a difficult place. I'm sure whatever made you leave wasn't easy. I mean, whatever it was—"

"He kicked me out. So you don't have to go all tortured-soul on me, all right? No big last beating, no death threat, no Hollywood escape plan," I say.

"You're right. No drama there at all."

I look at her, and she's got her arms crossed and is smiling at me.

"Jace, I understand if you're uncomfortable talking to me about it, but be sure you're talking to someone, okay? I mean, I'd prefer an adult. I'd suggest a therapist—"

I glare at her, and she puts her hands up and continues, "But I know how well that would go over. So, maybe Tom, or even Dakota."

I think of Dakota's house and how, even though it was

loud and everyone was laughing, I felt like there was something still and quiet, something unbreakable there.

"Christian never talks, and he's doing all right." *Better than me, at any rate.*

"Well, we disagree there. He has some real problems, and he—"

"Hey," I say and point the potato peeler at her. "There's a limit, all right. I'm his brother first."

That sad little crescent appears on her lips once more.

"Mirriam, are you all right?"

"Yeah. You just sound like him."

I do? "Thank you."

She looks at the clock again, helps me put the turkey in the oven, and gives me instructions for mashing the potatoes.

Mid-instructions, she breaks off and says, "She named her cat Kali?"

Before she gives me the lecture that I can see brewing, I say, "I always thought it was kind of cheap to name a cat after someone's God, but not my cat, not my call."

She gives me her proud-teacher smile, and I roll my eyes, which makes her laugh. She hurries through the potato instructions. But as she's walking out the door, she stops and says, "Your mom's going to love this. Imagine, making that trip and finding her family waiting for her, a turkey dinner all laid out. It'll be great."

I look at the kitchen and sigh. It *will* be great. As long as she can get here.

chapter 21

it's twenty days until my mom comes, and I forgot my cleats. Stupid, yes. But why not? The rest of the day has been so perfect—I shattered a test tube in science and spilled some kind of acid on my shoe, which left a big hole over my toe, and I can't imagine how much new shoes will cost. I didn't get lunch because I forgot to pack it. So I distracted myself in the media center, checking my e-mail. My mother's contribution to my day was, "O.K." In two letters, she was lying. I wanted to write a scathing e-mail about protecting my dad via silence, but instead I typed in, "Good to hear. Stay safe."

Then the dreaded one from Lauren. The Warrant e-mail came back to me once more. Previously, she had written "done." Now:

Undone.
Your father came to see me a few days
ago. I need to talk to you now more than
ever. What can I do to get you to call
me? To write? Confused and still in love
with you,
Lauren

Then, just before the game, I realize that I'm cleatless, so I race to the apartment, fly up the stairs, and unlock the door. This day has got to get better, right? I'm owed a little luck. After all, it is statistically improbable that we will lose every game this season. We're off to a ripping start of 0–8.

On the floor, slipped under the door, is an envelope with my name on it. Hmmm. I open it up and pull out three white sheets of paper that I unfold. A pink Post-it is stuck to the top sheet.

J,

Found this when I was cleaning out some old stuff. Thought you might like to know . . .

M

I rip off the Post-it and flip through the papers: "Statistics on Intimate Partner Violence or Spousal Abuse," "Resources for Domestic Violence Victims," and "Domestic Violence Centers." I hold my breath and scan the top sheet.

I never realized how much I hated statistics until this moment. How pleasant, how reassuring, how helpful to know that my family is not an anomaly, that all the times my dad has come after us can be reduced to fat black numbers and percentages on a page.

Oh, and good, what I did to Lauren is also represented here, in a special break-out section called "Teen Abuse."

I get a number, too. I'm four times as likely to become a fuckup and hit my own girlfriends because of where I've come from. How nice that I'm in rotten company. We should form a club. Is that what Mirriam meant when she wrote that she thought it might help? I have to remind myself that she doesn't know that I hit Lauren and isn't trying to piss me off. It was one of the many stats on the sheet. She's trying to let me know that I'm not alone and that I can "get help."

I clench my teeth until my head hurts and end up finding my cleats under the freaking bed in Christian's room. (Why did I put them there?) I drive back to the school at around ninety miles per hour. But I'm late anyway, so the coach benches me for the first half, and I watch Tom fritter away chance after chance. When I get in, I get no touches on the ball until there's less than two minutes left and we're down 2–1. The entire fight is downfield, and our defenders are digging it out. Finally, a midfielder gets it to Eric.

I'm open. I have a clear shot to take it up the sidelines and then cross it back to him in the box. On the left side, Tom has lost neither the midfielder nor the defender.

Eric scans the field and sees me. We make eye contact for half a second. I lift my hand. He turns and tries unsuccessfully to thread it through to Tom. He's been doing this all damn season. The opposing team picks up the ball.

I'm sick of losing and sick of his shit.

I pivot and push hard against the ground, seeing the cross the defender is going for. I sprint as hard and fast as I can. I trap the ball with my chest, dribble it up the center, and see Eric. I should pass to him, I know it. Not a chance. I take it up myself and fake a hard shot, expecting the goalie to go for it. My foot is already on the ball, swinging through for the strike, by the time I see that he did not bite. The ball soars, but it's an easy get.

After the game, we're in the locker room, and I'm avoiding Eric, and he's avoiding me, even though our lockers are three apart (another one of the signs that God has forsaken high school). Coach Davis slams the door open, and we all freeze.

"Out!" he screams. "Everyone but Jace and Eric, out."

Tom hops by, trying to get his shoe on as he hurries out of the locker room.

It is suddenly silent, and everything we say echoes a little.

"You two. You aren't leaving here until you get this worked out," Coach Davis says, and walks out the door.

I stare at Eric.

He stares at me.

We start at the same time and run over each other's words: I don't give a shit; I scream, he screams.

"You could have passed me the ball," he says.

"Your showboating cost us the game."

"Goddamn prima donna."

"Don't you ever get tired of losing?"

Even I can't hear what I'm saying anymore. I stop. When he's quiet, I say, "Just take out Caitlyn, bonk her until you can't see straight. I don't care. Leave it off the field."

I slam my locker closed and walk out.

When the coach steps in front of me, I say, "I've got to get to work so they can pay me next to nothing."

He's slower than me, so I get around him.

"Get back here and sort this out."

Before a backdraft, if you're looking for it, a little smoke leaks. I get a whiff of that now and say, "I can't be late or they'll fire me. You want that?" I am yelling it, I realize. "I've gotta go."

Gotta go before I punch your face in.

He gets in a final shot: I'll run laps at seven a.m. on Monday morning or I'm off the team.

Dakota is not at work when I get there; she has called in sick, and I've got a customer who seems to want to push each of my two hundred and seventy buttons in quick succession. Oh, wait, the universe missed one. Douglas sees me slamming cash register buttons and suggests the stockroom; I know he's right, but I swear at him before I go.

On the way home, I'm trying to figure out how Christian does it, remains calm. I remember him running his hand through his hair and his anger disappearing. Could I ever do that? I remember Mirriam's voice: *Those kids were broken.*

Can the broken be fixed? Is four times as likely equal to inevitable? It would be easy to say yes and have done. But there's Christian, who has never hit a girlfriend.

Undone, Lauren wrote.

When I get home, my brother has decided to make us . . . Oh my, mushrooms and soup. Can we live off something else? I remember my scanty paycheck and shut up and eat. He wants to have a brotherly talk.

"How was your day?"

Sucked. Remember high school? "Okay. Yours?"

"You know what, Jace? This isn't going to work."

I've already agreed to all your ground rules; I'm working my

job; I suck down soup and mushrooms without complaint, and keep the apartment in shape, stuffing everything of mine under the couch, under the desk, under the filing cabinet. Shall I just shrink into the woodwork? Would that be better for you?

I try to borrow his calm and place the spoon down gently, even though I can barely see it. "Okay, what do you need me to do differently?"

He looks at me funny. "Not you. This place. When Mom moves out here, we'll need something bigger. I won't be sending her money anymore, so we should think about moving."

You'd think that would calm me down, the idea that Mom is coming, the idea of both of us welcoming her in. Instead I see nothing but white for a second. I don't want to think about it right now. I push it off.

"What about Mirriam?" I ask.

"We broke up."

"You what? Why?" I say.

"She was not happy with me."

"Why on earth not?"

Christian stirs his soup, and I watch his Adam's apple bob when he swallows. *That bitch.* I remember how she was trying to avoid him the other day, and that sad smile that kept coming to her lips whenever we talked about Christian, and how she is showing up here, slipping notes under the door for me. I push the chair back and walk out the door.

"Jace!"

I pound on Mirriam's door. She answers it just as Christian catches up.

"What the hell are you doing?" I ask.

Her eyes flick over to Christian. He explains, and she tells me to come in so we can talk.

I refuse to take one step into that traitor's apartment. **177**

"*You* told *me* to be patient, that it was hard for him to open up, and here you are, ending it. You're a such a hypocrite, Mirriam. What's wrong? Is he a 'broken kid,' too? Too much for you to handle?"

"Jace," Christian says from behind me in the hallway. "Stop."

"He's played by your goddamn rules, and still you dump him. You fucking bitch."

Mirriam's face loses its unflappable teacher expression. She takes a step back, and as I'm taking one forward, Christian reaches through the doorway and pulls at my arm. My muscles are coiled. When I try to shake him off, he clamps down on my wrist.

"Jace." His voice is as firm as his grip. "Get back in the apartment." He locks my arm down, keeping me immobile until I look at him. His eyes pin me. "Right. Now."

I relax my arm. He lets me go, and I stomp back to the apartment and slam the door.

I can barely see where I'm going as I circle the apartment; I grab the back of a chair and slam it to the carpet. The metal back bounces with a thud. One, two, three chairs on the floor. We can't lose Mirriam; she's teaching me to cook. She's bothering to slide irritating statistics under the door and ask me questions, even if I don't want to see the damn stats or give her answers. She's the one who got Christian to let me stay.

I kick the couch, my bare foot slamming into the cast-iron bed frame. "Fuck!" I hobble over to my latest victim and sit down, feeling the cushions give under me.

Through the paper-thin door, I hear Mirriam say, "That's what I mean, Christian. Something is eating at him."

"We're doing fine, and you . . . You're not a part of it anymore."

"Oh, yes I am. He just came over here."

"He won't bother you again. I've got it," he says.

"You know I don't mean it like that. Has he ever talked to you about Chicago? Told you about the night he left?" she says.

"He doesn't have to. I know it."

"No, you don't. Neither of us has any clue what his life has been like for the last five years. It's more comfortable for you to think you know it, so you can continue to avoid it."

"No, I'm just giving him the space he needs. When he is ready, and not before that, he'll talk. It's not fair to push him, to make him get better on my time line."

I stand up, and my foot throbs in protest. I walk out the door. "Did you break up because of me?"

Christian is in the doorway in half a second, his body blocking me from her.

"No," they say together.

"Go back inside," he says.

I look around his shoulder at Mirriam. "This isn't right. How can you do this to him when he opens up to you?" I say.

He turns me around by my shoulders, ushers me back inside, and says sorry to Mirriam before he closes the door behind him.

"Don't you ever do that again. What happens between Mirriam and me is just that. Between her and me. You stay out of it. Got it?"

"But she isn't—"

He lets go of my shoulders, puts a finger up in my face, **179** and waits until I look down. He heads into the bedroom. I try to see something other than white. There's a door in front of my face, I know it. Something soft hits me in the head and then drops to the floor: running clothes.

"Put them on," he says.

"Christian, my foot is—"

"You wanted to know how I do it? How I keep calm, even when I'm so pissed I could put my fist into your gut?"

I blink in surprise. *Fist in your gut?* Whose language is that? Certainly not my brother's. My imperturbable brother.

He goes back into his room, and I change into the shorts and T-shirt. My foot is already swelling, but I stuff it in my shoe anyway.

He comes back, also geared up.

"Didn't you run already today?" I ask.

"Let's go."

We're about two blocks from the apartment building, standing on a parched dirt path next to a fenced-in golf course. The twilight has turned the grass into a green lake, the blades of grass blurring into one dark surface. The night air bites at my bare arms, and I wonder if he decided to toss me a sleeveless jersey as part of my punishment. He's wearing a long-sleeved shirt.

"Go," he says, and nudges my back with his shoulder.

I start jogging, in spite of my protesting toe. Christian jogs next to me; I watch him finding his rhythm, knowing he has shortened his steps for my pace. I open my mouth to explain, but he cuts me off.

"No talking," he says. "Just listen."

But he doesn't say anything. He gazes out, not looking

at me. I push the pace faster until I'm sprinting past him. I look back, and he is trailing at his own pace. When I stop, he strides by me, still silent. I catch up and keep his steady pace, not knowing how long we'll be running. Hell, this guy runs 26.2 miles for fun, but apparently he does it silently.

What am I supposed to listen to?

Half a mile of road later, I start to hear it: my footsteps striking in a steady rhythm; my breath in and out; the wind singing in my ears. I glance at Christian. He is mesmerized by the horizon. I focus on it too and watch the sky soothe itself into blackness.

Everything goes out of my head: my forgotten cleats, the stats, my fight with Eric, Mirriam's face stripped of her calm-teachery-mask, my mom's hand not touching mine when she promised to come out, Lauren crumpling on the ground . . . It all fades . . . all I hear are my steps, breath, wind . . . all I see are the changes in light as we run under the streetlamps . . . crossing from lightpool to lightpool . . .

bright . . . black . . . bright . . . black . . .

step . . . breath . . . wind . . .

finally, I silence my brain . . .

We are about three miles out when my breathing becomes panting. I don't want to stop, but my body is giving up. My legs quit. My toe throbs. It's probably the size of Africa. Christian loops around in front of me and blows back past me.

"There's only one way back," he says as he passes me.

I turn and start walking—limping, really. His back disappears toward the darkness. Above him, the moon is full, low on the horizon. It is large and the color of cream. I'm about to chase him down when he glances over his shoulder, turns again, and jogs to me, slowing to a walk as he gets nearer.

"Okay," he says, "you look ready. It's my fault that Mirriam broke it off. I didn't talk to her."

"Why not?"

"I don't like being pressured into it. It's the principal of the thing."

"Bull," I say.

He starts to object, but I talk over him.

"You want to, but you're scared. What's she gonna do? Break up with you?" I say, and he smiles. "You've faced down worse than this."

"Not really faced it down, Toad."

"Well, then, it's about time."

"I guess so."

His breath puffs into mini-clouds, reminding me that it is still cold. The wind blows my arm hairs to attention. Contrary to all logic, walking is harder on my toe than running. I take off again. About thirty steps into it, he catches up to me.

"What about you?" he asks. "What have you faced down?"

I shake my head and keep my eyes on the horizon. "No talking. No questions. Your rules."

He runs a little behind me and I can hear our footfalls in chorus. When we get back, I put my hand on his shoulder and hop up the stairs, since my ankle has gotten in on the throbbing action.

On the second-flight landing, he points to the top step. "Sit. Let me see it."

I sit down, and he jogs down a couple of steps, kneels, and works off my shoe gently. He does the whole doctor thing, watching my face while he twists my foot one way and then the other. It would be amusing if it weren't so painful.

"What did you do?" he asks.

"I just . . . I, uh, kicked the couch, hit the bed frame."

"Good choice."

I roll my eyes.

He says, "Seriously, better a couch than a person. You've gotta not do that with Mirriam, all right? Not with any woman. Not with anyone. You know that, right?"

I swallow and nod, casual-like. I go for the distraction technique again.

"Yeah, of course. Do you think it's broken?"

"You just ran six miles. I doubt it. Just give it plenty of rest, all right?"

Right, that's just what Coach Davis is going to let me do.

"Remember RICE. Rest, Ice . . ."

"Compression and Elevation," I finish for him. "I could have a PhD in first aid."

"I'll bet."

He grabs my wrist and hauls me up. I wait for him to pass me so I can put my hand back on his shoulder as we make it up the steps. At the top landing, he says, "You're sure you're okay?" When I nod, he says, "Then I'm just gonna . . ." He tilts his head toward Mirriam's door.

"Good."

While I'm limping through our door, I hear him knock on Mirriam's. "I have some things I want to tell you," he says. "Can I come in?"

Her door squeaks open, and I close ours. I sit down on the couch. I wait and watch our door handle. It doesn't turn. I take off my sneakers. My big toenail is puffy and red. Blood has crusted around and under it.

I get a sack of frozen peas from the fridge. I put it on my foot and stare at the door handle. It still doesn't turn. Not by the time I fall asleep, my body aching for the relief of a long night's rest, my foot raised up high on a stack of couch pillows. The door handle only turns the next morning, when Mirriam comes in for a change of Christian's clothes while he is in the shower.

"Thanks, Jace," she says. "You're a great brother. And a good friend to me, too. Christian told me that you were the one who got him talking."

No, I'm a broken kid. A little help here and there isn't going to fix that.

"Sorry I scared you."

She looks away, not willing to tell me that it's all right because we both know it's not. Finally she looks back and says, "If you take care of yourself half as well as you do him, you'll be all set."

monday morning, and I have three miles. Three miles my ankle doesn't want to run. I don't even bother showing it to the coach. I just tape it tight and take off. At least I got a couple of days off.

The early-morning air is cold, even though it's supposed to get hot today. New Mexico weather is a mystery. Who knew it gets cold in a desert? The soccer fields have a weird smell of dust and grass intermixed because beyond the fields you can see where the sprinkler stops and the ground goes back to its native survival mode.

"Next to each other," Coach Davis shouts.

I don't change my pace.

"Marshall, hurry it up," Eric calls back.

"You're both benched for the final game if you don't get in sync. It's not like our record would suffer."

I don't change my pace, which surprises even me. The last game of the season is usually a big deal for me. Especially this year, since I'm not lined up on an indoor team for winter. Somehow, I care less about soccer now than I did when I got out here. I wonder if I'll even go out for the team next year. Eric stares up at the sky, swears, and then jogs in place until I catch up.

"You're acting like a granny this morning, I see. Prima donna," Eric says.

"My toes are swollen up like sausages."

He glances at my foot and slows down even more. "What happened?"

"Nothing."

"Something happened."

I tell him about kicking the couch.

"What'd ya do that for?"

"I was pissed, all right? Do I have your permission to get angry, O Captain, my Captain?"

"I was just trying to be decent."

Decent this.

I set my jaw, and we jog in silence. I remember running the other night, when the world slipped away, and try to get back there, but with Eric's breath in my ear it ain't happening. I glare at him. He looks through narrow eyes at me for the rest of the lap. We pass Coach Davis in silence.

"God, you're an ass to make me say it. You're gonna make me say it, aren't you?" he says.

"Hey, how about you just don't talk to me unless you have to?"

"No, we blew the play because we didn't talk. So . . ."

He looks like a kid who is being forced to take medicine. "You were right. I was wrong. Any rivalry about Caitlyn should stay off the field."

"There is no rivalry. Caitlyn isn't even on my radar anymore. Would you just ask her out?"

The whole stand-in-to-make-him-jealous act is pissing me off and boring me simultaneously. My community service is done.

"Aren't you guys . . . together?"

"NO! Jesus, just ask her out already. People *do* get back together, you know."

That Friday, for our final game, Eric is no longer taking his romantic angst out on me. We're moving more like a unit; Eric is passing me the ball. The scoreboard doesn't show it (0–0 with only penalty time left), but we've been whipping their butts; the ball's been on their side most of the game, and if we could only get one around this goalie, we could win. The team is pursuing, pursuing, and I'm feeding off their energy.

I convinced Dakota to come. I try not to think about her watching me and wonder if I look good or like someone trying to look good.

For the throw-in, I jostle with the sweeper as he tries to find an adhesive remover to get me off his tail. The ball is passed high, and we fight it out in the air, both of us going up for it. Off my head. A pass to the Eric-ish region. On the way down, the sweeper bangs into me, and we both end up on the grass, my tongue on dirt and green. He uses my head for support as he gets up and drives his knee into my back. The bastard. I pull my face out of the dirt and stick my foot out as he's stepping forward. *Your turn to eat the grass.* I'm reaching for him when the crowd begins to scream and whistle. Eric streaks past, his hands in the air, and the ball is trapped in the net. The whistle shrieks three times, and the game is over. We won.

The guy waves an exasperated hand, but I can still taste the dirt and the anger in my mouth. Before I can get to the sweeper, half the team is around me, dancing on the field. I muster up a smile.

I promise Tom I'll be at his end-of-soccer-season party next week and ditch the team, opting for an olive and sausage pizza with Dakota instead. Once we're seated in the pizza parlor, Dakota tries to get me to call the highlights, but I switch topics.

She says, "You don't seem very excited."

I should be. Usually I'm a maniac at the end of a season, especially if we go out on a win. Last year, Lauren said if the winter soccer season didn't start soon, she would take me to therapy.

"I'm not sure I'll play next year," I say, and as soon as it's out of my mouth, I realize that I've been wanting to quit for at least a couple of weeks.

I haven't had fun at one game this year. I thought it was because we weren't winning, or because of Eric, but maybe not.

"Yeah? I thought you were all about soccer. It was soccer or bust, you know?" Dakota says.

I think of the guy who I tripped today and the significant self-control it took not to land on him. I thought all the fury came from playing with Eric, from losing all the time, but it wasn't that at all. Soccer was always about adrenaline.

188   "Maybe I'd rather run."

"I could see you in track."

I picture that. *Feet jammed in the blocks, the adrenaline pulsing through my veins as I wait for the gun, every muscle poised.*

"Nah, just running."

The solitude in running, the quiet, would be spoiled by the hope of kicking the other guy's ass. I want that rhythmic stride, not the competitive rush of soccer.

What would my dad say? For the first time, I wonder how often I was on the field just so my dad and I would have something to talk about.

It's ten days until Thanksgiving, and Mirriam comes into the store to get some Christmas shopping done. The lines are getting long now for the holidays, so I can't help her out, even when she asks me what I think Christian will like. She says she'll wait for me in the café.

When I head back there, Dakota and Mirriam are sitting together, each with a cup on the table.

I approach with caution. After hellos, I ask what they were talking about, and Mirriam says, "He's just worried I'll tell you all his secrets. Come back in ten minutes."

They turn back to each other as if I'm not standing right there, and Mirriam says, "So you didn't like the dye job?"

"He just doesn't look like himself."

"Yeah, I think that was the point."

Then she reminds me that I should skedaddle for ten and practically shoves me out of the café. I'm left remembering how I felt waiting outside parent-teacher conferences.

When they get back from the café, the lines are down, and I offer to walk Mirriam to her car.

It's cold out, but too dry to snow. She points out her car in the parking lot, and I wish I'd brought my jacket. When the wind picks up, it slices through my clothes and chills my skin.

"Dakota's really nice. Why don't you take her out?" she says.

"I'm on a dating hiatus."

We pass an SUV, a toy car, and a topless Mercedes that makes me wish I had a better car.

"So . . ," I say, trying to think of a subtle way to ask, but I give up. "Did she say anything about me?"

"Yes, but that's between her and me. All I'll tell you is that you should ask her out."

"Nooooo, I shouldn't. I like her too much to date her."

"That makes a lot of sense."

"It makes Jace-sense," I say.

"Which is the equivalent of nonsense," she says, smiling. "Family trait?"

"You noticed that, huh?"

"You do know that a 'dating hiatus' is not mysterious code for a 'bad breakup.' "

I throw my arms in the air. "Did I say to you 'Mirriam, I'd like to be interrogated on a weekly basis'?"

We arrive at her car, and she gets halfway in. With the door still propped open, she starts the engine, and we say good-bye. Just before she closes the door and pulls out, she says, "If I were you, I'd cut the hiatus short. Take it from someone who knows. It's not easy to be patient."

Before I leave work that night, I seek out Dakota.

"Hiya, stranger," she says.

"Have I been a stranger lately?" I ask, lifting half a stack of books off her arms and walking with her to Fantasy.

"No, you're just stranger each time I see you."

"Funny. Get that one off a cereal box?" I say, but I can't help laughing.

Dakota has this strange habit of enjoying how not-funny her jokes are. We stop in front of an empty shelf, and I feel a magnetic pull tugging me toward her. I want to drop the books on the floor, back her up to the stacks, and taste the cinnamon-rain on her neck. Instead I tilt the books and shove them wholesale onto the shelf.

"Did I tell you about the game?" I'm suddenly a tongue-tied geeky thirteen-year-old who is asking a girl out for the first time.

"Last week? The one you won? The one I was there for?"

"Did I tell you about the postseason party?" I ask, even though I know I haven't. "No parents, lots of booze, that sort of thing. Come with me."

"When is it?"

"Friday. You're not working."

She smiles. "Have you been stalking my schedule again?"

"Come on."

"Sure."

I go hot, and my brain jumps into panic overdrive. *In a few months, Dakota will come to work with a bruise on her face and a good story about tripping over a branch while hiking in the mountains. She'll be good at covering up by then.*

"Wait," I say, "It's not like a—"

"Date or anything," she finishes for me. "Yeah, I got it."

chapter 23

Christian's car is back in the shop, and when I pick him up at the hospital, he tells me the garage will take a few more days. Could I pick him up again tomorrow?

"No problem. You know what? I'll bet we could manage with just one car. It would save on expenses. Maybe you should just abandon the Pontiac in the shop."

"I don't know if it will be harder or easier when Mom gets here. Is she coming by car?"

"I don't know."

He says nothing, and I just grip the steering wheel tighter. The silence stretches out, as if she's here already, as if she, Christian, and I are working on becoming a family, a threesome rather than a pair. It will change everything.

"If she does try to leave him, it'll be risky, you know? Mirriam told me that that's the pattern. When she tries to leave, it's the most dangerous time," he says.

"You needed Mirriam to tell you that?" I say.

He is quiet, and I realize that I've been too sarcastic, but I don't know how to soften it now.

"Jace," he says quietly.

"Yeah?"

"She promised she'd come, right? She said that?"

"She said, 'I'll come to you.' "

"Oh. Can I ask you a question?" he says, finally breaching the rules that I've stomped all over this whole time.

"Just this once," I say, grinning, but he doesn't join me.

"Did she ever try to leave him again, since that one time?"

I shake my head. "I begged her not to leave him then. Did you know that?"

"You were only, what, six?"

"Five," I say. "She'll be smarter this time, right? I mean, more careful, right?"

"Only six more days," he says.

We're silent the rest of the way home. I turn on the music to make it seem more natural, as if we're both not thinking about the day she tried to hustle us off to a shelter, the day she decided that the lower-class life she grew up with was better than the abuse she was taking.

When I try to sleep that night, it's completely futile. I keep hearing my dad's voice, going from angry to icy. I keep watching an eleven-year-old Christian step between my dad and her.

She had told him that if he ever touched a hair on our heads she would be gone. I don't know; maybe that's why 193

Christian did it, to force her to get us out. But I think Christian just loved her too much to keep on watching silently.

Christian and I were sitting in his room while Dad was screaming at her downstaris. I don't remember about what anymore. We were trying to play Go Fish, but each time we said "fish" our voices were a little quieter, listening to my father spewing his acid. Then we heard a smack against her skin: open-handed, a slap. Where? Her face? Her arm? Christian got up and cranked up some music.

"Turn that shit down!" we heard.

He leaned over and turned down the music. I tried to listen to the woman in the music wailing instead; I tried to hear only the guitar screaming. Christian and I were both staring at the cards in our hands when we heard a crash. We looked at each other over our cards, and he put down his hand slowly, open-faced, so I could see the spades and diamonds, the hearts and clubs fanned out against the carpet.

In his eyes, I saw an unreadable look, maybe the first one I had ever seen. I always knew what to do when I looked at Christian; he would shift his weight, and I would know to step back; he would twitch his lips, and I would know to laugh. But this was enigmatic. It was the only indication I got that we were about to enter different worlds: him taking the hits, me still protected and watching.

He stood up and walked to the door. I watched him hesitate before he turned the handle. I didn't know if he was waiting for me. I stood up and went downstairs with him, each footfall just a little slower than the last until I was going right foot, pause, left foot, pause.

When we got to the bottom, he swept the air behind

him, motioning to me to stay back. But when he disappeared, I ran the length of the hall and peered into the archway.

My father had my mom by her shirt collar and was pushing her against the china cabinet. Her head was pressing against the glass. Christian stepped right between them, knocking Dad's hands to the side.

"You son of a bitch," Christian said.

"Christian, honey—"

"Don't talk to me like that," Dad said.

"Don't tell me what to do," Christian said, and I noticed that his head only reached our father's shoulder.

I edged into the archway, but Christian straightened up as if he could tell I was there without looking. He shook his head, and I knew to stay out. I crept over to the side and watched.

"I'm your father. I tell you what to do, and you do it."

"Not when you hit my mother, asshole."

"Christian, that's enough," my mother said, grabbing his arm and trying to ease him out of my father's way.

"What's the matter?" Christian said. "You want to hit me, but you can't because she's got you on a leash, doesn't she?"

Christian didn't see it coming. His head snapped back when Dad popped him, and Christian, not used to taking it yet, went down, hitting his head on the floor.

Fightology Lesson #6: To reduce the chances of a concussion, keep your chin tucked to your chest on your way down.

I screamed; I was not schooled in being a witness yet, either.

The next day, she packed while he was at work. I was 195

eating chocolate chips straight out of the bag for lunch when the taxi honked. Christian grabbed my hand. As we started out through the garage, I saw my bike. I grabbed the handle bars and started bringing it with me.

"No, honey," my mom said. "You can't bring that."

"Then I'm not going," I said. "I want my bike." A vision of a new bike made me hopeful. "Unless I'll get a new one at the shelter."

"Well, let's see when we get there."

"No," Christian said. "You won't. Jeez, Mom, at least be honest with the kid."

He came back and grabbed my hand. I clung to the open garage door.

"But Dad won't be able to find us."

"Yeah, that's the idea, stu—"

"Christian," Mom said.

He sighed and ran his hand through his hair. He could have pried my fingers off the door. He could have jerked me away. He only let go of my hand and walked on.

"I think it's better to leave, so I'm going."

I let go and ran to catch up, taking one last look at my bike.

When I turned back, my dad had appeared out of nowhere, his car blocking the taxi. My mom's face was deflated, her jaw open, her cheeks sagging. He paid off the driver, moved his car, and ushered us back.

"A taxi? Sometimes, Jennifer, I think you might actually be clever."

My mother bit her lip and didn't meet my eye. Christian and I both knew that the taxi wasn't her idea, that it had been arranged by the shelter.

196   "You were watching us? I can't believe you watched us."

"I don't have to watch you to know how that little mind of yours works."

Years later, I learned that this cryptic comment was not about a psychic connection. He *knew* because my mom made a big cash withdrawal, and he kept an e-mail alert on the account. After that, he took her name off the account and handed her cash for all purchases, which made for plenty of awkward moments.

We walked into the garage, and I felt my skin go from hot to cold in the space of a second. As the garage door closed, the sunlight disappeared by degrees.

Here's the thing that scared me the most: he was calm, he was deliberate when he reached for the hammer. I saw him extend his hand and choose a nail out of his blue toolbox. Usually there was screaming, name-calling before the blows began. But this time, he just walked toward her with the hammer and nail resting in his palm. She backed up, back, back, back, until her feet hit the wall.

"Walter."

"You know what I always said about taking my kids."

"You know what I always said about *hitting* my kids."

He raised the hammer and swung it. I shut my eyes and felt Christian's arm close around me. I crumpled, and he held me up as I buried my face into his side. I heard the crack of the hammer striking, and he exhaled in one great breath, his stomach pressing against my cheek, so I knew I could look.

My dad pried the head of the hammer out of the wall, not two inches from her ear. When he lifted it a second time, Christian let go of me and rushed my dad. The hammer clattered to the floor. He lifted Christian up and threw him to the cement.

Fightology Lesson #7: Sometimes you'll need to roll faster than a boot.

I wonder now why I stood there and watched. Why didn't I race to my downed brother, open the garage door, grab the hammer away, anything? No, I froze and watched him fire his foot into Christian's stomach, cock it, and slam it into his back and then his face. Christian's head hit the cement with the distinct *thud* that I came to associate with concussions. He curled up and rolled onto his side with his face resting in a blue-green pool of antifreeze. Incongruously, Mr. Yuk Face flashed in my mind: *Don't drink the poison.*

My dad regarded the blood on his black dress shoes. He swore. Then he picked the hammer up off the floor and walked to my mother. He grabbed her wrist, and her arm went slack, following Fightology Lesson #8: Relax when the hits are coming because it hurts less. He lifted her hand and pinched the flesh between her thumb and index finger, stretching it up. Pressing the thin flap of skin against the wall, he placed the point of the nail into it.

"Hold still," he said. "I don't want to miss."

"Walter, wait. I won't try to leave. Not ever again, I promise." She started sobbing.

But he raised the hammer again. She closed her eyes, her body tensed.

Fightology Lesson #9: Sometimes even the rules don't protect you.

It took him three slams to pin her skin to the wall. *Thunk*-scream, *thunk*-scream. *Thunk.*

"You'll leave only when I tell you that you can." His voice was like ice and I thought, *That's not my father. My father's voice is like a blanket.*

"Only when you say so," she said. "I'm sorry."

"You won't ever leave," he said in his ice voice.

"I won't ever leave."

He kicked Christian again, and I heard a grunt.

"My kids," he said. "My rules."

When he drew his leg back again, a wordless scream erupted from me. *Stop. Stop. Please, please, stop.* He whirled around to me and stared at me as if he had forgotten I was there. He tilted his head.

"Jace?" he said, his voice suddenly sounding like my father's again. "Go into the house," he said gently. "Go on."

In the sudden silence, I looked at Christian, who was propped on his hands and knees, antifreeze and blood racing each other to the ground. He lifted his hand and motioned to the door, protecting me still.

"Close the door all the way," my dad said. "And go on up to your room, all right?"

I went inside the house. Our kitchen, empty and clean. I clicked the door shut, but I didn't go to my room. I stared at the hinges, rust seeping out through the seams, and squatted on the floor, hugging my knees.

"Look what you did!" I heard my father screaming. "Did you see his face? How am I going to explain this to him now? He wanted to stay. He understands loyalty." I heard a muffled sound, Christian's voice. "What?"

"I'll talk to him," said Christian.

"You?" I could hear contempt thickening his voice. "You're as bad as her."

I heard his shoes striking the floor, coming toward me. *I should get up,* I thought, *I should go to my room. Like he told me.*

"Dad?" Christian said, and the shoes stopped. "Can I . . . May I please take her hand down?"

"No. She doesn't want to come home."

"I do, Walter. I'm sorry."

"No, don't rush into any decisions, Jennifer. Take your time."

I uncrouched and climbed the stairs to my room. No place seemed safe. I crawled under my bed, but that didn't work. I walked out and went into Christian's room. He had a prism hanging in his window, and I watched the rainbows bend across his wall.

When I heard her scream again, I knew that my dad had pulled the nail out.

When my dad found me, he carried me to my room and, I clung to him. I can't remember almost anything he said to me except, "I couldn't let her take you from me. What else could I do? Don't you want to stay with your dad?"

And I did. Even then, I did.

What would life be like without him? He was our glue. At the center of our lives, he determined what we would eat for dinner, where we would go for vacation, what school we'd attend. Wouldn't our family spin out of orbit, drifting away and lost, if we weren't charting our course around him?

At dusk, he dumped out the recycling bin, going through *Chicago Tribune* by *Chicago Tribune* until he found the one he wanted. He cut out an article from the newspaper about a man who was acquitted of killing his wife. I watched the scissors neatly snipping, and him smiling. He went into the garage with a flashlight and read it to her. I heard him telling her that he had his defense planned out and that he knew how to get off.

By dinnertime, I was starving, having only had chocolate chips for lunch, and I thought about how it was outside and how hungry Christian and my mom would be. He refused to take them anything to eat, but I asked if I could. He considered it and then said he was proud of my loyalty to them. So I spread peanut butter and jelly on some bread and poured them each a glass of milk. I peeled carrots, sloughing off their thin, frail skins, revealing the bright orange meat beneath. I put the food and drinks on a tray and carefully balanced it as I opened the door.

I walked into the windowless garage. In spite of the dark, I could make out my mom. She had sunken to the floor, but Christian was not visible, not even a shadow. I hesitated in the doorway until my eyes adjusted.

When I took my first step in, Christian appeared out of nowhere, and I jumped away as he reached for a sandwich. I stared into his eyes, which looked foreign and unknowable. Yesterday, before the card game, I knew every expression. This one was new. It was hunger and panic and desperation. When he reached again, this time for me, I dropped the tray. It clattered to the ground, and I heard glass shatter as I ran back into the house. My father was in the other room, and he came out as I came in. I ran straight into his waist, his belt buckle cold against my cheekbone. I smelled his Bay Rum as his arms went around me.

"Don't let them scare you," he said. "It's just weakness, but you're strong, right? Yes, you are. You're strong."

I nodded. I hoped I was. I hoped I couldn't end up like that, with hunger and panic and need in my eyes. My dad's arms gripped me, and I relaxed in them.

The next morning, he let them back in the house, and a few days later, a real estate agent came over. She was told my mother had cut her hand when cutting up a chicken. I don't remember how long it was until we moved, but our first night in our new house, I went to their bedroom. My mother was sitting in a rocking chair with his head on her lap.

He looked up at her and said, "Please don't leave me. I don't want to have to do that again."

She pushed his head back to her thighs and stroked his hair.

When she tucked me in that night, I said, "Let's stay here. It's a nice house. I like my room. Let's stay."

"Don't worry," she said. "We're staying."

Her eyes traveled over to the window. I thought she was just studying the new neighborhood, but now I think that that far-off look was about all the things she couldn't have. Now I think she saw her life shrink, contained inside a two-thousand-square-foot house.

When she looked back at me, she said, "I promise."

She wrinkled up her nose and waited for me to smooth it out before she gave me a kiss.

Now, as I lie in bed and stare at the ceiling, I wonder what I'm doing to her. Am I wrong to hope for Thanksgiving? Surely it's worse to stay trapped like that than to risk getting out.

The sky is unblackening in preparation for the sun. I go for a run, watching the horizon and listening to my blood pulse. I train my footsteps to a mantra: *She is com-ing. She is com-ing.*

at Tom's party, the music is pounding through the house.

Dakota says, "You brought me. Now you've gotta dance with me."

Tonight I have already touched her waist to guide her inside and her forearm while getting her a drink.

We walk out onto the makeshift dance floor. (Tom has pushed all the living room furniture to the walls). For a second, we face each other, neither of us moving. Then she takes a step toward me, slings her arm over my shoulder, and, with hips grooving, sinks down. *Oh, that kind of dancing. I can do that.* I put my hand on her hair, and as she comes up, I slide it down her back until my hand rests just above the curve of her butt. Under my fingers, her back muscles are working, keeping her hips on the move. I pull her toward me, and in one quick move, she straddles my leg. The beat drives us closer together, and her breath brushes my shoulder.

She leans back, her weight against my hand, and I see her stomach stretching long, her jeans dipping lower. I curl over her, my mouth by her collar bone, her cinnamon-rain scent everywhere. When she comes back up, I lean down so her lips come close to mine. Her eyes start to close, and I pull back.

"You want something to drink?" I say.

Tom, who has been watching us, says, "I'll keep her company. You go."

She asks for a beer, and I thread my way through flying arms and pounding feet as I head for the kitchen. A cooler sits on the table. After grabbing her drink, I rifle through a bunch of ice and bottles to find something non-alcoholic. (I'm driving.) I retrieve a Limonata and watch Dakota dancing with Tom. She keeps her distance, maybe a foot and half between them. The dirty dancing is just for me.

"Who's she?" I hear next to me.

I turn and see Caitlyn watching Dakota.

"Come on," I say, because I can barely hear Caitlyn over the music.

I catch Dakota's eye and gesture to the door. She nods and continues her moves while I lead Caitlyn to the porch. She hops up on the railing, and I rest Dakota's beer on the porch rail. Caitlyn launches into twenty questions: What's her name? Where did you meet? What is she like? But I become so monosyllabic, she switches topics.

She tucks her chin to her chest and snickers. "Tom's quite a dancer, huh? He's too uncoordinated even for that, much less soccer."

Tom's not a bad guy. Someone who you could trust with a girlfriend. Not at all like Edward. Tom isn't trying to use me as a ladder to get to the top of the social stratum. He has never seemed to care about that.

"Tom's okay. Leave him alone."

"Good thing he has a man to stick up for him."

"I get that you needed someone to play off Eric, and I was cool with that, but now . . . What, you've gotta put someone else down to lift yourself up?"

She lifts her eyebrows and crosses her arms; I'm out. I'm sure of it. Maybe not this minute, maybe not even this month, but slowly I'll be cast to the side. Maybe that's where I need to be to keep that bastard-no-longer pledge once and for all.

Eric comes out of the house, slamming the screen door behind him.

"Hey," he says, weaving a little already.

He puts his arm around her back, and she nuzzles into his shoulder. Their mouths meet for a second. Well, I guess that's why he has become Mr. Friendly Guy.

"So, who's your date?" Eric asks.

"Her name is . . . We're not dating."

"Yeah, right."

"How come no one believes me when I say that?"

They both laugh, and I push out a couple of ha-has with them.

"If you dance like that with someone you aren't dating, what do you do with your girlfriends?" Caitlyn asks.

My cheeks get hot, and they laugh again.

I feel a weight on my shoulder and turn to find Dakota, who is making me her chin rest. When I introduce them, Dakota and Caitlyn size each other up.

I hand Dakota her beer, and she offers me a swig. It's bitter and rich. Eric puts his arm around Caitlyn, and they go in for another long kiss. I exchange a glance with Dakota as their kissing escalates.

"Hey," I finally say. "There are rooms upstairs."

They separate, then look at each other and head inside.

"Ho-kay," I say. "Let's walk?"

She puts her arm around the porch pillar and leans out over the bushes, looking up into the sky. "Okay."

When we're on the sidewalk, I can't think of anything to say; there's too much residual heat in my mouth from the dance, from how close my lips were to her bare skin, from how she felt riding my thigh.

"How's your brother?" she asks. "It's funny. I would have pegged you as the oldest."

"Yeah? How come?"

"I don't know. You don't seem like someone who has relied on other people to take care of you. You know, you're bossy."

"My brother wasn't really around for a long time. College. And my mom had enough of her own problems to deal with. It was my dad who . . ." I want to say took care of me, but that doesn't sound right, does it?

"Who what?"

"Listen, how come no one believes us when we say we aren't dating?"

She shrugs. "Probably because we want to."

206

I don't say anything. She stops walking and takes my hand. She puts it around her back and then slings her arm over my shoulder again. I'm surprised I don't exhale steam.

"You want to dance here?" I ask.

We can still hear the music floating out of the house.

"No," she says. "I want you to make your move. Meet me halfway."

"No."

"Jace, I honestly don't get you. I know you want to date me. Hell, everyone knows you want to date me. So, what's the problem?"

"Yes, all right? Yes, I do."

A dog starts barking. I stop and wait until the dog's commentary is done.

"Your last girlfriend couldn't have been that bad."

"She wasn't . . . Believe me, it wasn't her. I'm just not a good boyfriend, and I don't want you to get hurt."

"Oh, really? What makes you such an awful boyfriend?"

I glue my lips together.

She waits.

Glued.

She waits.

Superglued.

She caves.

"So let me get this straight. You like me. You want to date me, but you think I shouldn't date you? Don't I get to decide that? There's a fine line between chivalry and control."

I shrug. "Sometimes people make the wrong decision, and if I can help it, you won't."

"Jace, that is so condescending. It assumes you know more than me."

"I do. I know more about me."

"Well, that's fixable."

She reaches up and draws a line with her knuckle from my temple to my jaw. I step back, out of her reach.

"I can't, okay? I can't."

"Know what?" Dakota says. "It's not okay. I'll get someone else to drive me home."

She turns, and I watch her walk away.

"**d**o you really think we need this much?"** Christian asks as I weigh a bag of green beans on the grocery-store scale.

This is the first time we've been grocery shopping together, and we're doing it on the Tuesday before Thanksgiving since both of us have the rest of the week off (him as a long Thanksgiving break and me because school was only a half day today). We were hoping to avoid the crowds, but they aren't cooperating.

I watch the red needle swing and then settle. "Recipe calls for a pound and a half."

"There will only be four of us, Jace. You're cooking enough to feed a homeless shelter."

I spin the plastic bag and twist the green tie around it. 209

"Mashed potatoes and gravy, cranberries, green beans, and turkey. Sounds reasonable to me."

"Twelve pounds of turkey."

"That's actually a very small bird."

"And then Mirriam is making, what? Four pies?" Christian says.

"You're exaggerating." I tick them off in my mind— pumpkin, apple, pecan, and peach—and then glance at him aslant. "Oh. Four."

"How much do you think Mom will eat?" he asks. He looks down at the cart and runs his thumb over the green plastic handle. Back and forth. Back and forth. "And we had to shop organic?" he says.

I put the green beans in the cart. "You're worried about the money?"

"I'm worried about the waste."

He pushes the cart. As we pass the mushrooms, he slows, but doesn't stop.

"You don't like the menu?"

"No, Jace, it isn't that." He picks up a lemon and passes it from one hand to the other.

"We need two lemons."

He doesn't reach for another one. "What if she doesn't come?"

"She'll come."

"Jace, she hasn't even left yet. Isn't it a day's drive from Chicago?"

I shrug and push the cart out of the produce department.

"You need onions," Christian calls.

I park the cart by the chicken breasts and head back for the onions. White, I decide, and pick up a bulb. The papery skin flakes off in my fingers revealing green lines that stretch like longitude marks. Christian has a plastic bag open and waiting. I toss three in.

"Sometimes I thought she would come out to New York."

"She'll come. All that time, I'll bet she stayed for me. Now there's no reason. The night I left, she told me she would come to me," I say.

I take the bag from him. Maybe she said that just so I would leave. Would I have left without that reassurance? Is that why she told me Thanksgiving, to keep me away? Did she know that I wouldn't want to return once I got settled here with Christian? I spin the bag too fast. It whips out of my hand, clunks to the floor, and rolls to Christian's feet. He picks it up and twirls it closed. When he hands it back to me, his forehead wrinkles with a sort of pity-worry look. But then it smooths out.

He sighs and says, "Does she still like cherries? Maybe we should have some fresh fruit on the table."

I choose to believe that I've convinced him, that he's not indulging me.

When we get home, I drop my four bags on the table and go straight to the computer. She's supposed to be here in two days. Christian's right; unless she's driving straight through, she should have started. But I get a two-word e-mail from her.

Just fine.

I sit down, Google her route, and find hotels every four hours on the trip. I drop the links in an e-mail and write:

Thought this might be helpful. When are you leaving?

Christian is watching me while unloading the insanely expensive winter cherries. He takes out the green beans and sets them beside the cherries on the chair. His way of unloading groceries: dry and crunchy items on one chair, bathroom stuff/tissues/cleaners on another, and fridge and frozen goods remain on the table. That organized. That much like my mother. If she was coming, she would have planned out her own hotels, I know. I stand up and start helping him.

"Anything?" he asks.

"She hasn't left yet."

We are silent so my words dog us. They follow me around as I kneel down to find the herbs for the rub. They cling to my ear as I put the spice jars on the counter. I decide to shake them off.

"But she will," I say, while he continues to organize frozen from fresh.

"What?"

"She will come."

When the silence falls again, I start making the brine, pouring a steady stream of salt into a pot of water. I measure out and dump in the herbs: small dried sage leaves; sharp, unforgiving rosemary. He comes in, opens the freezer door, and begins to fit the new food in.

"You don't think so," I say.

"Maybe we should call."

"I'll just finish this first," I say. "We've bought the groceries, anyway. And the brine alone takes twenty-four hours."

I'd rather keep thinking she's on her way.

I reach for a knife to start cutting the flesh-toned plastic off the bird, but he catches my hand.

"Make the call," Christian says.

I dial and hear it ring. *Please don't pick up. Be gone. Be on the road already. Be in a hotel.* I want my dad to pick up and say in a breathless voice, "Jennifer?" I want to hear that desperation.

Ring.

"Judge Witherspoon." My father's voice comes, gruff and angry.

"It's me."

I hear something behind him that makes it sound like he's on a train platform or something.

"Why are you calling us again? You need money?"

Sometimes I wonder why words can't actually make us bleed.

"What's that sound?" I ask.

It clicks off, and I can hear him more clearly now.

"The vacuum cleaner," he says, and my stomach tightens.

"Mom's cleaning?"

"Of course."

"Can I talk to her?"

"She's busy right now," he says. "She decided to scrub the floors by hand this morning, instead of asking the maid to do it. She's doing everything herself for the party we're having."

"For the what?"

"Thanksgiving party. We're having the judges over."

There's a pause while I try to absorb what he's saying. She's not going to walk out on him before a party with his colleagues.

"Can I talk to her?" I say.

"Who is it?" I hear her ask in the background.

"It's Jace."

There is a long pause, and I know what's happening. They're doing the post-abuse dance. My dad is judging: How many minutes can I let her talk to earn her forgiveness? How close can I stand? If she comes on the line, I know he's back in charming mode, know he has something to make up for.

"Jace?" she says, but her voice is shaking, and she hits the sibilant sound too long. "How are you?"

My throat tightens up. "Are you all right?"

I grip the phone tighter. I know we won't really be able to talk, not with him hovering over the phone. But I wish she could say, *Never better. I'm heading out tomorrow and I can't wait to see you and your brother.* I wish she would say, *We'll be okay now.*

"I'm fine, honey. Don't worry about me, okay?"

Her vowels are flat; it hurts to move her mouth.

"When are you leaving?" I ask.

"No, he's doing fine, too. Lassst night, he thought that I wasss trying to find you. How ssstrange that you called usss today. Where are you?"

"Say 'that far?' " I tell her.

"That far?" she says.

"Does he know that you're leaving?"

"Not ex-ss-actly. You can't call usss again, okay, honey? It'sss not good for you to think we can be a family again."

"What does that mean?" I ask.

"Jennifer," I hear him say.

"I have to go now."

"He doesn't know about the e-mail account, right? Has he found it?"

"No, no. I should go. Bye, honey."

"Are you coming?"

Click.

Christian is waiting in the kitchen doorway. Characteristically, he doesn't ask. He just walks beside me.

I step back. "Something's wrong."

"What do you mean?"

"She's in trouble, Christian. Real trouble. She just took one from him, but he hasn't let up. He's suspicious, but he can't find proof yet. Calling was . . . I just made things worse."

I cup my forehead in my hand, my thumb pressing into my temple. I know what I need to do. I put her at risk when I drove off without her. I put her at risk when I hit my father, knowing full well that he would not tolerate me in his house anymore. I can't leave her there unprotected. I need to go back. But Christian isn't going to react well. I'm going to have to argue.

I'll say, "I have to get her."

And he'll say . . . My imagination stutters.

It doesn't matter. Anything he says, I'll have the same response: "I have to."

I take a breath, drop my hand, and turn around.

When he sees my face, he sighs.

"Okay," he says, his voice tight and his elbows pasted to his sides. "Let's go."

I hadn't realized I was holding my breath, but now it comes out in a rush. He'll come with me? My eyes start to sting.

"Really?" I say.

"Really."

chapter 26

he's driving my car, and we're in Oklahoma. As we pass each state line, his elbows shrink closer and closer toward his sides while his hands stay glued at ten and two. I probably should have told him I'd get Mom myself.

I try getting him to talk.

"Mirriam is okay with this?" I ask.

"She said she'd make the turkey for when we get home," he says, absently. "Do you still know Mom's schedule?"

"Well, I know *his,* if that's what you mean. No packing this time, all right?" I say. "Let's just get her and go. I want her to be a ghost."

I grimace at myself. I wish I hadn't chosen that word.

He is silent.

"What kind of fast food do you like?" I ask, trying to distract him.

"What if she won't come?"

"KFC? There's one up ahead with a really grumpy window boy, so maybe we could go for Arby's."

"Should I pull over for this conversation?" he asks. " 'Cause we are having it."

"No, let's keep moving." I pause. "She'll come."

He is silent again.

"Okay," I say. "So you were right; she wasn't going to show up for Thanksgiving dinner."

"It's not about an 'I told you so.' I just want you to prepare yourself."

"She's just kind of confused, is all. She doesn't want to go back to being lower-class."

"She's not worried about money, Jace. She's committed to him, and I don't know if she can change anymore. She was only twenty when they got married, and they'll be celebrating their twenty-fifth anniversary this year. She's spent more than half her life with him. She has never lived as an adult without him. How easy would it be to leave that? I just mean that if either of us could decide for her, we wouldn't be here, right?"

"She'll come. Both her sons, no more worrying about all the little things that could set him off. We just won't mention how small the apartment is."

He smiles.

I continue, "If you don't think she's coming back with us, why are you here?"

He looks in his sideview mirror. "What do you think, Toad? That I'd let you walk back into that by yourself?"

My throat tightens up again. I don't know how to tell him how much I needed him to come, how much it means that I'll have backup, that there is actually someone else on this island of one, so I skip it.

"Let's think positive, okay?" I say.

"No, let's be realistic. If she doesn't come with us, you're going to have to let it go. You can't keep putting yourself in the line of fire for her, all right? I did that—we both did that for too long."

"She's your mother too, Christian," I say.

His jaw muscles jump, and he runs his hand through his hair.

"I don't mean it like that," I say. "You're coming inside with me, right?"

"Right."

"So you're putting yourself in the line of fire too."

"No, I'm not. We're making damn sure he's nowhere around before we set foot in that house, got it?" he says.

"Got it."

"No chances."

"No chances."

Even though it's nineteen hours both ways, it seems longer going back, while I watched the clock and decided that seventy-five in Texas, then eighty in Oklahoma, eighty-five in Missouri, and ninety all the way up I-55 could only garner me a speeding ticket, so who cared? While Christian was asleep, I went ahead and did a hundred. When he woke up, I dropped my speed to ninety. He looked at the speedometer but didn't say anything about it. Instead we talked about everything Albuquerque, keeping it light— better for morale. But I noticed he started to lean forward as if urging us closer to Mom. *See, he cares about her.* I told myself. *Because if he doesn't, if he really can cut her out of his life just like that, then what could he do to me?*

As we get close, he becomes quiet and stares out the side window. When the skyline comes into view, he smiles; that's a good sign.

I change paths, taking Lake Shore Drive a little earlier than necessary so we can see the water and so we can slow down. I miscalculated before. I want to make sure that Dad's out of the house by the time we get there, even if he's running late. It's the day before Thanksgiving, so the traffic is lighter than usual; already people are taking the day off.

As we're passing Hyde Park and the University of Chicago, Christian leans against the door, watching the lake rush and break in a spray along the concrete blocks. He points as we pass the Museum of Science & Industry. "Right there," he says. "Can you see the really tall white apartment building over there?"

I nod.

"I lived in that little brick one, next to it." He pauses. "5649," he says softly, to himself.

"What?"

"Street address."

"Where did you work?"

"In Greektown? Greek Islands Restaurant."

"Really?" I think of the white stucco-like walls and the blue aprons on the waiters. "I love their lamb."

He looks at me and smiles—strange to share a memory that we have in common, if not together.

"I didn't realize how much I wanted to see it again," he says.

I nod. Maybe that's how he'll feel when he sees Mom, too.

"You guys are in River Forest now," he says, and rubs his fingers together, making the beaucoup-bucks sign.

My dad only made it to the bench after Christian left. The Seventh Circuit has been good to him.

"My bedroom is obscenely large. Probably bigger than our entire apartment."

We're quiet as we pass downtown, and I revert to big-city driving. Break, gas. Break, gas, and then the traffic begins to break up and it's gas, gas, gas.

"The Costacoses are in Berwyn," he says, looking south as we pass by the neighborhood on our way.

When we get to my house, I coast around the block once, hoping no one will recognize my car. The thin covering of snow is custom-fit to the lawns.

"Which one?" Christian says.

"There." I jerk my chin at the house. "The brick one."

I watch his face. No jumping jaw, no wistful remembering. That's just me.

"No cars out front," he says when I don't stop.

"I'm looking for his car. You know, just to make sure."

As I approach the house, I look down our block. The branches of the elms form a canopy of sharp points that pin the gray sky up. As I pull in to park, my wheels slip on the leaves that lie in wait under the snow. I kill the engine and stare at our two-story house. I don't understand why places that felt like acid can work like salves after you've been away. I don't know why seeing the patio swing, used only once since we moved in, makes me want to throw the door open and declare that I'm back.

Christian is watching me. "Are you all right?"

"Yeah. You ready?"

"Yeah," he says, but we stay seated and stare at the house.

I hear a car engine approaching. I sink lower, just in case, and watch an unfamiliar blue sedan speed by. I put my hand on the door handle but don't pull.

"We can just drive home if you want. It's up to you," he says.

But what if my dad knows that she was planning on leaving? What if she's pinned to some wall? What if she isn't breathing? I push the door open.

"Wait," says Christian, grabbing my arm. "Are you sure, absolutely sure, he isn't home?"

"Yes. It's like ten." I double-check it on my watch, making sure I've adjusted for the time change. "He leaves for work at seven-thirty. Gets back at five-thirty. We have a big window."

"What if he's sick today?"

"Let's check the garage first."

He nods and follows me around the house, past the bare Mock Orange bush to the garage. We peer in windows and see the empty concrete. My mom's car isn't there, either.

"Come on," I say.

Christian lags behind me as I walk around to the front and up the six steps to the house. I insert my key, hear the tumblers slide and then pop. I flash on the last time I was here, screaming around my father for my keys. This time I'll drag my mom out by her hair if I need to.

It is utterly quiet. I glance around the foyer. My stuff—my jacket, gloves, hats—are gone. I see my mother's blue coat and touch the wool.

Christian starts to close the door, but I shake my head

at him, and he pushes it back open. I want a quick escape route in case he is at home and his car is in the shop or something.

I step inside and look through the living room, into the dining room. Behind me, the oak floorboards creak under Christian's weight. My breathing is shallow, and I can practically feel my adrenaline glands pumping. We split up—him to the left, into the living room, and me to the right. Out of habit, I knock on my dad's study door. Empty. Files lay in stacks. One is splayed open, and his pen is resting on a page. I look at the leather chair in the corner where I used to do my homework.

The leather squeaks under me when I sit down. I slide my fingers around the cushion stitching, and they catch on something. From between the cushion and the arm, I dig out my dad's old money clip. It's empty. I pocket it. It isn't exactly stealing; he intended to give it to me when I turned sixteen anyway, but he lost it. Is it so wrong to keep a piece of him?

I continue my sweep. In the downstairs bathroom, the one off the kitchen, I see a clear glass jar of Q-tips, identical to the one I broke the night I left. I stare at them until Christian says, "She isn't here."

I jump.

"Do you know where she is?" he asks.

"For all I know, she's on her way to Albuquerque."

I finally think to pick up the phone and dial, talk to the clerk: Is Judge Witherspoon there? He's on the other line, would you like to hold or leave a voicemail? I opt for voicemail and then hang up.

"I guess we've got the place to ourselves," I say, making a bad joke, Dakota-style. His elbows release slowly.

I say, "Come on," and head for the stairs.

As we walk up the steps, Christian stops, looking at the photographs on the wall: my mom on their wedding day (hard to believe they were so young); my dad when he was about seven, sitting on a pony with his cowboy boots on; me, leaping for a header, the soccer ball in midair, my blond hair flying; a shot of my mom in profile at the beach. As we walk up, it's like walking back through the years; I young-ify—standing with my dad at Soldier Field when I came up to his shoulder; with my mom at the lake when I was skinny, but I was trying my best to make a bicep pop up; middle school graduation, purple cap in hand, the closed smile of junior high, hiding my braces; and my toothy pre-braces, fifth-grade grin. Finally we reach early elementary school, and Christian stops. He puts his hand on the frame.

"I took this one," he says.

There isn't a single picture of him on these walls.

"Mom has a whole box of pictures of you in the base-ment," I say.

"It's okay," he says.

At the top of the steps, I turn and walk into my parents' bedroom. So much order. The bed is made and laid beside it are my dad's slippers. I walk over and open her closet. Everything is hanging. Except for her brown boots, all her shoes are lined up.

In the bathroom, I crouch before the vanity, yank it open, and see the tampon box. I open it up: an envelope, thick with greenbacks, is taped to the inside.

"She hasn't left," I call out.

And Christian was right; I've been a total fool, relying on her. My cheeks go hot. I should have known she'd need help to get out. I sit down on the bed and look out the window.

Christian says, "Can I see your room?"

"Sure. I guess you haven't gotten a tour."

We walk to the end of the hall and push open the door to my room. I stop.

It is empty.

The mattress is stripped and lies naked. The walls are bare, and all that's left is my furniture. Gone are my trophies, my poster of Beckham, the picture of Lauren and me at the Brookfield Zoo. Even my Cindy Sherman prints. Gone. I scan for anything that looks familiar.

It's not like I wanted to live here again or anything, so why does the emptiness feel like a slap? It's like I don't exist anymore.

"Jace." Christian puts his hand on my shoulder.

I shake him off, remembering something. I slide my hand between the mattress and box spring. My fingers reach fabric. I clamp down on it and pull—my queens. I sit on my bed and scoot them out into my hand. Ally, Guinevere, the whole crew. Their carved faces never changing, immobile and frozen. At least I can take them with me.

"Jace?" Christian says.

"Yeah."

Christian sits down beside me. "Did you . . . You stole those?"

I look him in the eye. "Yeah, but I don't anymore."

"Why don't you leave them here, then?"

"No," I say, pulling them away from him. "This time, they're coming with me."

He sighs and looks around. "I'm sorry about your

room."

I suck in a big breath and am ashamed of the way it shakes. "It's not a big deal or anything. It isn't my room anymore, anyway."

Short bars of rainbowed light start to float around the room.

"What is that? That isn't my—?" Christian asks.

"Yeah, your prism." I stand up and pull it from the window, the suction cup kissing loudly.

"I can't believe you kept it. How many times did you move since I left?" he asks.

"Only twice. Mom figured out that whenever she made friends, he'd move us. He was clever about it; kept work close and friends far. Triangulated, probab—"

"Twice," he says, his eyes still on my hands, "and you kept the prism?"

I pause, my focus shifting to the cut glass in my hand. "Yeah. I kept it."

It was kind of stupid, I guess. When we moved right after Christian left, I freaked, afraid he wouldn't be able to find us. I took his prism and hung it in my window, thinking that if he happened by our house, he would recognize it and know where we were. Now I hand it to him.

"No," he says. "Leave it. I don't want him to figure out we've been here."

I hesitate, but I guess I don't need it now. I return it to the window, trying to stick it back in the dustless circle.

"So . . . ," I say.

"Should we wait?"

"I guess so."

We sit in silence for a minute.

"Hungry?" I say. "Come on."

We go to the kitchen, and he stands, not knowing   225

where anything is, while I hit the fridge. On the door, I see our white board. Scribbled in blue ink:

> 10:00 Get stuff for party
> 12:00 Cake ready, pick up at 1:00
> 2:00 Season turkey, boil potatoes . . .

I show it to Christian.

"She won't be back till two," he says.

On the microwave, the clock reads 10:15.

I say, "Well . . . Now what?"

We knock on the door to the Costacoses' mini-brownstone. Through the green stained-glass window, I see a shape moving toward us. I glance at Christian, who is less than three inches from the door. I'm hanging back behind the welcome mat.

A short, white-haired man opens the door, and Christian throws his arms around him. He slowly embraces Christian and then closes his eyes.

"John," Christian says when he has disentangled himself. "This is my brother, Jace."

John steps forward and shakes my hand. "Good to see you both after so many years." He turns and screams, "Effie!"

I take a step back while he shouts to her in Greek. The only word I catch is the untranslated "Christian."

A rotund little woman comes barreling to the door and engulfs Christian. He laughs and kisses her cheek. They walk inside, heading through the house. I follow behind them and hesitate at the kitchen entrance. Christian sits down at the table while Effie disappears into the fridge and pulls out a platter of dolmades and three kabobs.

"What can I make you? What can I get you? Are leftovers okay? Everything in the fridge is for tomorrow's dinner, but leftovers feels a little, well . . . ," she says.

"Leftovers are perfect."

"Really? Do you like Greek food?" she asks me. "Come in, come in. Sit down."

Christian looks around the kitchen, beaming. I haven't seen him beam once in the almost three months I've been in Albuquerque. This, I see, is the gap between the brother I knew and the brother I know.

"You've redone the curtains," he says.

Effie walks over to Christian and puts a hand under his chin, looking at his face like a mother checking for dirt.

"I'm all right. I'm good."

"Fair enough," she says, and I know where that phrase came from.

She starts dishing out yellow rice onto Christian's plate, her head turned toward him. They've enveloped him within seconds and have not asked one question. I can see why he's so at home here.

John pulls up a chair. "Should I call Paul and Henry to come over for dinner? How long can you stay?"

Effie practically bounces. "Oh, wouldn't it be fabulous to have a real family dinner, all of us together?"

"We can't stay long." Christian glances at me.

She comes over to me, grabs my sleeve, and tugs me over the threshold onto the linoleum floor. "Jace, it's so good to see you. Come in, tell me what you'd like."

I ease my sleeve from her grasp. "I'm fine. I'm actually not going to stay."

Christian's head twists toward me, his eyebrows furrowed.

"I have someone I should see, too."

After a few protestations, Christian says he'll walk me to the door, as if this is his house.

I remind him that Dad gets off the bench at four-thirty and is usually home at five-thirty. So we agree on one-thirty to go back to the house. When I put my hand on the door-knob, he says, "Stay. I want you to meet them."

"Nah, you've got a whole thing going on here."

"You're not going to be in the way."

"It's not a fifth-wheel thing. I really do owe someone a visit."

He looks at the stairwell. The couch. The ceiling. He doesn't ask. I can see it on his face—he's here in this house, with people who never asked him anything; how can he ask me who I need to see, and why? It's a pay-it-forward attitude that, I now see, I've been taking advantage of.

He looks down, and I scurry out the door before he changes his mind and decides to press me.

chapter 27

Lauren's red Celica is in the driveway, parked across both spots, blocking the garage. Her mother must be on a bender. Tomorrow is Thanksgiving, debauchery in prime time.

Their maid answers the door and lets me in without question. She tells me that Lauren is upstairs.

As I climb the steps, I hear music pulsing from her room. The song switches from Eminem to U2, and I know she's listening to a mix I gave her. Through a crack in the door, I can see her. She is reading a magazine, lying on her stomach, her knees bent. Her calves curve up toward the ceiling, and her glitter-green polished toes tap the air in time with the music.

I feel something brush my leg. Kali is curling around

my jeans. She meows at me. I pick her up and push the door all the way open. Lauren sees me and freezes, her finger paused in her magazine, her toes stopped. She looks exactly the same.

Kali twitches to get down. I gently toss her onto the bed next to Lauren, and she goes padding by, her paws sinking into the comforter.

Lauren's room is the most familiar thing I've seen since I've come back. I recognize the maple furniture that rests against the rose-colored walls, the white picture rail that runs from door to window to door with a prayer stenciled in black over it: GRANT ME THE SERENITY TO ACCEPT THE THINGS I CANNOT CHANGE; THE COURAGE TO CHANGE THE THINGS I CAN; AND THE WISDOM TO KNOW THE DIFFERENCE.

I've been here so many times, showing up like this without warning after I watched a beating or took one. I'd just stand in her doorway, raw and wrecked, with a well-practiced smile, covering up. She'd always open the door for me, even between the times we were dating. She'd take me to bed. Now I want to stay here, in this familiar room, with familiar her.

Lauren stands up and slinks over to me. She pulls me inside, closes the door behind me and leans toward me. I'm not sure who kisses whom, but when her lips press against mine, I am right back. I pull her hard toward me, and she leaps, wrapping her legs around me. I fold my arms under her butt, and she dives in for another kiss.

Everything slips away. I put my tongue inside her mouth.

She yanks on my neck, and I carry her over to the bed. I lay her down, and her hair splays across the pillow. She

scoots down and peels the hair off her neck so I can kiss it, but when I see the curve of her throat, my memory intrudes. *Her larynx pressing against my palm.*

"Lauren." I pull back. "I can't do this anymore."

"All right."

She grabs my hand and drags me down next to her. She arranges me around her. I lie with her on her single bed; we are curled into one smooth shape. After a while, I feel her breathing change under my arm. Inhale, and hold, and then breaking. I pull her tighter, and she hangs on.

She pushes up again and turns to me so I can see her face. No makeup today, just plain Lauren. My thumb wipes her cheek, and we sit up.

"You asked me to come. Maybe I shouldn't have."

She reaches up and puts her finger to my lips to shush me. God help me, I want to take her wrist and kiss the spot between the two blue veins running up her arm.

"What you did that night"—she touches her cheek and then her neck—"I'm okay now. It's okay."

"It's not."

She pauses, as if thinking about whether to tell me something. Finally she says, "I know about your dad."

I put my hands on my knees and lean into my thighs. I breathe. She knew all along. She knew that I would take beating after beating without defending myself, without manning up. I look at her.

"How did you find out?" I say.

"You remember that time you broke your nose?"

"God, that was over a year ago," I say.

"You told everyone it was in your soccer league, but I watched that game. No one threw an elbow."

I drop my face into my hands, and she leans her forehead on my shoulder and then plants a few quick kisses. I   231 should have guessed she'd know. She was like that, picking up on little cues. Unless . . .

"Did Edward know? Did everyone?" I ask.

"He's so clueless. I wanted to tell him so I could explain, but I—"

"No explanation, Lauren," I say to my lap, my palms pushing against my eyelids. "No excuses. Get that, okay? Please, get that."

She pushes my hands out from under my head, and I jolt upright.

"It makes a difference. It does. Damn it. It means that . . . it wasn't my fault," she says.

"It *wasn't* your fault."

"It means that I wasn't, that I'm not stupid to want to be with you still."

"I didn't know that I could do that . . . ," I swallow and then say it. "I didn't know I could hit you. You really didn't do anything wrong."

"Except seduce your best friend," she says.

I take a breath; I don't know how to untangle that night for her. I can barely untangle it for myself.

"Listen, when you issued that warrant, I was really impressed. I'm sorry about my dad."

"About your dad?" She shoves my shoulder. "What about what you did?"

"Lauren, I am . . . so . . . so sorry. What I did to you, that was unforgivable."

"But I do forgive you, Jace."

She reaches for me, and I spring up off the bed.

"But I don't want you to forgive me, okay? You don't get to forgive me. If you do . . . Lauren, it gets so ugly. I don't know what my father said to you about love and second chances—"

"He said that forgiveness is how you get to go on loving someone after they've done something you hate."

"You can't listen to him, all right? Consider the source. He's fucked up," I say.

"Sure, but so what? He has a point."

Kali hops back on the bed, and Lauren takes her in her lap. She draws her fingers down Kali's back.

"I'm tired of this, Jace. I just want to go back; I want us to be us again. I'm tired of feeling like I *should* hate you. If I don't get to forgive you, then I get stuck." Her voice goes cold and iron. "I. Won't. Get. Stuck."

"I'm not trying to . . . We can't go back."

She acts as if I haven't spoken. "I mean, look at my parents, your parents. They can't really walk away, they can't really forgive each other. They're stuck. Well, not me." She yanks on my hand and pulls me down so that I'm kneeling before her. She cups my face, and I feel her palms, hot against my cheeks. "I forgive you, Jace. Whether you want it or not. And if you don't forgive yourself, then you can run halfway across the world, but you'll still be stuck on that street outside Starbucks."

My throat clenches tight, and I swallow again. I pull away from her and stand back up. *Isn't it too convenient just to forgive yourself, let yourself off the hook? What will keep me from doing it again, then?*

"Jace, I love you." She looks up at me and waits for my response, but I don't say it back to her. Finally she asks, "Don't you, too?"

"I don't love how screwed up we got. That night outside

Starbucks, that's not love. It's way darker than that, like obsession."

"I like the sound of that. Like you can't live without me."

"No, it sounds like addiction." I'm talking like Mirriam now. Great.

She reaches for me again, but I step back. The word *addiction* is still going through my brain when I find a way in.

"You always said that the difference between you and your mom was that none of your addictions were bad for you. Well, this one—me—is. Hate me, don't hate me. Forgive me, don't forgive me. But don't let me back in, don't ask me back in."

I start to walk away. She grabs my wrist, and her fingers squeeze and release, squeeze and release.

"Jace," she says, her voice small again, "I should be the one breaking us up. Don't you think?"

Please.

She stands up and cocks her arm back. I see it coming; I could block it, but Lauren is nothing if not proud. And it's easy to take one more if it means that Lauren can be Lauren again. I let her slap me, and my skin burns. It's been so good to be blow-free for over two months. I grit my teeth as the immediate pain passes.

"We're even. Now get out." Her voice is thin, and I wish I believed that it was shaking in fury.

I wish for so many things as I walk down the steps: that we had never met, that I had not taken her back after she screwed other guys, but most of all, I wish she was right—that her slap made us even.

Bastard evermore.

chapter 28

I **spend the rest of the morning** at my haunts. I stop
at my old school, running the snow-covered soccer
fields, my sneakers leaving my last footprints. I pass Edward's house, consider stopping and explaining, but what
could I say? I could lie, sure. Easy enough. I could let him
take a swing at me, too. But our friendship ended the night
he decided that sleeping with Lauren was a good idea. The
rest is just dragging out what's done.

I do end up with my longed-for pizza, but it tastes thick
in my mouth and sits heavily in my stomach. Maybe I'm just
nervous about what's to come.

When I drive back to the Costacoses', Effie comes out
on the stoop. She tells me Christian called the house and
my mom had gotten back early. They just dropped him off. 235

I race over to my house and screech into the driveway. As I enter, I hear a man's voice, loud and pissed off. I freeze before I recognize it as Christian's.

"Do you have any idea what he's been doing since you promised him, you *promised* him you'd come at Thanksgiving, Mom? He's been making turkeys. I swear, if I have to eat another bird, I'm going to gag on it. You can't do this to him."

I rush to the archway and see Mom. Her hair is in two braids that hang beside her ears, like a schoolgirl's—something she does before a full day of working on the house. She is wearing blue jeans and a sweater that my dad gave her for Christmas last year. Her cheek is so swollen it looks like she's sucking on a Gobstopper. He never hits her in the face; he knows better. And now she'll have to explain it away at a party, no less. It is getting worse; it's getting worse because of me.

"What's going on?" I say.

"Jace!" My mother comes up to me and hugs me.

I'm seven again and looking to Christian for clues. He shakes his head at me, and I don't return my mother's hug, but I do get a waft of her strawberry shampoo. I want to bury my face into her shoulder.

"Oh, honey. You look so different. Your hair."

I pull on an end of it. It is looking pretty weird these days, with the blond growing back in and the black starting to fade.

"Let me have a good look at you."

"Mom," I say, taking her by the shoulders. "You have to come with us."

"I'm sorry that I said Thanksgiving, but I can't come out now. I e-mailed you yesterday, but you must have left by then. Aren't you sweet to drive all the way—"

"Mom, you have to come with us."

"It's just that your father is giving a party. All his colleagues will be here, and he'd be so embarrassed if I—"

"I don't care about his colleagues. You have to come with us."

She pulls away from me.

"Jace." Her face starts to slide into that look of pleading that she gives my father before he hits her. "Please don't ask me for things I can't give you."

"That you can't give me?" I can feel the anger igniting. I need to go for a run. I need to hear my heart and nothing else. "What am I supposed to ask you for? Am I supposed to say, 'it's okay that you're wrecking your life'? Am I supposed to say, 'thanks for choosing that bastard over me'? 'I'm grateful that you're fucking me up'? Things you can give me? What have you ever given me?"

My mom reaches for me, but I step back.

"This is my problem, Jace. Let me solve it."

"But you don't solve it, and so we get stuck in this circle of hell with you. Do you even get what Christian has been through? He's lucky he didn't lose Mirriam because of that silence that you taught him. You practically stitched his mouth shut. Do you get that Lauren is sitting in her room right now, wanting to take me back? How did I manage to school her into this hit-sorry-forgive cycle so fast? Do you think she deserves that? It's not just your problem."

She is crying now, and I barely care. I can't stand it in here anymore. One more second, one more breath of oxygen, and I know where I'll go with it.

I spin on my toe and bolt out the back door. I breathe the November air and try to listen for my pulse like I do 237 when I run, listen for my breath. I put two fingers on the inside of my wrist and feel the fast bumping of my blood.

I lift my chin up to the sky. I did it. I walked away when I wanted to belt her; I chose to come out here instead. I want to believe I've passed some sort of test, that I won't turn into my father, but I know better. I know that I won't have to make that choice just once.

The door swings open, and my mom and Christian come out.

Christian is saying, "Mom, let him get his breath. Just give him a minute."

I turn around and look her in the face.

She glances at Professor Coe's house. "Come inside. It's freezing out here."

Right. That's what you're worried about.

I walk back into the kitchen, and its warmth smothers me. Christian stops beside me, and we face her together. He rests a hand on the counter and gestures to me to finish.

"He will kill you. Can't you see that it is getting worse? You have a party, and he's hitting you in the face? You have to come with me," I say.

She clutches her hands together. Her thumb rubs the scar on her palm. "And what happens if I try to leave, Jace? He found Christian in New York; he can find me. And if I'm with you, then he'll find you, too. I'm safer here."

"We'll protect you," I say.

She shakes her head, and I see it on her face: she doesn't believe we can. Why should she? We've never stopped him from hitting her. We've never really protected her. All we've done is delay it now and again.

"Jace, I'm sorry, so sorry, but I can't leave him. I can't see my life without him; I can't even imagine it anymore."

"Mom, please."

I grab her wrist and start to pull, but Christian puts his hand on mine, gently. I turn and look. He shakes his head, and I let go.

"Jace, it's not going to work. If we drag her out, she'll just come back. She has to walk out on her own or we're putting her in more danger when she returns," Christian says.

"Your dad will be home soon. The courts close early today," she says.

"Jace," Christian says, his voice high with panic. "No chances."

He puts his hand on my arm, and I shake him off, my eyes still on my mom.

"Screw that. Go back to the Costacoses', okay? I know you didn't sign on for this."

He doesn't move. "You and I . . . We're walking out that door together. I will not leave you here again."

"Christian, please go," I say. "If he sees you . . . I can't watch that again."

"You won't have to," he says.

Beside me, I hear a long, metallic sliding sound, like a shovel going into dirt. I turn, and Christian has a knife in his hand. His elbows aren't at his sides. His mouth isn't in a tight line. He's relaxed, ready.

My mother lets out a gasp.

I close my eyes.

Christian in an orange jumpsuit standing before the court, begging for mercy, but refusing to admit regret; Christian sentenced for murder one in a death-penalty state for my own stubbornness.

I close my hand over his on the knife handle and guide it to the counter. He releases it and looks at me.

"Let's go," I say. "We've done all we're going to do."

I look at my mom with her braids still up, with her face still pleading. I can't manage to say good-bye because I know this is the last time I will see her.

We walk through the house, and Christian has to take my elbow to lead me since I can't see anything clearly. By the time we get outside, I am bawling, chopped-breath sobs. Christian takes the keys from me and guides me to the passenger side.

"I'm sorry, Jace," he says, "but we've gotta go."

I watch my house as we pull away.

I'm a mess through Illinois. Christian keeps his hand on my shoulder when he's not shifting or fishing out tissues. By the time we hit the Missouri border, I've dried up and all that's left is that hiccupping-after-sobbing thing that I haven't done since I was like nine. I'm leaning my head back, my eyes closed, but I can feel Christian glancing over at me every couple of minutes.

"I'm okay," I say.

"Sure?"

"Well, I'll be okay. I'm sure." I open my eyes and look over at him. "How about you?"

His elbows are in, hands gripping the steering wheel; he looks worse than he did on our way out here. "I'm . . . uh . . . I don't know."

"What's going on?" I say.

Christian pulls the car over. I wait, but he doesn't move. He slowly turns to me. He puts his hand out as if to shake mine.

"I'm Christian Marshall," he says. "When I was seventeen, I ran away from an abusive home and left my little brother behind to take what I couldn't manage. I don't know who that turned you into. So why don't you tell me?"

I knock Christian's hand away and try to smile at this strange sort of joke that I'm not getting.

"Who's Lauren?"

I pull my knees up to my chest, wrap my arms around them, and rest my sneakers on the seat. "She's a girl I used to date," I say.

"Why did you break up?"

My instinct, to lie, to speak in half-truths and talk about her infidelity, is tempered by my memory of him standing in our kitchen with a knife because he refused to leave me behind again.

"We broke up because I punched her in the face, pushed her against a brick wall, and then started to strangle her."

Christian's face stays exactly the same. Not a muscle twitches. He swivels his head, puts the car in gear, and pulls back onto the road.

I watch the trees on the side of the highway rushing past the car window. We pass a blue billboard that promises McDonald's, Burger King, and lodgings at the next exit. We pass a green billboard that gives us distance: St. Louis 253 miles. We pass the Burger King exit. We pass a Texaco gas station sign floating like a bubble above us.

"Christian," I say. "I'm sorry for what I did, for lying to you about it, for everything."

He nods, but he doesn't look at me.

We pass a mile marker and go under a bridge. When we flash back to sunlight, his face does not change; his eyes don't even blink.

"Say something," I say, finally.

"I want you out of the house."

nineteen hours of silence. We didn't talk when we pulled over to switch seats. We didn't talk when we ate at an Arby's. (I'm surprised he sat at the same table with me. If we weren't driving my car, I'm sure he'd leave me on the road.) We didn't talk when we stopped for gas, not even when he needed to get the bathroom key from me at a gas station. Instead of asking me for it, he let me return it to the counter and took it from the clerk.

And something inside me snapped, like a traveling ice pack. Break it, and it gets really cold.

Fuck him.

When we get to the apartment, he clears his throat and says, "Leave your key on the table," and knocks on Mirriam's door.

I am standing in the hallway when Mirriam opens the door.

"Aww, Christian, you were supposed to call me from the road. I haven't even started the turkey." She sees me standing in the doorway of Christian's apartment. "Jace," she says, "where's your mom?"

I walk into our—his—place and close the door.

The small apartment is bloated with my things. I get my backpack and take it into Christian's bedroom to start loading it up. I open the bottom drawer and look at my jeans, my clothes lying there neatly. My eyes are dried out.

When my backpack is overflowing, I pull out a garbage bag and stuff in the rest of my clothes and books. The bag stretches thin around one of my textbooks.

For the last time, I call up the Internet on his computer and search for emergency homeless shelters. I'll have to lie about my age or I'll get put into the system. The printer fires up and rasps out a set of directions. I pry my key ring open and slide the gold key off. I leave it on the table. Just like that, I am erased from this place, too.

I'm about to go, but I remember one thing that I want to do. I pull the closet door open and take out his NYU diploma. I whip it like a Frisbee across the room, and its frame takes a little chunk out of the wall. I leave it on the floor, broken.

I am halfway down the steps when I hear Mirriam's voice.

"Jace?" She comes running down the steps. "Where are you going?"

I show her the directions as I hear another door shut
upstairs. Our door. Christian's door.

"What's this?" she asks.

"The only place I can think of."

"Come inside. Come with me. Let's figure this out."

"Mirriam, I'm done with him. I'm done with this place, and all of it."

"Are you done with me?"

I sigh. "No."

I haul my bag back onto my shoulder, she grabs the garbage bag, and we walk into her apartment.

I put the bag down inside her door, but I don't close it. "I shouldn't be here. He wouldn't want me here."

"It's not up to him."

She takes my hand and pulls me into her apartment. I smell eggs and green peppers. I want to pretend it's just another day, another cooking lesson. Maybe Mexican.

"Did he tell you?" I ask.

Yes, he told her about Lauren. Is there anything else? she wants to know. I tell her I hit my dad.

"Well, that's a little different, don't you think? Sit down, okay?" she says.

When I'm sitting on her couch, she looks me over and then says, "You've had a long trip."

I shrug. "It'll be longer still."

"Jace, try to understand; he is torn apart by this."

I stand and pick up my bag. *Right. I need someone defending him.*

"Okay, I'm sorry. This isn't about him. Please sit down and tell me what I can do for you."

"You really want to help me? I need to find a place to live. Maybe I can get a room around the university."

"You're going to stay in Albuquerque?"

"Yeah. I still want to graduate from high school if I can 245 manage it. Maybe I'll test for my GED or something, so that I can go to college."

She smiles. "You never give up."

Oh yeah? I left my mother there. Again.

Fightology Lesson #10: It hurts worse the next day.

"Jace," Mirriam says. "Why don't you stay here? I mean, those shelters can be . . . a hard place for a kid on his own, and you're not in any shape for that."

"But . . . Christian?"

"You won't have to see him, I promise. Just stay until we can find you a place of your own."

I probably should say no, but I'm as sick of protecting Christian as I am of seeing him. I'm about to say yes when I narrow my eyes at her. "Why would you help me? Now that you know."

"You're not going to like my answer."

I cross my arms over my chest.

"All right," she says. "Because you *are* a kid-at-risk, but you're not hopeless. Yet. And because I think Christian will regret it if you disappear from his life." I open my mouth to object, but she keeps going. "And because I think you deserve a break. Christian told me that you let your mom go. And that's a step in the right direction."

"It is? For whom?"

"For you, Jace. For you." She sighs. "I think you should stay, get your bearings, and make your decisions in your own way. And I'm in a position to help, so why shouldn't I?"

"Because of what it might cost you," I say, looking at the wall that separates her apartment from Christian's.

"I won't lose anything."

"You *hope* you won't lose anything," I say.

"If Christian were to break up with me over this, I wouldn't want to know him. I won't lose anything." She doesn't even blink.

Who'd have thought that I could be a deal-breaker?

"Thanks. I'll try to keep out of your way."

"All right. I'm going over there now, but I want you to stay here. Can you promise me that you'll stay here?"

"Yeah," I say and put my backpack on the floor.

"I have a TV in my bedroom."

I've been here for months and there's been a TV next door without me knowing about it? That is just so wrong.

I kick off my shoes and head into her bedroom. It is cluttered, clothes spilling out of the hamper, and the dresser carries more gadgetry and makeup than I've seen anywhere: brushes strewn, a hair dryer and its attachments littered, a compact left open with its sponge lolling out. I flip on the TV. My brain glazes over with commercials and black-and-white *I Love Lucy*.

Through the walls, I hear Christian and Mirriam.

Blah, Blah, Blah, Jace! BLAH, BLAH, BLAH.

Whatever. A pair of headphones sits on top of the television. I plug them in and turn up the sound.

After a little while, Mirriam appears in the doorway.

I say, "You shouldn't fight about me."

She says something, but I can't make it out. I pull the headphones off. "What?"

"You couldn't hear us?"

I wave the headphones at her.

"Well, thanks for the privacy," she says. "We didn't really fight."

I raise my eyebrows at her.

"I mean, we aren't breaking up over it."

I don't know why she would want to stay with him, but I doubt I'll ever really understand women.

"Well, if that's what you want, I'm glad for you," I say.

I put the headphones back on. Lucy is wailing because Ricky Ricardo is making her feel like a useless idiot again, and I listen to the laugh track.

chapter 30

When I wake up the next morning, I forget where I am, but the citrus smell reminds me that I'm not next door, that I've been ousted again. The worst part is that the one person I want to turn to is the same person who has shown me the door. I can't go back, so my only option is to keep going. And to keep going, I can't think about Christian anymore.

I push myself off Mirriam's futon and fold the blanket she gave me last night. After digging through the garbage bag of my stuff, looking for my camera, I realize that I left it at Christian's. *Oh, that's just great.* I consider knocking on his door for about two seconds.

I'll get Mirriam to ask him for it.

I put on my soccer shorts and jersey. It will be cold for a   249 run, but at least I'll be outside. The apartment feels over-heated, just like my head. I peek in Mirriam's bedroom, but she is dead to the world. I leave her a note, grab the key, and take off.

While I'm on the run, I try to let the images of my mom and my house be driven out of my brain. But my hands are so cold, I need to turn around before I get relief. *Someday,* I tell myself, *I'll have my own place, and I'll come home to it day after day after day. No one will be able to tell me that I can't live there anymore, and I won't have to live by anyone's rules.*

When I get back, Mirriam is just coming out of the bed-room. Her eyes are not blinking in sync yet. She can't be-lieve how long she has slept, she says, and looks away when she gets that I've already been out and back. She asks how I'm doing. I don't answer because I don't want to lie and I don't want to get into it, either.

"Jace," she says, "you don't have to answer me today, okay? But maybe tomorrow."

I can't think that far ahead yet. All I can think about is how to manage the ache I've got right now.

After a shower, I tell her I'll make some coffee and an omelet while she takes her turn in the bathroom. My homeless-person cardboard sign could read WILL COOK FOR RENT. I am ripping up cilantro for a spicy omelet when a knock at the door interrupts. Gotta be Christian. I go for the pretend-no-one-is-home strategy.

He pounds a second time.

"Mirriam!" His voice is panicked. He's probably wor-ried that I killed her or something.

"She's in the shower," I yell back.

"Open the door, Jace. I have something for you."

"Slide it under."

"It's your camera."

"So leave it there. I'll get it in a minute. I'm cooking," I say.

"I'll just . . . ," he says, and I hear a key slide in the lock. Of course he has a key. Why didn't I think of that?

I sigh, put down the cilantro, and open the door before he can. A wave of overheated hallway air pushes its way in. I grab the camera, but he won't let go of the strap.

"I wanted to say I'm sorry," he says. "You know, that it turned out this way."

"Whatever."

"And to give you this." He pulls a check from his pocket. "It's what I owe you from your last paycheck."

I've been depositing my checks into his account. I don't know how he has calculated what's mine and what's his.

"Give it to Mirriam for letting me stay."

"Well, it's a lot . . . How long are you staying?" He peers past me into the apartment.

"Until I can find another place."

"Can I come in?"

"I'll tell Mirriam you came by," I say.

"At least take the check. You'll need it for a security deposit."

I start to close the door, but he pushes his palm against it.

"Take it," he says. "It's yours."

Sure, hand me money, hand Mom money, pay off your conscience. You're gonna have to break the bank. I grab the check, rip it in half, and drop it on the floor. Mirriam will have to do her own prep work. I pick up my backpack and try to head out the door, but now Christian roadblocks me.

"Excuse me," I say through clenched teeth.

"Where are you going?"

251

"Siam."

"You know what, Jace? Why don't you try, for a change, telling me the truth?"

"Okay. I don't know where. I'm finding a room in Albuquerque; I'm keeping my job; I'm finishing school. Happy? Now get out of my way," I say.

He separates his legs—shoulder-width apart, ready for anything.

"Christian, let me out of here."

He still doesn't move but pushes his jaw out. I go and sit down on the futon. He closes the door behind him, and I remember the way my dad would draw the shades. But no one's kicking my butt today.

"Well, what then?" I ask.

"Explain."

"Not a chance," I say.

"Now whose mouth is stitched closed? What? Is there more? Is there a whole string of ex-girlfriends?"

"No."

"Was this the first time?"

"Yes. Is this interrogation over?"

"Interrogation?" His shoulders fold, and he studies his shoes. He is tied to his "don't ask" policy. *Figures. God forbid he should actually extend himself for anyone.*

But then he looks me in the eye and says, "It's past time."

I grind my teeth together and stare at him. Outside, the wind would feel good against my face. Outside, I would get in my car and start driving. I wouldn't even glance in the rearview.

"What do you want?" I ask.

He stands there.

"Well?" I say. "Open your fucking mouth."

"How come *you* get to be pissed off at *me*? You can honestly tell me that you would choose to live with another abuser now, after you've gotten out? That you would sit down to a game of rummy and a plate of sandwiches with him? You're the one who beat up his girlfriend and lied about it so you could weasel your way inside my door. So how come you get to be pissed at me?"

Oh, gee, I don't know. Maybe because you're such a stand-up, reliable brother? Could it be, just maybe, because you dump me on my ass whenever you don't like the scenery?

I'm kindling, but this time it is hotter than it ever was with my dad, with my mom, even more explosive than with Lauren. I can't believe I spent so much time trying to be like him. What a waste. I stand up, and he steps so close to me that I know he had oolong with breakfast today. My hand clenches into a fist, and I dig my nails into my palms.

"I've gotta get out of here." I step to the side, and he steps with me, his face close to mine. "Jesus. Lemme out."

"Or what? You're gonna hit me, too?"

He's baiting me, like he used to with Dad. Bring it on, get it over with, control what you can. We're close enough that I could easily take two swings before he could bring his long arms into play. I could get the advantage, knock him on his ass, and kick the shit out of him.

Smoke wisps.

I put my fingers on my pulse, close my eyes, and try to breathe. I can't even feel my blood. All I can think about is that crystal in my window. I keep one wrist locked inside my own grip. *I am not my father.*

"You're gonna tell me what I did to piss you off, 'cause

253

you've been on edge since day one," Christian says. "I kept Mirriam off your back with a stick, nearly sacrificed our relationship, so you wouldn't have to talk about it. God, Jace, of all things . . . You had me protecting an abuser, again. And I was stupid enough, trusted you enough, not to ask. So now I deserve better from you."

Backdraft.

The sucking sound deafens me, and I can't even hear myself screaming at him, but words are shooting out of my mouth.

"*You* deserve better from *me*? Two years, Christian. Two fucking years. That diploma from NYU was dated two years ago. Where have you been? And don't give me that Dad-had-never-hit-you-so-I-thought-you'd-be-all-right bullshit. Did you check? I mean, good God, it couldn't have been that hard. We were listed in the goddamn phone book. He nearly killed you in New York, and you never thought about me? I Googled your name seventeen thousand times; I hunted state by state on whitepages.com for you. You sliced me right out of your life and left me to sink without a second thought. I mean, have you considered, have you thought about what a difference it would have made if you had come back for me? I hadn't even met Lauren when you got out of college."

And, in that instant, I see how I'm most like my father; I'm blaming someone else for what I did. But the words keep coming.

"And now you do it again? You pull out so hard and fast that I'm left on my ass again? So Fuck You. But you've gotta know, Christian, that I would never have done that to you. You could commit murder, and I would offer you an alibi. I

would fucking confess."

I lift my hands, my palms open, and stare at them. No more fists. That was it. That was my backdraft.

I go back to the couch and sit down. I drop my head into my hands and feel my pulse thumping through my temples. I count the pulses. One. Two. Three . . . When it slows, I take one big breath and look up.

"Well," he says, "don't hold back on my account. Tell me how you really feel."

A short bark of a laugh escapes me.

"I couldn't go back, not even for you. I couldn't think about Dad or Mom or that house. None of it. I just buried it, and yeah, I buried you with it. You're right, Jace. Everything would have been different for you."

I grab a red throw pillow off the futon and fold my arms over it.

My dad always had excuses: she had it coming; he had a hard day; no one understood the pressure he was under—the usual, the flimsy. And here I am, making the I-had-a-hard-life excuse.

Finally I say, "No. Beating up Lauren . . . that's all on me."

Christian inhales sharply and holds his breath. He comes over and sits next to me. When he speaks, his voice is lower, his words thoughtful. "I've heard Dad say he's sorry, I've heard him promise he won't do it again, but I've never heard him say it's his fault."

I take a breath and close my eyes. The tears push out. "Really?"

"You're not that much like Dad. No blaming everyone else, no pushing Lauren to come back, not nearly enough charm. Short."

He's got me crying and laughing at the same time.

He continues, "I'm not excusing what you did to her—" 255

"Nothing could—"

"Exactly, nothing could. But . . . if anyone could see the difference between you and Dad, it would be me, right? I mean, when you messed up, you tried to fix it. He's still using guilt and charm and everything else to win Mom back just so he can do it again."

I crush the pillow to my chest. He's right; it's the one thing I've done that was good. I've never blamed Lauren, never guilted her, or tried to trap her in my mistake.

"But how come you went through the same thing, and you wouldn't hit a woman, not ever?"

"See, that's what I thought, too. That we went through the same thing. But we didn't. For one thing, you and Dad were close, and everyone always said you were alike. You looked up to him, wanted to be like him for a long time. I always had Mom."

"But that's not—"

"And then last night, I couldn't stop thinking about what you said when I pulled that knife. You said that you couldn't watch him hit me *again*."

I go back to that moment and replay it in slow motion. What was I thinking about when I said that? My brother's face lying in a pool of antifreeze, dropping the tray of food in the garage, and racing to my dad, burying my face into his stomach.

I begin ripping at the pillow's tassel. He frowns and takes the pillow from me.

"So?" I say.

"So, I never saw him hit you. And let's be honest, it was easier to take his crap than to watch Mom take it, right? That's why we both stepped up."

"Not for me," I say. "Just once I wanted her to take a blow for me."

"She did, Jace, for years and years. Once he got to me—well, once I left—you never had a chance." His lips curl inside his teeth—a gesture I haven't seen in years, but I do recognize it. He is trying not to cry. He doesn't look at me, and when he talks his voice is so quiet and shaky, I have to lean in to hear him. "The truth is I never checked up on you because I knew it was only a matter of time until he started in on you, but as long as I wasn't sure, I could tell myself that you were okay."

I exhale. I didn't know that an apology could actually help; I always thought saying sorry was more about alleviating guilt, that apologies were designed for the mouth, not for the ears. I nod slowly.

The shower water turns off, and the silence is louder.

"So . . . ," I say. "Now what?"

"Well." He starts nodding. "We've pretty much established that we're both screw-ups, right?"

"Yup," I say, bobble-heading in time with him.

"But brothers, right?"

I stop, while his head stays in motion.

I say, "We'll always be brothers, by blood, at any rate."

He stares at his knees, puts the pillow to the side of him, and stands up. "Okay." When he is at the door, he says, "Will you let me know where you land?"

"Sure, okay."

His lips curl over his teeth once more, and his Adam's apple bobs in his throat.

"I mean," I say, "I promise."

He twists the door handle and then stops. "Jace, I could

never live with another abuser. I worked too hard to get away from one."

"Yeah, I know."

"But considering that you're not going to do it again . . . that you're an ex-abuser . . . I made a mistake when I told you to leave. I painted you with the same brush as Dad. I'm trying to say that you could land with me." He waits as if it is a question, and I don't answer. "So, if you want, I'll be around, all right?"

I nod, and just before he leaves, I stop him with, "Hey, Christian? Maybe for Thanksgiving, I could come over and cook you something decent to eat?"

"Jace," he says, "Thanksgiving was yesterday."

I feel my throat tightening up, but I ignore it. "Well, our own Thanksgiving, then. The thanksgiving-for-screw-ups. Maybe next week?"

"What's on the menu?"

"No more turkey," I say.

He brightens. "How about pizza? Could you make that? I love pizza."

"You do?" I ask.

There's so much we don't know about each other.

mirriam is over at Christian's, and I'm finally alone. Three long holiday days here. I'm tired of hanging around, watching TV, and avoiding Mirriam's I'm-here-if-you-need-me support. Every single morning she asks me how I'm doing, if I want to talk, and when I don't respond, she tells me to answer her tomorrow.

When she goes, I stretch out on her bed and watch movies on TV. In the middle of a second one, I head into the kitchen to make some popcorn. As the microwave is beeping, Mirriam returns.

"I thought you'd spend the night at Christian's," I say. "I wouldn't mind or anything."

"No, Christian needs to go to work." She hands me a letter. "He wanted me to give this to you."

He lives like thirteen feet from me, and he's sending letters? Oh, this can't be good. I lift my hand to take it.

Mirriam says, "It's from your mom."

My hand stops in midair, hovering for a minute.

"It's addressed to both of you. Christian already read it."

I take it from her, place it on the counter, and stare at her until she leaves. I'm right back on the roller coaster of *Is she okay? Is he about to kill her? Is she trying to get out?*

But I don't open the letter because I know the answers to all of those questions. I can't read my mom's reasons for not saving herself, for choosing him over us. No more excuses. I toss the letter in the trash under the sink, remember that it was addressed to Christian, too, and dig it back out.

After a few minutes Mirriam comes back into the kitchen. She is in her bathrobe, her hair is pulled back, and her face has that just-washed look: strangely pale, except her cheeks. She is carrying two bottles of nail polish—one white and one clear—and sits down at the table. She glances at the empty space on the counter where the letter was.

"I don't want to talk about it."

She draws an arc of white paint across the tip of a nail and goes to the next one.

"Jace, you blew this off before, but how about talking to a professional?"

"Go to a shrink? Yeah, I have that kind of money."

She looks up when she hears my tone, which, oddly, feels like a victory.

"I actually meant the school counselor."

"And what would you have me say to him? That my

mom stayed with the husband who beats her? That she wouldn't come with her kids, who've taken beatings for her? What difference would it make, Mirriam? I mean, really? Would talking to a school counselor magically change my mom's mind?" I slow down. I take a deep breath, and another, until I can talk, not yell. "There's no point in talking about her. There's no point in talking *to* her. She made her decision, and there's nothing I can do about it."

She goes back to her damn nails and finishes the left hand. Finally she says, "I'm not sure you understand how hard it would be for her to leave him."

"Really? Christian did it. I did it."

"It's different for her, and you know it." She jams the nail brush back in the bottle. "I'm sure he's told her he'll kill her if she tries to leave, and every time he hits her, he proves he's as good as his word. She's trapped, Jace."

"It's not entirely unheard of, you know. Other people do it every day with less than she's got."

"She's scared, Jace."

"She's a coward? That I can believe."

"It's not that simple," she says, shaking her head.

"I'm not saying it's simple, and I'm not saying it's easy. I'm saying it's necessary." I pause, knowing that I'm being unfair to my mom, knowing that necessary doesn't equal possible. "And I know the law won't help. I'm not entirely naïve."

"That's your father talking. He's got you and Christian and your mom thinking that the law can't help you, but that's what it's there for. Cops, DAs, even judges . . . Whether your dad says so or not, that's their job."

I think of my dad cutting out the news story and   261

reading it to my mom with a flashlight in the garage. It hits me—getting off can't be common if it made the paper. You never see a story on TV about how a shelter helped or an order of protection worked, because that's not news; it happens every single day. I wonder if I could convince her otherwise, but he's got the advantage: legal knowledge and years of molding her reality.

Mirriam looks as though she is reconsidering. She returns to her bottles. She takes the clear one and shakes it up and down. A little black ball goes ping-ponging within the walls of the bottle.

"You're right, Jace; other women do it. She should have left him years ago. She should have put her sons first. A good mother—I guess she's just too weak," Mirriam says.

"God, Mirriam. She isn't weak. She can stand a beating you couldn't imagine and then pretend like it doesn't matter. She can forgive him, and that's not a weakness. It's a kind of . . ."

I trail off, cluing in to Mirriam's trick, showing how I attack my mom one second and defend her the next. How's that for confused?

"Jace, it's okay to get mad, even to hate her a little."

"Thanks, 'cause I needed your permission."

"You're welcome, because you do need someone's, and right now, you can't get Christian's."

The blood drains from my face so fast that it goes a little numb. I have no idea how Mirriam would know this. Hell, I didn't even know it.

She goes on. "You get to be mad because she didn't look out for you, like a mother is supposed to. You got stuck looking out for her. But you're in a catch-22 because you can't really blame *her.* You're too smart to think it's her fault she can't leave."

I know that staying there isn't exactly a decision. If someone's got a gun to your head, there's no choice. It was up to me to get her out. I think about her standing there with her hair in braids and her swollen cheek. He's killing her by degrees.

"Oh, Jace," Mirriam says, "I'm sorry."

"For what?"

"I shouldn't tell you how you feel. I get too invested and . . ." She looks at her hands and screws the nail polish bottle tight. Then she looks up at me, her lips puffed out in an embarrassed apology.

I sit down next to her.

"I just wish I could have gotten her out of there."

"It's not your fault, either."

"Yeah? Then whose fault is it?"

"You know the answer to that."

I slump back in the seat, my cushion soft against my back.

I always thought I was supposed to keep my dad off her, that every time he hit her, I failed.

But I'm not the one digging her grave; I didn't open her hole in the earth when I drove away that night or when I couldn't make her come with us. My dad dug it years ago; he forced her to lie down in it and kept her there by fear and beatings. And when she tried to get out, he stomped her back in. She has been lying there for twenty-five years. Her muscles have atrophied, her joints have stiffened, and she can't see anything except him and the tight little space she calls home. I don't know how she'll get out; I can tug and pull and yank, but it won't make any difference. She was right: she's gotta solve it her own way.

I've heard that some people who suffer from chronic pain only get how bad it is when they are finally cured. Muscles that I wasn't even aware of go slack. I lay it down.

Mirriam continues, "This whole time you've been wondering why your mom won't leave him, right? But that's the wrong question."

I nod slowly. I know the right question: Why is my dad hitting her in the first place? Isn't that where I need to start? Start with him, with myself.

"I'm working on that question, too," I say.

She smiles that so-proud-of-you teacher smile. This time it doesn't bug me so much.

"So, are you going to read that letter?" Mirriam says.

It may not be so bad that she can see right through me.

"I don't know," I say.

"That's fair."

We nod at each other, and I walk into the living room. The light outside is unusually somber. The sky is gray, instead of the intense blue I've gotten used to. I see two—wait, three—snowflakes sidling by, carrying with them the promise of winter. I wonder if here the earth will go quiet after big snows, the way it does in Chicago, as if the world is soothing itself. I think I can feel it coming on.

chapter 32

On Saturday, I'm digging for digs. Mrs. Ortiz, who I've talked to on the phone, swings open the door to the rental room. The walls shine bright yellow, contrasting oddly with a pink comforter. Could be worse. It's pretty small, but it's clean and furnished. Mrs. Ortiz tells me her brother vouched for me, so she's sure I'll behave.

"What does that mean? Behave?" I ask her.

She says she has some policies, and I'm immediately frustrated. I won't live underneath anyone again. It's level ground from here on out. But Mrs. Ortiz's policies are simple enough. She just wants the rent on time, no messes, and no late-night noise.

She leaves, so I can take a look around.

It is small but has everything I need: closet, bed, night table, and lamp (even though a porcelain squirrel is perched on the base). I walk over to the small window, which opens horizontally. The back "garden" is a winding path with a large, lonely cactus standing guard, front and center. Even though it's native, it looks out of place.

I sit down on the bed and bounce on it a little, as if I could tell whether it's a good mattress this way. My camera bag could sit under the bed; my books could line the top of the dresser; my shoes could be tucked inside the closet. This room could work.

I look at the bare yellow walls; they are nothing but potential. Christian's walls are bare, too.

I hurry back to Mirriam's, and we finish up the pizza dough and spread out the toppings. Once I'm all set to bake it, she lets me into Christian's apartment (he has the better oven) and tells me he'll be here, but he can't get away from work just yet. I bring over my mom's letter and place it on the table. Then I put the pizza in his oven to bake and hop on the computer, surfing until he comes home.

When he walks through the door, he just nods at me and then stops. He chuckles. "For a second I forgot you'd moved out."

"Mirriam thought it would be all right," I say, getting up.

"Of course it's all right. Don't be an idiot," he says, his voice light and casual. He stops. "I mean, thanks for coming over."

"The 'idiot' remark said it all," I say.

Christian sits down on the couch and leans back. He slides his shoes off with his toes while I pull the pizza from the oven. When he sees mushrooms on his half and pepperoni and pineapple on my half he says, "Good choice."

To make room for the pizza, he pushes the letter out of the way. I put the pan down and stare at my mom's handwriting on the envelope.

"I'm not that interested in . . . I haven't read it. Do I need to? Does the letter change anything?"

"No."

"Is she okay?" I ask.

"Yes."

"What's it about?"

"Do you want to read it, after all?"

I hesitate.

"The pizza needs to cool for a few minutes anyway, and I'm right here," he says.

My stomach is tight when I pull out the letter and read, but there is practically nothing in it. Just a bunch of junk: the party was fun, and everyone loved the stuffing, and they've decided to go away this year for Christmas. Not a single thing about us going out there.

"What the hell?" I say, turning it over to see if I'm missing something.

"I'm going to start e-mailing her. You okay with that?"

My instinct is to lie, to *Sure, okay* it. Instead, I think about the calmology lessons I've been developing: #1: Run every day; #2: Speak if you have something to say; #3: Fix what you can and accept what you can't.

I apply lesson number two and say, "Look, I'm not going to tell you what to do, but . . . I can't do this anymore."

"I'm not e-mailing her in the hope that she'll leave. I don't want to talk about that at all. I'm not even sending her money anymore. If she was going to leave, she would have."

"Then . . . why?"

"I don't have to agree with her to love her."

I dig my shoe into the shag carpet leaving a little valley. I wonder if someday I could write to her without asking if she's okay or when she's leaving. But not now. Maybe not ever, but still maybe.

I say, "I can't be with you on this."

"I'm not asking you to. I don't even want you to."

"Really?"

"Really."

He gets out the plates and sets them down. He stares at me for a second and then looks away. He begins the fish-mouth move, the I-want-to-ask-but-won't. Only this time, words pop out.

"On the phone, Mirriam said you're going to move. Have you signed anything?"

"Not yet. I'm supposed to let the owner know on Monday. I really was going to tell you," I say, and get cheese from the fridge. "Do you want Parmesan? How do you like having your place back?"

He reaches for the container and shakes it over the pizza. Parm snows down.

"I might not renew the lease. I'm thinking about moving to a bigger place. Downstairs. A two-bedroom. You know, if you wanted to. An apartment on the third floor is opening up."

He puts the Parm down and looks at me, his eyebrows up.

I finally say, "I don't know, Christian. We've both gotta move on. I'm not sure how best to do that."

"I think we've done too much on our own already."

He plates the pizza. His place looks sterile without my stuff cluttering his desk and creeping out from under the sofa. The steam from the pizza drifts and, as he puts the plate in front of me, the smell catches up. I lean down and inhale.

"Since when did you start liking pizza?" I ask.

"I've always liked it. Where have you been?"

"Here. You have not had one slice of pizza since I showed up," I say.

"Oh, that. I'm just too picky to order it here. I've been spoiled by Chicago and New York pizza, I guess."

I take a bite. The crust is gummy. I guess I still have a ways to go on this cooking thing. But the quality of the ingredients (and I paid a lot for those) saves it.

"So . . . ," he says. "If you're game, and you want the small bedroom, we'll share expenses. No more ground rules. No more lectures about how to contribute. Brothers."

I look at his blank walls. I know what I want to do, but what if Christian does another 180, like he is prone to—like he does, I realize, when *he* panics? Well, I know what to do with panic. Panic, I can handle. I'll talk him down, or crack a joke, or take him for a run. He would do it for me.

"Besides," he says, "I need someone to beat at gin rummy."

The last time I saw that dopey grin on his face, we were at the Costacoses' and he was among family.

I say, "I wonder if the Salvation Army sells beds."

"Consider this one on me," he says.

My stuff is already packed, anyway.

"Okay," I say. "It's on you."

"Okay."

chapter 33

three days later, Dakota is at the customer service desk, typing something into the computer. When she sees me, she stops. We haven't talked since the night of the party. When I got back to work on the Monday after Thanksgiving, expecting to see her, she had changed her work schedule. To avoid mine, I'm guessing. So I waited another week and then showed up while she was working. I walk around the Christmas book displays and stop in front of her.

"Hello," she says.

I go behind the counter, put my hands on her hips, and turn her around. I lean in and kiss her long and soft. She wraps her arms around my neck and slides her tongue between my teeth. Mid-kiss, she lets go and pushes back.

"Okay, I like that, I do. But I am working. I get off in an hour. Wait for me?"

I say yes and head to the café with a photography magazine. I sit and leaf through the pages, thinking about what she will say. When she comes in, she puts her hand in my hair.

"Your hair is fading back to blond."

"I'm okay with that. I don't really like this half-and-half look, though."

"It does look pretty bad," she says.

"Oh, there's that great feature of yours. That unadulterated honesty. Don't worry. I'm going for a crew cut until it's all blond again."

"So . . . ," she says while she sits down.

I look around the café. On one side of us, a boy is sitting next to his dad, a book in front of them, his finger tracking the letters and his mouth trying to work the sounds into words. On the other side of me, two women in black shirts are gossiping, and without even trying, I could find out why their "friend" is getting a divorce.

I say, "Not here."

Dakota follows me into the storeroom. We walk between the rows of boxes to a little dusty table-and-chairs set that must go outside in the summer.

"I want to go out with you," I say.

"Yeah." She puts her fingers to her mouth. "I got that."

"I'm sorry about before. You were right. You get to decide whether to date me, but you can't make an informed decision until you have all the relevant facts."

"You sound like a lawyer."

"I'm sure I do. Know why? My father is a judge."

I dust off one of the seats with my shirt sleeve. I gesture to it, and she sits down.

When I open my mouth, it's like I can feel the thread that has sewn my lips shut tearing out. I half expect to suck on that coppery taste of blood. I sit down on the other chair and tell my story.

I begin with the night Christian first started taking blows for my mom. I tell her about the hammer and the anti-freeze; how everything changed when Christian ran; how I hung that crystal in my bedroom, praying for his return while I took as many of my mother's beatings as I could.

I pause. I wipe my sweaty palms against my jeans. I don't want to finish because I know that I am defined by what I've done, not by what's been done to me.

So I tell her about Lauren.

Dakota's mouth opens wide, and I'm sure she will walk out. Why wouldn't she? I look down so I don't have to watch her leave. But when I look up, she's still there.

"I'm not telling you about my dad to excuse what I did," I say. "I'm telling you because it is where I've come from, but not where I'm going. I decide that."

"Finish," she says.

I take a breath, and I go on to the Q-tips; attacking my dad; nineteen hours on the road; seeing Christian again. I tell her everything: the turkeys; Lauren's warrant; the trip to Chicago and all I left behind; even those queens that got lost somewhere.

Finally I'm out of words. She fidgets with her sleeve and won't look at me. The silence stretches out. She's too polite to get up and walk away. Maybe she wants to run.

Then she says, "I don't know what to say. I didn't expect . . ."

"Yeah, I know."

"This is in a whole different class. I thought that you were just bitter about your last girlfriend, just scared."

"I know. I didn't mean to string you along. I couldn't bring myself to tell you, and I couldn't trust myself to ask you out, either."

"But now?"

"I'm rewiring."

With her finger, she draws a design of squiggles in the dust.

"You were right." I say. "You get to decide whether you date me, but only after you knew this. That's why I—"

"What you've told me is amazingly honest," she says.

"I promised to work on the honesty thing."

"You've been working on a lot of things. You're into confessing, aren't you? Stealing, lying, now this. Anything else?"

I shake my head.

"I always thought that as long as someone was honest with me, I'd . . . But this is . . ."

"It's okay to say no, Dakota. I'm not sure that I—"

"I really don't know what to say, Jace. I need to think about it, okay?"

"Okay."

"And you've got to know that I'm not like Lauren. I wouldn't forgive you; I would bring the law down hard and fast, and I would make it stick."

That's an assurance that I used to need.

"Okay."

I take a big breath, compensating for all the shallow ones since we walked in here.

"You're taking this pretty well," I say.

"Yeah, I am."

Her eyebrows draw together, and she looks both surprised at herself and a little worried.

"Well," I say, resisting an urge to touch her hand, "you know what I want, and I'm not going anywhere."

"Take my time?"

"Yeah."

She nods. "Good."

"Okay. But can I keep stalking your schedule?"

"Yes." She pauses and not-a smiles at me. "Sir."

Even though the air is practically crackling between us, I'm not back in the street outside of Starbucks. I'm right here, right now.

When I get home, I walk into our new apartment. Christian's boxes are still packed up. I walk through the cardboard maze and look at his labels on them: BOOKS (C), BOOKS (J), CLOTHES (C). A pile of assorted junk lies behind an empty box. I glance in my bedroom and see the covers lying neat and untouched. A yellow Post-it is stuck to my door. In Christian's perfect, un-doctor-like print, it reads, *Meet us on the roof.*

I climb the last flight of steps and push on the long metal bar to open the door. The cold night air settles on my skin. Something about it reminds me of the time Christian and I climbed the mountain and sat at the top.

Christian and Mirriam have dragged up chairs from our apartment. They sit with their backs to me, looking out over the lights of Albuquerque. She leans against him, and her long black hair curtains his shoulder blade. When the door closes, they turn around.

"Hey, Jace," Christian says, lifting a plastic martini cup filled with bubbly amber liquid. He sips it and stands up. "Come here. We're celebrating. We had a good mail day."

"What, no bills?"

They are giddy enough that even this makes them laugh, and I chuckle along.

"Even better," says Mirriam.

From an empty chair, Christian lifts an envelope, scattering the gravel that had been holding it down. When he hands it to me, I open it.

The return address is from Phoenix—the Phoenix Marathon. I pull out the insides and read.

CONFIRMATION OF PARTICIPATION

He is scheduled to run in October of next year.

"It's a qualifier for Boston," he says.

Mirriam hands me a plastic martini cup and fills it from a green bottle. I sip and am startled by the sweetness. Not champagne—sparkling apple cider. I should have known they wouldn't give me alcohol. It's fizzy, and the bubbles pop on my tongue and ricochet off the roof of my mouth.

"What about Dad? He watches the Boston Marathon on TV," I say.

He hesitates and looks at Mirriam. "He does, huh? I guess the likelihood is low the camera would air me." His voice is steady, but he pulls his elbows into his sides, and I get that he's terrified, but he's trying. "Maybe he'll find us, maybe he won't, but I can't let him dictate what we're doing anymore. You okay with that risk?"

I think of Christian crossing the finish line. "More than okay."

I hand him the letter back, and our knuckles knock together. I look out over the lights of Albuquerque. They are lined up, neat and ordered.

"I've got some serious training ahead of me," Christian says, "for the marathon."

"Yeah?"

"Tomorrow morning?" he asks.

"Aren't you working the early shift?"

He hesitates. "Yeah."

"You have to be at the hospital by six?"

"Well . . . yeah."

I imagine us running together in the dark. "If I'm gonna haul my ass out of bed that early, I get the first shower."

He glances at me aslant. "Sure, okay."

I look at him and know I'll have to race him for it.

a **week later,** my body has adjusted to his early shift. It's still dark when I wake up, hearing Christian in the bathroom that sits between our two rooms in our new place. The boxes are unpacked and heaped in a corner.

When we moved downstairs, our shag carpet upgraded from pink to green. The kitchen has an island, so we've ditched the table and chairs and have only the couch and desk in the living room. Our furniture looks like an archipelago in a shag green sea. On the wall over the couch, I've tacked up a shot that I took from the mountains. There's still a lot of work to do, but I suspect that this apartment will come together.

While I'm threading my legs into my running shorts, 277

Christian leans in the doorway and throws me a pair of running tights that he shrunk in the laundry, and a new pair of running gloves.

"Thanks."

I peel off the label and snap the plastic thing that keeps them stuck together. They are light and warm.

When we're both ready, when our watches have been strapped around our wrists, our gloves drawn over our hands, and our keys tucked into our pockets, we head out the door at a jog.

It doesn't take long for us to get into our rhythm. There are few cars on the road, so we hit the asphalt for the even surface.

At first, my thoughts are still firing: Will the bookstore be packed with Christmas-frantic customers? How am I going to finish the three papers I have due this week? What if my dad does spot Christian, checks the number on his jersey, and gets our last name online?

But I focus on my breathing, and the little panicky thoughts recede, clearing the way for bigger ones. The road slopes downhill and curves away out of sight. The sky is changing at the horizon. The sun isn't up yet, but color is coming anyway, a sort of whitish-gold. Beyond our path, I can see the smaller mountain ridges in the west. I don't know their names yet.

Maybe I'll ask Dakota to head out there with me, and she can draw while I shoot. She gets a focused quiet when she draws, all her thoughts attuned to the swoosh on the page. I wonder if I can capture her concentration in a photo. I hope she'll let me try.

The sounds of running start to dissolve my thoughts, and I know soon I'll hit the step, breath, wind rhythm that quiets my brain. For now, my thoughts interrupt in unrelated bursts.

. . . step . . . step . . . step . . .

I think about the October mornings so long ago when Christian and I would head out, him on foot and me on my bike. I didn't know how much those mornings would mean to me once Christian left.

. . . step . . . step . . . step . . .

Last night Christian apologized again for not coming back for me. When he finished berating himself, I told him that I get it. We all screw up. We all wish we were stronger than we are, and not one of us will get through this life without regret.

. . . step . . . breath . . .

When we get back, Mirriam will be in the apartment. She has taken to coming over in the morning and eating breakfast with us. She will have made tea and will be perched on a counter stool, grading or reading. We'll sit down together and eat before we splinter into our respective worlds, have our days, and then return again.

. . . step . . . breath . . . wind . . .
. . . step . . . breath . . . wind . . .

In the light cones from the streetlamps, snowflakes fall. My breathing becomes controlled and regular, and the chest-squishing elephant never shows up. Instead, the air slips through, in and out of my lungs, carrying on it the scent of dust and sage and frost.

We run and run and run until there's nothing but sound and my brother beside me. I don't know who is cuing off of whom, but when we've gone far enough, we turn around and head back, up the long rise toward home.

acknowledgments

there's a consensus that writing is a solitary act, but it took a village to grow this book. I am indebted to the insightful and wise Mary Logue, who guided me on this project from the first word to the last and who always knew what to say to keep my pen on the paper. Julie Schumacher helped me see what this book was about and, more importantly, what it was not about. Pete Hautman helped me call myself a writer, always treating me as a professional.

H. M. Bouwman, Brian Farrey, Heather E. Goodman, Charlotte Sullivan, and Scott Wrobel have read this book repeatedly, commented astutely, and helped me keep my faith in my writing. Nicholas Kaufmann told me that I could make this career work.

Rosemary Stimola's swift and patient responses made bringing this book to market and beyond a pure joy. My editor, Nancy Siscoe, gracefully led me through the long maze of publication. Her sharp eyes and acumen helped me give my characters the ending they deserve. The good people at Knopf—marketers, publicists, and designers—supported this book's creation.

The Loft Literary Center provided me with rich experiences as a member and as a recipient of the Mentor Series award and, along with Hamline University, defined my writing community. The University of Minnesota's creative writing faculty presented me with intelligent lessons on language and structure, and the English department provided me with the Graduate Research Partnership Program Fellowship so that I could complete *Split*.

The brave clients of and dedicated staff at Domestic Violence Legal Clinic (formerly Pro Bono Advocates) helped me frame the questions of this book.

Deepa Dharmadhikari, Patrick Hueller, Amber Vangen, and Lois and John H. Yopp cheered loudly with me when I got good news and were appropriately despondent when I didn't.

My children's patience astonishes me. They not only braved days of maternal absence while I attended conferences, classes, and presentations, but also endured the innumerable times when I was lost in the world of the book.

For three years, John Yopp, my husband, ideal reader, and portable dictionary/thesaurus, listened intently to every single thought about this book, whether whole-book concepts or comma placement. He knew when I needed a sounding board and when I needed more. Now he can channel Jace's voice so clearly that I sometimes eye him suspiciously, baffled by how he has constructed a direct line to my subconscious.

Thank you all.